SOMETHING OLD,
SOMETHING NEW

Also by Beverly Jenkins

Fiction

A SECOND HELPING
BRING ON THE BLESSINGS

DEADLY SEXY
SEXY/DANGEROUS
BLACK LACE
EDGE OF DAWN
EDGE OF MIDNIGHT

MIDNIGHT
CAPTURED
JEWEL
WILD SWEET LOVE
WINDS OF A STORM
SOMETHING LIKE LOVE
A CHANCE AT LOVE
BEFORE DAWN
ALWAYS AND FOREVER
TAMING JESSI ROSE
TOPAZ
INDIGO
VIVID
THROUGH THE STORM
NIGHT SONG

SOMETHING OLD, SOMETHING NEW

A BLESSINGS NOVEL

Beverly Jenkins

wm

WILLIAM MORROW

An Imprint of HarperCollins*Publishers*

This book is a work of fiction. The characters, incidents, and dialogue are drawn from the author's imagination and are not to be construed as real. Any resemblance to actual events or persons, living or dead, is entirely coincidental.

HarperCollins books may be purchased for educational, business, or sales promotional use. For information please write: Special Markets Department, HarperCollins Publishers, 10 East 53rd Street, New York, NY 10022.

Library of Congress Cataloging-in-Publication Data
Jenkins, Beverly, 1951–
    Something old, something new : a blessings novel / Beverly Jenkins.
      p.   cm.
    ISBN 978-0-06-199079-3
    1. African Americans—Fiction. 2. Weddings—Fiction. 3. Family secrets—Fiction. 4. City and town life—Fiction. I. Title.
PS3560.E4795S43   2010
813'.54—dc22

                                                    2010037385

11 12 13 14 15   OV/RRD   10 9 8 7 6 5 4 3 2 1

Reverend Stacy Salles
for her friendship, faith, and cowboy boots

PROLOGUE

Miami, Florida

Reverend Paula Grant walked into her small, cluttered office and sat down tiredly in her tattered brown leather chair. She'd just come from a meeting with her bishop, where she'd been informed that her inner-city church, named after Absalom Jones, the nineteenth-century founder of the nation's first Black Episcopal church, would be closing in a month. The city wanted the land for razing and regentrification, and the bishop wanted the profit from the sale to shore up the diocese's ailing coffers. It was a win-win situation for everyone involved, except Paula and her congregation.

Her protests on behalf of the homeless and indigent who made up her congregation had been anticipated by the bishop; she wasn't know as Rev. Pesky Paula without reason, so he'd countered her arguments by showing her data on just how much keeping Absalom open was costing the diocese in terms of costs, salaries, and insurance premiums. She'd be the first to admit that Old Ab, as it was known in the neighborhood, hadn't pulled its financial weight in the decade she'd been at the helm, but she didn't remember Jesus having to meet budgetary expectations in his ministry. His work had been about saving souls, and so had hers. However, the church of the twenty-first century needed money to do what Jesus instructed his followers to do, and since Old Ab was worth more shuttered than open, she and the crumbling edifice had to go.

She sighed audibly. It hurt knowing that in thirty days the doors would be padlocked, and those in greatest need would have to find somewhere else to go to sing their off-tune praises on Sunday mornings—not that the homeless, addicts, prostitutes, or felons that filled Old Ab's pews would be welcomed at any of the other nearby houses of worship, but apparently that wasn't anyone's concern, either. The bishop had even offered her a severance bonus if she followed her church into nonexistence. "You're close to retirement age," he'd pointed out gently.

Paula was fifty-five years young and hardly ready to be put out to pasture. It had taken her many years to answer God's call. After finishing college at Spelman, she'd taken her BS in psychology and turned it into a master's in child psychology. She then added a doctorate. As Dr. Paula Grant, she began her new career teaching graduate students, but when that no longer satisfied her, she opened a private practice, treating the moneyed and oftentimes spoiled African-American teens of Atlanta. However, always in the back of her mind and in the front of her heart was the joy of Christ, so fifteen years ago she'd surrendered to the call and given herself over to God.

After completing seminary and her ordination, she was

handed the keys to her own church, Old Ab, in one of the seediest neighborhoods of Miami. Days later, she learned that she'd been offered the parish because no other priest wanted it, but that didn't matter. From the moment she set eyes on the half-a-century-old place with its crumbling spires and Gothic bones and met its eccentric, transient congregation, she knew she was home.

Now home was being yanked out from under her feet like a threadbare rug, and she was out of work. The bishop assured her that had he another position to offer her, he would, but economic times being what they were and with more people spending Sunday mornings online than in church, she'd have to leave Florida if she wanted to continue as an Episcopal priest.

She dropped her head in her hands. It was her belief that when God was in the mix, things happened for a reason, but as with most movings of the Spirit, she had no idea what that reason might be. She got up and walked over to the window. In the years since her arrival, the neighborhood had changed. Gone were the mom-and-pop stores and small businesses that once offered everything from fresh bread to dry cleaning to shoe repair. Now the church and its struggling neighbors were surrounded by graffiti-sprayed storefronts sporting security bars in faded buildings that seemed to sag under the combined weight of weariness and neglect. Even the church had been broken into more times than she'd ever reported to the authorities, but soon the whole area would be bulldozed and prettied up for the moneyed latte crowd, with their imported cars, time-shares, and 1.2 children.

She asked forgiveness for her bitter thoughts and knew that God was upstairs shaking His head. Paula asked for forgiveness a lot, but He was patient with her, so she supposed she had to be patient with herself. In thirty days, life would begin anew, and she couldn't help but wonder where the call would lead her next.

CHAPTER
1

September

At 6:00 a.m. Lily Fontaine was awakened by the ringtone on her phone crooning "Reunited," the old-school tune by Peaches and Herb. Smiling sleepily, she rolled over and picked up. "Morning."

"Morning. Did I wake you?"

The sound of Trent's voice filled her up like she was seventeen all over again. She turned over onto her back. "Yes, but there's nothing better than hearing from the man I love. How are you?"

"Wishing we were already married so I could wake up with you. You always sound so warm and soft in the mornings."

Lily's heart skipped. "For a country boy, you're pretty seductive at the crack of dawn."

"Only with you."

Was it any wonder she loved him? "You want to come over for breakfast?"

"Can't. Meeting with the Dads at the Dog in about an hour. Did you sleep well?"

"I did, but I'll sleep better once we say 'I do.' "

"Now who's being seductive?"

"Just trying to keep up with you." She told herself for the five hundredth time how blessed she was to have Trent July in her life.

"Well, hold that thought, the wedding date'll be here before you know it."

"Can't we just elope?"

He chuckled. "Not if we want to come back and live here."

"There is that." An elopement would definitely disappoint everyone in town.

"Anything special on your agenda for the day?"

"Not that I know of, but this is Henry Adams. No telling what may have jumped off by the time the sun sets."

"True, so let me let you go. Just wanted to give you your wake-up call. I love you, girl."

"Love you back. Bye."

Sighing contentedly, she lay there for a moment, then set the phone aside and left the bed to begin her day.

The Dog and Cow was the only dining establishment in Henry Adams, Kansas, and at 7:00 a.m. the booths and tables were just beginning to fill with construction-crew members, businessmen in suits, and a few casually dressed locals. In another hour the place would be bustling. The young waitstaff would be weaving in and out of the crowd, carrying piled-high plates of some of the best food in the county, while old-school music blared from the diner's fancy red jukebox.

Now, however, the place was quiet, the satin voice of Sarah Vaughan floating on the air.

In one of the back booths, Mayor Trent July was presiding over the weekly Thursday meeting of Dads Inc., an organization formed over the summer to provide a way for local fathers to get together and talk about the challenges they faced raising their children. The local women, led by town owner Bernadine Brown and Tamar July, Trent's grandmother, were forces of nature, and sometimes the dads needed the male bonding time to weather the storms.

In attendance was: Colonel Barrett Payne USMC, retired; Dr. Reggie Garland, town pediatrician; and Jack James, Henry Adams's only schoolteacher.

"So how's everybody doing?" Trent asked his comrades.

Reg sighed aloud. "Still missing Roni."

They all nodded understandingly. Roni was Reg's wife, and an award-winning R&B singer. She was in New York, working on her newest CD.

"I thought she was going to record in the studio you all were building here," the colonel said.

"So did I," Reg replied, looking out from behind black-rimmed glasses. "But she decided to stay with the studio in New York. Said she didn't want to mess up the groove, and dealing with the building of the studio here was going to take time away from recording. She'll do the next CD here."

Trent sipped his juice and asked, "How's Zoey handling Roni being gone?"

Reggie's smile showed the fondness he felt for his mute but musically talented eight-year-old daughter. "She's a trooper. She's been real patient, but she's missing her mama big-time."

Trent understood, and seeing the way Reg had been moping around, it was obvious that Zoey wasn't the only one missing Roni big-time.

"Not to change the subject," Colonel Payne said to Reg, "but do you think it's okay for Preston to run laps in the mornings before school? He says he wants to get in shape." Preston was the foster son of the colonel and his wife, Sheila.

"Since when?" Trent asked, his surprise echoed in the faces of Reg and Jack.

"Since Leah."

"Ah," they all said.

Jack quipped, "Nothing like discovering girls to make you want to change your look."

Leah was the eldest daughter of Gary Clark, one of Trent's old high school buddies. The overweight Preston and the stick-thin Leah had been introduced last summer, and upon discovering they both loved physics as much as they did breathing, the two had become instant friends.

"Can Preston do laps with his asthma?" Jack asked, adding more ketchup to his eggs and hash browns.

"Olympian Jackie Joyner-Kersee has asthma, and she does okay," Reg replied. "Preston just has to listen to his body." He directed his next words to Barrett. "Bring Preston into the clinic and let me give him a quick once-over and share some dos and don'ts. Losing weight will help him physically as long as you don't push him like one of your boot camp recruits."

Barrett got the point. "I won't."

Trent knew that Barrett would be the first to admit that parenting Preston had been difficult during the first year of their relationship, but in the past few months he had made tremendous strides bonding with his son.

Rocky Dancer, the Dog's lady manager and head cook, walked over to their booth carrying a carafe of hot coffee. "Anybody need a warm-up?"

Jack's cup was full, but he held it out anyway. Trent smiled inwardly. Jack considered himself in love with the drop-dead-gorgeous, stacked-to-the-max Rocky, but getting her to give him more than a warm-up for his coffee was proving difficult. She and Trent had grown up together, and she remained one of the toughest women he knew. Although Trent kept telling Jack he stood a snowball's chance in hell of getting next to her, the schoolteacher remained focused and undeterred.

Rocky poured an inch of brew into Jack's full cup and turned away. "Anyone else?"

Her frosty attitude caused Jack to shoot Trent a knowing smile, and it occurred to Trent that Jack was actually enjoying the challenge.

"If you need anything else, just holler," she said. After giving Jack a grim look, she and her carafe departed to serve the other diners.

As they all watched her walk away, Reggie asked Jack, "So how's your campaign going?"

Amusement lit Jack's black eyes. "She can run, but she can't hide."

The men laughed loud and long.

"What's so funny?" The question came from Malachi July, Trent's father and owner of the Dog and Cow. He and his coffee cup were standing in the spot Rocky had just vacated.

Jack explained, "We're laughing at my quest to win the hand of yon fair maiden."

They could see her now talking with a small group of construction workers seated in a booth up front.

Mal shook his head. "Be easier to catch the wind, son."

Jack shrugged. "I got nothing but time."

Mal sat down next to Trent. "We'll put that on your headstone."

Trent checked out the letters on his father's black tee. The shirt appeared to be new. "GD Inc.?"

Mal glanced down at the big gold letters emblazoned across his chest. "Yeah. Thought I'd form my own support group and get my own shirt."

Reg grinned. "I'm almost scared to ask, but what's GD stand for?'

"Grand Dad, of course." Mal swiveled around so they could see the letters *OG* emblazoned on the back of the shirt.

Trent chuckled. "I keep telling you OG stands for Old Geezer."

"And I keep telling you—quit hating," he retorted with humor in his voice. Mal was a retired veterinarian, a recovering alcoholic, and a former ladies' man. Before falling hard and fast for town owner Bernadine Brown, the sixty-plus-year-old Vietnam vet had spent his days and nights hanging with women young enough to be mistaken for his granddaughters. In the past year, he, too, had made tremendous strides.

Barrett asked, "Are you planning on having your own GD meetings?"

"Nope. Coming to yours so I can give you young bucks the benefit of my advanced wisdom."

"Uh-huh," Trent tossed back with a doubt-filled laugh.

A grinning Jack raised his juice. "To dads and OGs everywhere."

"Hear! Hear!" they shouted gleefully.

Once things had settled down again, Mal asked Trent, "So how're the wedding plans going?"

Trent sipped his coffee. "If we can keep Bernadine from renting Buckingham Palace or flying in the bishop of Canterbury or the pope, Lily and I should be good."

Mal shook his head, a knowing smile on his face. "She is something, isn't she?" Bernadine had a bank account as wide and as deep as the Grand Canyon, and she was happiest when sharing it.

Trent agreed. "Love her to death, but Lily may have to wrestle her to the ground and tie her up in order for us to have the nice, simple wedding we both want." He eyed his dad and asked innocently, "How about telling Bernadine to save all that bling for when you two get married?"

Mal spit coffee across the table.

Snickers followed.

Mal wiped his mouth and looked Trent's way. "Don't even go there. We are not talking marriage."

Trent loved teasing his father. "Maybe not today."

The chuckles of the others made Mal grouse, "Stop encouraging him."

Heads and eyes dropped, but the amusement remained.

The conversation moved on to the all-family trip to the

Grand Canyon the colonel wanted them to take next year, but everyone went still at the sight of Riley Curry and his new lady friend, Texas millionairess Eustasia Pennymaker, being escorted to a booth by the hostess.

Riley was the town's former mayor. He was wearing a nice black suit that sported his signature fake red carnation on the lapel. His thinning hair was plastered on his head with pomade, and the way he was smiling and waving, you'd've thought he was campaigning. Eustasia, with her big Texas hair, was decked out in leopard print from her headband to her stiletto heels.

Mal whispered, "Well, I'll be damned."

The two had been in town for a few months now, but as far as Trent knew this was their first visit to the Dog. Eustasia was footing the bill for Riley's legal battle with the county, and they were living in an expensive double-wide trailer on the edge of town.

They'd just taken their seats when Riley's ex-wife, Genevieve, entered with Cliff Dobbs. Cliff, Mal, and Genevieve had grown up together in Henry Adams. Cliff had quietly loved Genevieve since their teen years, but when it came time to marry, Genevieve had chosen Riley. Now they were divorced, and after all she'd endured at the hands and hooves of Riley and his six-hundred-pound pet hog, Cletus, no one could much blame her. While once Genevieve had been the epitome of decorum and good taste, Riley's antics had so changed her personality that the sight of him was liable to send her around the bend. Mal and Trent exchanged a look of worry.

Trent asked, "Has the court date been set for Cletus and Riley?"

"Not so far. Judge is still viewing the case law."

Two summers ago, Cletus had sat on a man and killed him. The county planned to put the hog down, but before the paperwork could be finalized, Riley had helped Cletus escape, and the two went on the lam. Earlier this summer, the two were finally apprehended down in Louisiana and extradited back to Kansas. No one knew how or when Riley had first hooked up with Ms. Pennymaker and her huge sow, Chocolate.

Mal added, "Word is, Judge Davis may not hold the hearing until next spring. Me, I can't wait. Plenty of folks around here would love to put that hog on a spit with lots of barbecue sauce."

Trent hoped Genevieve would ignore the couple, but no. Apparently this was her first sighting of her ex, too; upon seeing him, she went stock-still and flames seemed to leap from her eyes. Riley had always been clueless about her moods, and to prove it, he stuck out his tongue at her and with a dismissive air turned his attention to his menu.

Trent shook his head sadly.

"Doc, do you have your medical bag?" Mal asked Reg.

The chuckling Reg hoisted it up for Mal to see.

"Good. We may need you. Excuse me, fellas." Mal left the booth and headed over to intercept Genevieve, now barreling down on Riley like a tank. When she spied his approach, she yelled, "Stay out of this, Malachi!"

The story of Riley, Genevieve, and Cletus had become the stuff of legend, and everyone in the Dog stared on, riveted.

Apparently Cliff had been told to stay out of it, too, because he was still standing at the hostess station up front.

Trent saw displeasure on his face, but it was impossible to determine whether his ire was directed at Genevieve, Riley, or both.

Genevieve walked over to the smug-looking Riley and for the moment ignored him. Instead she politely introduced herself to the wary-eyed Ms. Pennymaker, who replied, "Um, pleased to meet you, too."

Genevieve gave her a tight, fake smile before she turned blazing eyes on her ex, who had the nerve to say, "I hope you're happy, Genevieve. Cletus and me wouldn't be in this mess if it wasn't for you."

The onlookers slowly shook their heads.

The outdone Genevieve rared back and decked Riley with a punch so hard he was already out cold when he slid beneath the table and disappeared. The wide-eyed Eustasia cried out, "Riley! Honey!" and immediately ducked her head beneath the tabletop.

Reg grabbed his bag.

The seething Genevieve stood over the booth.

Trent figured that the force of the blow had probably broken her hand, but she didn't appear hurt. Too mad, probably.

As Reg saw to the knocked-out Riley, Rocky hurried over to offer Genevieve a bowl of ice to stick her hand in. Trent glanced around, taking in the shocked but amused faces of the other diners, and wondered if other small towns in America started their mornings this way.

Lily Fontaine frowned as she sat at her kitchen table and slowly leafed through a large stack of bridal gown catalogs.

The fancy designer gowns were absolutely gorgeous, but money to buy them could feed a family of four for a year. She and Trent were scheduled to tie the knot on Thanksgiving Day, so she needed a gown, but not one so pricey that she'd feel guilty wearing it, and that's what would happen if she decided on one of the gowns featured in the glossy pages of the catalogs. Frustrated, she closed the book and pushed it aside. Her gown dilemma could be laid at the Jimmy Choo–clad feet of her good friend and employer, Bernadine Brown. With the way Bernadine had been carrying on since Lily and Trent announced they were marrying, you'd think she was the one preparing to walk down the aisle. Lily loved her boss like a sister, but Bernadine wanted to open that bottomless checkbook of hers and turn the wedding into a Bernadine Brown production, complete with doves, white horses, and a six-foot-high cake. All Lily wanted was a gathering in the school's kiva or maybe the rec center's auditorium, followed by an old-school reception and dinner over at the Dog. She knew that Trent wanted a small, homey wedding, too, but how to convince Bernadine? The Boss Lady was big on giving out blessings, and the fairy-tale vibe she was trying to promote was a part of that. But it wasn't what Lily wanted, and no matter how many times she'd tried explaining that to Bernadine, the woman would just smile and suggest another pricey frill Lily might want to include.

Lily walked to the patio door and looked out at the day. It was the end of September, and fall was in the air. The grasses on the plains were taking on the rich golds and browns of autumn, and the temperatures were markedly cooler. She was sad to see the season end. It had been an eventful summer, what with Crystal's no-good daddy, Ray, kidnapping her, and Bernadine's ex-husband, Leo, showing up trying to win her back. In the end, Crystal had been saved, and Leo told to take a hike, only to have him show a romantic interest in Lily's godmother, Marie Jefferson, and begin building himself a mansion over in the neighboring town of Franklin.

So far, Lily and Marie hadn't discussed Leo. Lily supposed that had to do with the bond she shared with Bernadine. Marie probably assumed Lily was on Bernadine's side, and frankly, she was. Had Marie met Leo under different circumstances, she'd be the first to congratulate her godmother on finally having someone who loved her in her life, but Lily had yet to be convinced that Leo did. When Bernadine refused his offer to reconcile, he'd suddenly become interested in Marie. It didn't sit right. Still didn't.

Lily wanted her godmother to be happy, but all she saw ahead was heartache, and lord knew, Marie had already experienced more than her share. Lily made a mental note to call her later and suggest they get together. Marie had been the best friend of Lily's late mother, Cassandra. This semi-estrangement they seemed to be having didn't sit right, either.

"Morning, Ms. Lily."

She turned to see her nine-year-old foster son, Devon Watkins, entering the kitchen, and the sight of him brightened her mood. He was dressed for school in the outfit he wore every day: black suit, white shirt, blue clip-on tie. "Morning, baby boy. How are you?"

"I'm fine, Ms. Lily. How are you?"

"I'm fine, too. Did you sleep well?"

"Yes, ma'am." He took a seat at the table and poured out a helping of cold cereal into the bowl she'd set out for him earlier. While he did that, she walked over to the fridge and withdrew a carton of milk and a bottle of orange juice. He added the milk to the contents of his bowl and helped himself to a piece of toast and a few slices of bacon. After pouring some juice into his glass, he started in on breakfast.

Lily took a seat and watched him with all the affection she felt inside. He'd been in Henry Adams for over a year now, and although he seemed to be adjusting outwardly, he continued to hang on to his shy ways, along with the suits he insisted upon wearing all day every day, and his dream of becoming the town's preacher. He'd been raised by his now late grandmother, Willa Mae, in a small town down in Mississippi, where he'd been an ordained minister. Last summer, Lily and everyone else in town witnessed his preaching for the first time. He'd blown them away, and the public attention had been immediate. People began driving in from all over the state to hear him give the Word. There'd even been a few so-called managers wanting to sign him to contracts and take him on tour. She sent them packing because first and foremost, Devon was a child.

Lately though, the crowds had been dwindling, so she supposed the novelty had worn off. As a result, she and Devon had agreed that this coming Sunday would be his last public appearance. In a way she was glad attendance had dropped. Although she was convinced he had a gift, she was concerned he'd never be the carefree nine-year-old that he should be.

"Did you find a wedding dress?" he asked, seeing the stack of catalogs by her spot at the table.

"Not yet. They're all too expensive, but I'll keep looking."

"Zoey and I want to be in the wedding."

"And you will be. You and Davis'll give me away, and Zoey's going to be the flower girl." Zoey and Devon were best friends, and Davis was Lily's twenty-four-year-old son. He lived in California.

Devon said earnestly, "I really want to marry you and Mr. Trent."

Lily paused over her raised glass of orange juice. "I know, baby, but you aren't a licensed preacher in Kansas. We talked about this before, remember?"

"I do, but why can't you and Ms. Bernadine get me a license?"

"You're going to be in the wedding, Devon. You'll have to be content with that. Besides, I want you to help give me away."

His look of disappointment made her sigh with a disappointment of her own. This whole preacher business had to be resolved, but she had no idea how to make it happen. All she wanted was for him to be a real little boy, not this polite wooden rendition that reminded her of Pinocchio.

After breakfast, he put his dishes in the sink and went up to his room to get his backpack. School started in less than an hour. She could tell he wasn't happy, but she wasn't going to change her mind about him performing the wedding.

A few moments later, he returned ready for school.

Trying not to be affected by his sad brown eyes, she asked

brightly, "Do you want a ride to school, or are you and Zoey going to walk?"

"We'll walk, Ms. Lily. Thank you."

"Okay. Give me a hug."

In spite of his brooding, he gave her a hug that was filled with love, and she kissed his cheek. "Have a good day."

"You, too, Ms. Lily."

Once he was gone, Lily pondered over him for a few seconds longer, then went to get her car keys so she could drive to work.

CHAPTER
2

The flat-topped red brick building where Lily worked was called the Power Plant. It had been constructed last year and held all of the Henry Adams administrative offices. Her official title was Henry Adams COO. Bernadine's hand turned the world, but Lily's job was to make sure that world turned efficiently and under budget. On the short drive in, she marveled at all the changes Bernadine had wrought since buying Henry Adams off eBay two summers ago. Armed with an eye-popping divorce settlement from the aforementioned Leo Brown, Bernadine had taken the sleepy, near-destitute town and turned it into a twenty-first-century showplace. She'd added roads, new buildings, and Wi-Fi sites, providing construction jobs for a community that had been economically slammed by the recession. When the initial building phase was finished that first summer, Henry Adams, founded in the mid-1880s by freed slaves, stood as the envy of every other town in the county. Newspaper articles and cable news reports chronicled Henry Adams's rebirth and Bernadine's unique foster child program, which centered around the five children she'd brought in from cities all over the country. They were thriving under the loving care of their new parents, and although Henry Adams seemed to have enough drama going on for three towns lately, Lily didn't want to live anywhere else.

When she entered the eco-friendly Power Plant with its atrium and thriving potted plants, Bernadine was already in her office and seated behind her cluttered desk. No matter how early Lily arrived, Bernadine managed to beat her in. Many of the town's residents swore the woman didn't sleep, and Lily agreed.

She stuck her head in Bernadine's office. "Morning, Boss Lady."

"Hey, Lil. Morning. How are you?"

"I'm okay. You?" Lily came in fully.

"Doing fine. Have you decided which gown?"

As always, Bernadine was dressed to the nines. Expensive gray suit. Tasteful gold hanging from her earlobes, around her throat, and on her wrists. The hair was perfect, makeup, too. By society's standards she was a big girl, but she was the classiest woman Lily knew.

"Nothing yet."

"All those catalogs?"

"They're too expensive."

"Lily—"

Lily said softly, "Bernadine, look. I appreciate the blessing, but if you want to buy my gown, get me something I won't feel guilty wearing. I'm marrying Trent July, not Prince Charles."

Bernadine's disappointed face reminded Lily of Devon's

as she came to her own defense. "I just want you to have a fabulous wedding."

"And I appreciate that, but Trent and I just want nice and simple. You can save all this fabulousness for when you and Malachi tie the knot."

Bernadine rolled her eyes. After a year of denial, she'd finally surrendered her heart to the retired veterinarian. In spite of Mal's sometimes crazy ways, he seemed to be as good for her as she was for him, even if Bernadine did continue to hang on to portions of her denial in much the same way Devon continued to hang on to his suits and clip-on ties. "Mal and I aren't even thinking about marriage."

"Maybe not this second," she teased.

Bernadine's eyes rolled again with amusement. "Okay. Let's change the subject. I'm flying down to Miami this afternoon. Do you want to go?"

"What's in Miami?"

"A piece of property. The city is buying up the area, and my investment people think I should get in on the ground floor before everything gets snatched up."

"Are you coming back this evening?"

"Yep."

"Then sure, I'll go with you."

"Okay, good. We'll leave in a little while."

Bernadine owned a private jet, which made it easy to take quick spur-of-the-moment trips.

"I have another reason for going to Miami," Bernadine added. "I want to show around pictures of Zoey and her mom, Bonnie. Maybe we'll get lucky and run into someone who knew them. Hiring detectives hasn't worked."

When the Miami police found Zoey living under an expressway, her mom's newspaper-shrouded corpse had been discovered there as well. Bernadine had hired detectives to try and find someone who might be able to tell them whether Zoey'd been mute before her mother's death, and maybe more of her story, but so far nothing. She'd made contact with Zoey's only known relative, Bonnie's sister, Yvette, but because Bonnie had been a crack addict, Yvette wanted nothing to do with her niece. On the upside, though, no one could love Zoey more than Roni and Reg, and they provided the perfect home environment for her and her awesome musical gifts. Lily asked, "Do we have anything else on the calendar today?"

"Other than you finding a gown, no."

"Don't start," Lily warned, smiling. "Find me one that's lower than the price of the Taj Mahal, and I may just bite."

"Party pooper."

"That's my name. Don't wear it out."

Bernadine laughed. "Go to work."

Lily loved Bernadine very much. "I'll see you later."

But before she could make her exit to her office next door, Bernadine said, "When His Honor gets in, if you see him before I do, don't let him sneak out again without stopping in to see me. I need his autograph on some construction bids."

"Will do."

Trent was still trying to get over Genevieve and her mighty right hand when he parked his black truck in the Power Plant's parking lot and got out. She had broken it on Riley's glass jaw.

Walking now toward the building, he passed Bernadine's Baby, a bright blue Ford F-150, and Lily's army green Chevy SUV, Nemo, which in Latin meant "no name." The two women always beat him to work, mainly because he wasn't as driven as they. Life in his hometown had moved at a much slower pace before Bernadine's ownership. Back then, if he wanted to spend the day at his garage lovingly restoring his old cars and holding council meetings while Mal and Cliff and the rest played checkers and drank Tamar's lemonade, it was allowed. Not anymore. Then again, under his rule, they'd wound up selling the town, lock, stock, and barrel, to allay a massive debt. Bernadine had the place running as smoothly as an old-school Chrysler engine, so he'd be the first to admit that her version of town leadership beat his, hands down.

However, he still chafed at being mayor. The only reason he held the office was because no one else wanted the job. Riley Curry had been mayor for decades, but when the town went broke and Riley wanted to solve the problem by having their historic town annexed by the neighboring city of Franklin, the voters booted him out. Trent was a July. His Black Seminole family had been in Henry Adams since the 1880s. When first elected, he'd felt a certain responsibility to his lineage and to the dreams of the Exodusters who had founded their small community, but now it appeared as if he might hold the office for life, mainly because no one else wanted the job.

As Trent entered the quiet building, the hushed air held the faint lingering notes of Lily's perfume, and thoughts of her made him admit that coming to work wasn't so bad after all.

His office suite was across the hall from the ones occupied by Bernadine and Lily. Lily's door was open, so he paused outside it for a moment to observe her unseen. She was wearing a pearl gray twinset, and her eyes were glued to her computer screen. He loved watching her; the way she moved, the way she bit her bottom lip when she was concentrating on something. They were sixteen when they first met at Henry Adams High. Her mom had recently passed away, and Lily had come to town to live with Ms. Agnes and Marie Jefferson. The memory of seeing her that first day at track team tryouts was still vivid. She'd been wearing a white tee and a pair of burgundy track shorts that showed off her gorgeous gams. No one knew anything about her, but when her timing lap came, she blasted her way around the track and hit each hurdle with such power and grace, Coach Bing Shepard's eyes nearly bugged out of his head. Trent and everyone else looked on in amazement, and when she hit the last hurdle, he knew he was in love.

Over the next two years, she broke every high school track record in the book. The newspapers called her Fabulous Fontaine.

Trent walked into her office. "Morning."

She turned from the screen and greeted him with a tender smile. "Morning, yourself—and before I forget, make sure you stop in and see Bernadine before you sneak off."

He grinned, and they spent the next few moments silently drinking each other in. That they were back together and in love amazed them both. "The girl who punched you during the state relays senior year. What was her name?"

Lily's eyes went cold. "Wendy Allman. I'll never forget."

"Bet she hasn't forgotten you, either."

"After the beat-down I gave her, she's probably still cursing me to this day."

While he chuckled, she added, "I couldn't believe she slugged me like that."

"You were going to win the race. She didn't like it."

Lily's best track event was the hurdles, but she was also fast enough to run the anchor leg for the Henry Adams girls' relay team. She and Franklin High's Wendy Allman were neck and neck and stride for stride coming through the last turn. Lily began her kick and was starting to pass her opponent, only to have the frustrated competitor reach over and punch Lily in the shoulder so hard it sent her flying into the infield. While the crowd looked on in horror, Lily got up. Eyes blazing, she took off after Wendy.

Trent grinned as his memory took him back to that day. "I remember you running her down and the crowd cheering like crazy."

"And when I caught her I went crazy."

"Yeah, you did. Tamar said it reminded her of roller derby."

"I wanted to knock her into next week, I was so mad. I couldn't believe the judges disqualified me, too."

"The girl did need five stitches in her lip, Lil."

"She should've been glad I didn't break her legs."

"To look at you now, no one would ever know you were a hotheaded teenage Wonder Girl."

"You didn't tell any of those old Wonder Girl stories to my son, Davis, when he visited Marie during the summers when he was young, did you?"

Trent quieted and studied the face of the woman he'd never stopped loving. "You and I weren't exactly pen pals back in those days, remember?"

She stilled. Guilt claimed her face as she dropped her head and said quietly, "You're right. I forgot."

Their relationship had shattered after she went away to college, and the ugly way it happened left him with a battered heart and a vow to never speak to her again. The change in her mood now made him say, "Didn't mean to bring you down."

"I know."

He added softly, "But I'm glad we worked it all out."

"So am I."

Lily was still humbled by the size of his heart. Even though she'd stomped all over it, his love for her had remained buried beneath the hurt and pain she'd caused. She acknowledged it by whispering, "I love you."

"Love you back, Lily Flower."

It was the name he'd given her back in the day, and the sound of it on his lips twenty-five years later still made her insides do flips.

"How about you and Devon come over for dinner tonight?" he asked.

"I should probably take a rain check." She explained why and added, "Hopefully it'll be a quick trip, but I'm not sure what time we'll be back. Bernadine also wants to show Zoey's picture around while we're down there."

"She's the most optimistic woman I know."

"Me, too."

Trent ran his eyes over the sweep of her throat and thought about the kisses he'd placed there whenever they managed a moment alone, which was not very often. He dragged himself back to the present. "Then how about Devon hanging out with me and Amari until you get back? I know he usually goes home with Zoey after school, but we're all going to be family, and I'd like for us to start connecting."

"That's a good idea, Mr. Mayor. You are so smart," she replied, sounding pleased. "I'll run by the school before the Boss Lady and I leave for the airport and let him know to go home with Amari. Not sure how he'll take not being able to hang with Zoey. He's already pouting about not being able to marry us."

"He's still asking?"

"Yep. Not changing my mind, though. The boy's a kid. I need him to stop acting like he's ninety. He wants to be a preacher so bad, and I can respect that, but I don't think he's ever been given a choice to be anything else but that."

"You could be right."

She sighed. "Not sure what I'm supposed to do. I feel like I'm making it up as I go along."

"You love him, he loves you. That's half the battle."

"I suppose so."

"Tell you what. Give me a kiss, and I'll let you get back to work."

"That's quite a segue, Your Honor," she said saucily.

"Have to keep you motivated." He walked over and braced his hands on the edge of the desk. "Don't want you slacking on the job."

"Can't have that," she agreed, and rose from her chair. When he took her into his arms, she placed her head against his heart. "I say we elope and run off to Tahiti."

"Be nice, but Bernadine will just find us and book the Sistine Chapel anyway."

"Probably."

He looked down into her eyes. "Did I tell you today that I love you?"

"Hmm. I think so, but be nice if you showed me."

And so, after a kiss that was slow and sweet, Trent went into his office. Grumbling about being mayor was the last thing on his mind.

A short while later, Lily drove over to the school to talk with Devon. The children were outside, working in the sunshine. Crystal, sporting her new short, feathered do, was hunched over a table with her ever-present shadow, Eli James. They appeared to be drawing something. When Crys looked up and saw Lily, she waved happily, and Lily waved back. The new hairdo was an offshoot of the injuries Crystal had suffered at the hands of her biological father, Ray Chambers. Ray was ultimately killed during a tornado, and the badly injured Crystal had to have her head shaved for the doctors to treat her concussion. Her hair was growing out, and Lily had to admit that their resident teen queen looked very fly.

Devon and Zoey were seated at another table, working on math problems along with Amari and Preston.

As she walked up, Devon turned and beamed a smile her way. "Hi, Ms. Lily."

"Hey, Devon."

She nodded in greeting to Amari and Preston. "Amari, may I talk to you and Devon for a minute, please?"

Amari went stock-still. "Are we in trouble?"

"Not with me, but is there something I need to tell your dad?"

He grinned. "No, ma'am."

Enjoying him as she always did, she led him and Devon a few steps away before she explained why she'd come.

Amari didn't seem to have a problem with her request and replied, "Sure. I told Dad I'd meet him at the garage. I can take Devon with me."

Lily turned to Devon. "Is that okay?"

He nodded, but asked, "After that can I go to Zoey's?"

Lily chose her words slowly and carefully, "I think this time you should stay with Mr. Trent and Amari until I get back. We're all going to be family soon, Dev. Be nice if we could get to know each other better."

Amari nodded as if he agreed, but Devon didn't seem convinced. "What if Zoey gets lonely? She misses her mom."

Lily could see Zoey watching them. Those big dark eyes of hers were Lily's undoing, so mentally, she threw up her hands. "Okay, Amari, take Zoey, too. I'll let Dr. Reg know."

Amari shrugged off the addition of another person to his entourage. "No problem."

"Thanks, Amari. Devon, I'll see you this evening."

As she turned to walk away she heard, "Ms. Lily. Hold up a minute. I need to talk to you." It was Preston.

When he reached her, she asked, "Hey, what's up?"

He moved a few steps farther from the others before saying quietly, "Just wanted to let you and Ms. Bernadine know that I'm searching for my birth parents."

That was not what she'd been expecting to hear, but

having lived with these exceptional kids for two years, she was learning to expect the unexpected. "Have you talked to the Paynes about this?"

He shook his head. "No."

"No?" she asked gently. "Why not?"

He shrugged as if not knowing what to say. "I don't want them to think I don't appreciate them."

"Then tell them that. They'll appreciate the honesty. Do you want to live elsewhere? Is that what this is about?"

"No," he countered quickly. "Not at all."

"Then you should tell them that, too."

He looked down at his shoes and then back up into her eyes. "Okay."

"When did you decide to do this?"

"A few nights ago. Leah thinks it's a good idea, too."

Lily scanned him for a silent moment. "So are you doing this for you, or for her?"

"Me," he replied without hesitation. "She just helped me think some things through, like what if my parents are both dead, or if they turn out to be bad people like Crystal's dad."

Lily nodded understandingly.

"But I wanted you to know in case an e-mail comes through, or something comes in the mail to Ms. Bernadine, or somebody shows up from CPS. I already registered my name on some of the sites I researched, and I posted my birthday and place of birth. That's all, though."

"Are you sure you're going to be okay with the outcome? This might turn out to be wonderful, or something that breaks your heart."

"I know, but I want to know. I'm tired of not knowing

who I am. Zoey knew her mom, and so did Crystal. Devon had his grandma. Amari and I are the only ones who don't have a clue."

Lily's heart went out to him. "Does Amari know about this?"

"Not yet. I haven't told him either, but I will. Maybe later tonight on the phone."

"Okay. I'll let Ms. Bernadine know, but I want you to promise me that you will sit down with the Paynes and tell them what you're doing. They're your parents, Brain. They should know, and will probably want to help. Promise me," she echoed, making sure he met her eyes.

He nodded tightly. "I will. I promise. I'll talk to them after school."

She gave him a quick hug. "I'm rooting for you on this. If there's anything Ms. Bernadine or I can do, let us know."

He gave her a smile. "I promise that, too."

She gave him another quick, tight squeeze. He nodded good-bye, and she resumed her journey to her car.

But as she crossed the parking lot to where it sat, someone else called her name. Once again, she stopped and turned. At this rate, Bernadine was liable to fly off without her.

Gary Clark was waving at her from the driver's side of his sweet new Buick. He'd gone to high school with her and Trent, but lived now over in Franklin. He drove slowly over to where she stood.

"Hey, Gare. How are you?" The last time she'd seen him had been over the summer at the dedication of the new school.

"Been better."

"What's the matter?"

"Just enrolled the girls in school here. We're moving back to Henry Adams."

Before Lily could form a reaction, he added, "And you may as well know, Colleen left me. She wants a divorce." His pain was obvious.

"I'm so sorry." Colleen was his witch of a wife. Lily had known her in high school, too.

"How in the hell am I supposed to raise two teenage girls alone?" he asked, and ran a hand wearily over his tired face.

"She's not asking for custody?"

He blew out a breath of disgust. "Please. No."

Lily didn't know what to say.

He shrugged. "I'm broke, Lil. The company shut down my dealership. Between that and the way Colleen has been spending, and the hits I took on the company stock . . ." His eyes were bleak. "We have no place to go, so the girls and I have to move back into my parents' old place. I drove out and looked at it yesterday. It's been empty for so long, it's a mess. Mice nests, snakes. Rotting wood. We're staying out at a motel on 183 for now."

Lily's first reaction was to whip out her phone and call Bernadine, but something stopped her. Gary talking to Trent might be better. "Have you talked to Trent about this?"

"No."

"You should."

He shook his head. "A man's got his pride."

"And this pride is going to clothe and feed your daughters how?"

The pointed question made him turn away and stare sightlessly off out into the plains.

Lily waited.

He finally met her eyes and gave her a soft smile. "You haven't changed a bit, have you, Fontaine? Always straight to the point."

"No sense in messing around."

"Or putting lipstick on a pig."

"Or anything else. Talk to Trent, please, Gary. You were best friends. He'll figure out a way to help you."

"And if I don't talk to him?"

"Then I will."

He sighed and chuckled. "Okay."

"Today, Gary," she warned as she walked to her car.

"Okay. Lily. Okay."

She gave him a wave before she drove back to the Power Plant like a bat out of hell. Her quick trip to the school had taken longer than she'd planned. First Preston and now the Clarks. She and the Boss Lady were going to have a whole lot to talk about on the flight down to Miami.

CHAPTER
3

When it was time for Lily and Bernadine to head off to the airport, Trent walked them out to the waiting town car, where the hired driver, Nathan, dressed in a sharp blue suit, stood at the ready. Lily gave Trent a kiss good-bye.

Bernadine gave him a hug and a humor-filled warning, "Tell folks I expect this place to be still standing when I get back."

"With Genevieve on the warpath, that might be hard."

Both women responded with puzzled looks.

"You haven't heard about the Thrilla in Manila at the Dog this morning? Genevieve knocked Riley smooth out."

Lily tried to contain her chuckles but failed.

"What?" Bernadine asked, as if maybe she hadn't heard him correctly.

"Out cold." He gave them a quick rundown of the morning's drama, and when he was done, they both sighed.

"Okay," Bernadine said, shaking her head. "If Riley

presses charges and she's arrested, take care of the bail if she needs help."

"Will do. Have a safe flight."

Lily quipped. "Keep your head down."

"And my dukes up."

Nathan closed them in and drove them away.

Trent went back to his office and used the rest of the morning to pore over the paperwork tied to the new sewer system planned for the spring. The project was necessary if the dream to revitalize the once-thriving Main Street was to be achieved. Presently, the only building from those glory days still standing was the sagging hulk that in the 1880s had been the Henry Adams hotel. There were hopes to revive it, too, someday, but pipes for water and sewage had to be laid first.

"Knock, knock."

He looked up to see Rocky standing in the doorway.

"Got a minute?" she asked.

"Sure. Come on in."

She took a seat.

Trent waited for her to tell him the reason for her visit, but she remained silent. Wondering if she was waiting on him to begin the conversation, which didn't make any sense, he asked, "How'd the mess with Riley and Genevieve turn out?"

"Soon as Reg got him back on his feet, Gennie knocked him out again. Crumbled like a wet cotton sheet."

In spite of her answer, Trent got the impression that her mind was elsewhere. "Rock? You okay?"

"No," she replied and turned to meet his eyes. "Why does he keep asking me out?"

"Who?"

"Jack."

"Ah."

"Don't ah me. I've told him no a hundred times, and he keeps coming back."

Trent viewed her with humor and affection. "Man's sweet on you."

"I need him to be sweet on somebody else."

"What's wrong with him?"

She folded her arms tightly across her chest and sighed with frustration. "In truth, nothing. And that's why I keep trying to run him off."

Trent never claimed to understand the women in Henry Adams, or anywhere else, for that matter; after all, he'd been divorced twice. "I'm sure there's logic behind that answer somewhere, but you'll have to explain it to me."

"He's nice, Trent."

"And?"

"I'm vulnerable to nice."

He still didn't get it. "More logic, please."

She rolled her eyes. "Never mind."

And before he could say anything else, she got up and walked out.

He wondered if there was something in the town's water that made the females around him so special. First Genevieve, and now Rocky. The only woman who seemed relatively sane was the colonel's wife, Sheila, and that was because she'd yet to show any personality at all, but Tamar, Bernadine, or Lily could always be counted on to take up the slack.

He was still pondering Rocky's visit when another knock

sounded. Seeing Gary Clark standing in the doorway, he stood up and said with surprise, "Hey. How are you?"

Gary shrugged. "Need to talk to you about something."

The emotion on his old friend's face was plain. "Come on in."

Gary glanced around the well-furnished office. "Nice place you got here."

"I think so, too. Blame it on Fontaine. She picked out most of the stuff. Have a seat."

Gary chose one of the plush brown leather chairs.

Trent rested his hip on the edge of his desk and folded his arms. "How're things going?"

"Not so good."

"What do you mean?"

Trent listened as Gary told him the same story he'd told Lily, and finished up by confessing. "Only reason I'm here is because Fontaine threatened to tell you all this if I didn't."

"Kudos to her. It's what friends are for."

"You'd think she'd've grown out of being so bossy."

Trent laughed. "I know, but that's part of her charm." He brought the conversation back to the topic at hand. "How much work do you think your parents' place is going to need before you can move back in?"

"More than I can afford, that's for sure. Thousands more, probably."

"Then let's take a ride out there. Once I get a look, I can make a rough estimate of what it's going to cost."

"Doesn't matter, Trent, I can't afford it."

"Who said anything about you being able to pay?"

Gary went still.

Trent said, "I know you'd rather eat rat poison than take charity, but let me make a phone call. I know a place where you and the girls can probably stay until we get your place back in shape."

"Trent—"

Trent turned away and called Tamar. After a short conversation with her, he closed his phone. "Okay. Found you a place."

"Where?" Gary asked with wonder on his face and in his voice.

"The town owns some trailers out on Tamar's property that are used for emergencies like this. They're fully furnished, and Tamar's on her way to the grocery store in Franklin to fill the fridge."

His mouth dropped. "But—"

"No buts allowed. Your family has been here longer than mine, Gary. You're my friend, and you need help. I'd hope you'd do the same for me and my family if the shoe was on the other foot."

"You know I would, but I can't pay for any of this."

"We'll figure out something when the time comes. For now, consider yourself and the girls guests of the mayor. You want to drive, or shall I?"

Gary seemed frozen by the generosity. He finally said, "You."

Trent picked up his keys and walked to the door, but Gary still hadn't moved. He was still staring at Trent with wonder.

"You coming or not?"

Gary shook himself free. "Yeah. Yeah, I'm coming."

*   *   *

The old Clark place was in as bad a shape as Gary had predicted. Everything from the roof to the support beams to the storm cellar needed replacing. Walking carefully over rotting floorboards and through spiderwebs the size of bird's nests, Trent used the beam of his flashlight to assess the interior as best he could. The small two-story home hadn't been occupied since Gary's folks died within days of each other back in 1992.

Outside now, Trent grabbed a hand towel from his truck and ran it over his hair to rid it of the dust and cobwebs. He handed one to Gary, who did the same.

Gary asked, "So what do you think?"

Trent tilted up a bottle of water to wash the dust out of his throat. "Depends on what you want to do." He handed a bottle to Gary. "If you plan to stay here, I see two choices. We can either have everybody pitch in to rebuild it, or you can have Bernadine build you a new place in the sub."

He stared again and croaked, "A new place?"

"There are plenty of plots."

"But I don't even have a job, how am I going to pay for a new house?"

Trent sighed. How to explain Bernadine to someone who had yet to benefit from her blessings? "Money is not the issue here right now. Getting you and your family up and running is. We can work out payment sometime in the future, if that's what you want."

"But—"

"No buts allowed, remember? Do you have any job prospects, or is there something you always wanted to do?"

"Like what?"

Trent shrugged. "If a djinn gave you a wish, and you could be anything in the world you wanted to be, what would it be?"

He laughed. "I don't know."

"Think about it, and if it benefits the town in some way, all the better."

Gary shook his head. "The way you talk, it's like Henry Adams is made out of money."

"You don't know the half of it."

They stood silent for a moment and scanned the old house. Trent smiled at a memory that came to mind. "Remember when we had your sixteenth birthday party here?"

Gary laughed and choked on the swallow of water he'd just taken in. "Twenty minutes after the party started, my mother found out we'd spiked the punch and shut us down. Sent everybody home."

"Shortest sweet sixteen party in town history."

"Maybelle Clark was a pistol."

"Your old man was no slouch, either. Remember the day he head-butted Mal during the Super Bowl because Mal said Terry Bradshaw couldn't read?"

Gary laughed. "Forgot about that. He was something." Gary quieted for a moment, as if thinking back. "Pops would say I'd made a mess of my life."

"I don't think he would."

"He wanted me to be the first Clark to study law. And then I met Colleen."

Trent stayed quiet.

"Who knew that hiding beneath all that beauty was the Wicked Witch of the West?" Gary asked bitterly. "When she told me she was pregnant, I stepped up. It's what a man's supposed to do, right?"

"You did the honorable thing."

"Some honor. Told me three days after the wedding that she'd lost the baby. I should have split then, but when her father offered me part ownership of the dealership . . ." His words trailed off as if he didn't need to explain more. "My father never liked her or her family."

Trent hadn't either, but he kept that to himself. "So now, you get to do what you always wanted to do, whatever it is."

"I'll have to think on that one. When can I see this trailer?"

"Now if you like. Tamar said she'd leave the keys out. Rocky lives in one of the other trailers, so you'll have her as a neighbor."

"What happened between her and Bobby Lee? One minute I hear she's married. Next thing she's divorced, gone, and now she's back."

"You'll have to ask her." No way was Trent going to reveal that Rocky had divorced Bob because she found him wearing her underwear. If she chose to share with Gary, she would.

"It's going to be strange living here again after all this time away. When you and I were growing up, we swore we'd leave Graham County and never come back, remember?"

"I do. Glad to be back, though."

"Me, too."

They spent a few more minutes looking at Gary's old house and talking about the past before he turned to Trent and said in words that sounded like they came from deep in his heart, "Thanks, man."

"It's what friends are for. Now let's get over to Tamar's

and pick up your keys so that you and your girls can get out of that motel."

Gary nodded solemnly.

As they got back in the truck, Trent didn't remark on the tears standing in Gary's eyes, because that's what friends were for, too.

After spending the flight discussing Genevieve, Riley, Preston, the Clarks, and the rest of the Henry Adams goings-on, Lily looked out the window as Bernadine's snow-white jet touched down at a small private airport outside Miami. Once they deplaned, they entered a sleek black town car and were whisked away.

The meeting with the banker was to be held not in an office building but at a beautiful estate on the water. As the hired car moved slowly past the armed security guards posted at the entrance of the elaborate wrought-iron gates, Lily could feel her eyes starting to bug at the surroundings, but she took her cue from Bernadine and acted as if she traveled to swanky places like this on a regular basis. Inwardly, however, she was awed by the riotous colors of the lush tropical flowers lining the cobbled drive, the beautiful fountains, and the glimpses of the blue ocean that dotted the way. "Who lives here?"

"Tina Craig."

Lily paused, surprised. "Your friend Tina, who helped us get Tamar's land back from Morton Prell before Cletus sat on him and killed him?"

"Yep. She heads up the investment committee for the Bottom Women's Society, and this land buy is her baby."

The Bottom Women's Society was an organization whose members were the divorced first wives of some of the wealthiest men in the world. Collectively they had their expensively manicured fingers in every pie, from technology to real estate to micro loans awarded to female business owners in developing countries. The society also threw one heck of an annual convention, as Lily found out when she and Crystal attended last summer's bash as Bernadine's guests.

The car eased to a halt at the front entrance of the pink brick mansion, and all Lily could do was stare, impressed by the sprawling beauty of the home and the lush surrounding grounds. "You all live very, very large," Lily noted aloud.

Bernadine's eyes twinkled. "Have to do something with all this money."

The driver opened the door and politely handed them both out. A tall, tanned, dark-haired woman dressed in a flowing white tunic and matching capris hurried out of the front door to meet them. She had gold hanging from her ears, neck, and wrists, and jeweled sandals on her bare feet.

"Bernadine!" she screamed. The two embraced with affection and glee while Lily looked on with a smile.

Bernadine introduced Lily.

Tina said, "Lily Fontaine. I talked with you on the phone when we were dealing with that old thief Prell."

"Yes. It's nice to finally meet you."

"Same here. Love that name. Lily Fontaine. Like I said before, sounds like one of those old burlesque queens."

They were led through a covered brick archway that opened out onto a large outdoor room facing the ocean.

"Oh, my goodness," Lily said, blown away. "Would you look at the view!"

The water was as blue as a jewel, and the white sails of ships could be seen off in the distance. It was so quiet you could hear the breeze.

"Main reason I purchased this land," Tina confessed. "Told the architect, if she couldn't build me a house on this bluff, then find me someone who could." Tina then went silent for a few moments before adding, "Lots of peace here."

"It is beautiful," Bernadine replied.

Lily agreed. She imagined standing arm in arm with Trent and looking out at the view while surrounded by the beauty and silence. If Bernadine could find a place like this for the honeymoon, Lily would gladly let her foot the bill.

When Lily came back to the present, Tina was directing Bernadine over to a table that held a full-scale model of a sprawling, Vegas-style hotel and apartment complex. Curious, she strolled over to join them.

"This is nice," Bernadine declared, slowly walking around the rendering to get a full view. "Very nice. How much are we throwing in apiece?"

Tina quoted a number that made Lily's eyes roll back in her head, but Bernadine didn't even blink.

"The city has already purchased the property," Tina told her. "Soon as all the legal beagles are done barking at each other, we just have to sign the contract and transfer our funds to the developer's account."

Bernadine looked up from the model and asked quietly, "So why do I get the impression that something's not quite right?"

"You are good, B," Tina declared, smiling.

Bernadine inclined her head as if acknowledging the fact. "So what's up?"

Before answering, Tina gestured them to take seats and then poured three glasses of ice-cold sangria from a chilled glass pitcher sitting on top of a tea cart. She passed them their drinks and sat down with her own. "Everybody knows that profit is my middle name. Always has been."

"True," Bernadine replied.

"But the older I get, the more I wonder if maybe pursuing profit with a lowercase p instead of a capital P is better for my soul." She looked Bernadine's way and asked, "Do you know what I mean?"

"I do. It's sort of what I'm doing with Henry Adams."

"Yes, exactly."

"So what is it about this development that has you second-guessing yourself?"

"One of the places the city will be demolishing is an old church. Can't be good karma in that," she noted sagely before taking a sip from her glass.

"Is the church closed or occupied?" Lily asked.

"Services every Sunday."

Bernadine looked to Lily, who simply shrugged in reply, but Lily had to agree with Tina. Bulldozing a church so that a bunch of developers could put up a luxury hotel just didn't seem right.

"Have you talked to whoever the pastor is?" Bernadine wanted to know.

"No, but I did talk to the head bishop."

"He going to fight the city over the plan?"

Tina shook her head. "No. He said the diocese, I think he called it, thought they were given a fair price for the land, and that they looked forward to doing good things with the payment."

"Sounds reasonable, but I understand what you're feeling. I'm willing to let you make the call on this. If you want to take our money elsewhere, that's fine with me."

"That's what the other members said, too."

"Then take some time and think it over. All this peace here—you'll make the right choice."

"Thanks, Bernadine."

"No problem. Maybe I'll have our driver take us by the church so I can get a look at it, too."

"It was probably gorgeous in its prime, but time hasn't been kind. You'll see why the bishop was so willing to sell."

They spent a few more minutes talking about the model's potential and catching each other up on some of the organization's doings and gossip, and then it was time for Lily and Bernadine to leave.

Tina shared a long tight hug with Bernadine and gave Lily a hug as well.

"I hear you're getting married, Lily."

Lily shot Bernadine a questioning look.

"Guilty as charged."

Tina said, "Congratulations."

"Thank you. He's a very special man."

"You've been a godsend to Bernadine, so if there is anything I can do to help make your wedding-day dreams come true, just let me know."

All Lily could think was now she had two got-rocks

women wanting to help, but aloud, she said genuinely, "I will, Tina. Thank you."

Tina walked them to the car and waved until they were out of sight.

Bernadine gave the driver the church's address and said to Lily, "Let's do that first, and we'll tackle Mission Zoey next."

Lily agreed, but she didn't hold out much hope for getting answers on Zoey. On the flight down, they'd talked to Roni in New York, and she was sending them lots of luck and love. Lily promised her she'd call right away if anything turned up.

They settled in for the ride, and Bernadine glanced her way. "Tina meant what she said about the wedding."

"I know, and I'm not sure who scares me most, her or you."

When the driver pulled up in front of the church, Lily looked out at the crumbling old building and the desolate neighborhood its weathered spires rose above. She agreed with Tina that it probably had been grand in its heyday, but now the Gothic carved doors looked to welcome only the tired and poor.

"It is in pretty bad shape," Bernadine remarked solemnly.

"Yes, it is. What do you want to do?"

"Not sure, but let's go in and see if we can find somebody to talk to about the sale." She asked the driver, "Is there a parking lot?"

"Yep."

"Pull in, then. We're going to run in."

"Not the best neighborhood."

"No, it isn't," Bernadine agreed.

They could see young men lounging in doorways. They

and everyone else moving along the trash-cluttered street were eyeing the big fine car.

Lily asked the driver. "Will you be okay?"

"Ladies, I am armed and dangerous. You two go on in. I'll be fine here until you get back."

With those words of assurance, Lily and Bernadine left the car and walked across the lot to the nearest door. Due to the questionable neighborhood, Lily expected to find the steel door locked, but it opened easily.

Inside they were met by an echoing silence that seemed to resonate to the soul. To their left lay the sanctuary with its dark wood pews, but instead of rows of pews leading to the altar and the pulpit, there were only five pews, and none were near any of the others.

"Look at the cross, Lily."

Bernadine's soft voice drew her eyes up to the large cross hanging on the wall high above the simple altar. It appeared to be made from two old pieces of wood that might have come from an alley or from someone's garage. "Found wood" is what Trent would have probably called it. The sight of it was both moving and heartbreaking.

"Whoever is in charge here has been making a way out of no way, Bernadine."

"Amen."

From somewhere within the building came the sound of a woman's voice singing Yolanda Adams's "I'm Gonna Be Ready."

"Nice voice. Alto."

Bernadine nodded with agreement before calling out, "Hello!"

The singing stopped, followed by, "Hold on. I'll be right there."

While they waited, Lily looked around the sanctuary again and took in the peeling plaster, the three boarded-up windows, and the two intact ones guarded by security bars. Tina said there was a service held every Sunday, but Lily couldn't help but wonder how many people attended.

Around the corner came a fast-walking, short, thin, brown-skinned woman. She was wearing a ball cap, a black short-sleeved shirt topped by a white clerical collar, dust-covered jeans, and red cowboy boots. She appeared to be in her forties, but women of color aged so gracefully that it was hard to determine if the estimate was true or not.

The woman glanced curiously between Lily and Bernadine. "Good afternoon. Can I help you?"

"Are you the pastor?" Bernadine asked.

"Yes. I'm Reverend Paula Grant."

Bernadine introduced herself and then Lily. "Would it be okay if Lily and I talked to you about the sale of the church?"

The women studied Bernadine for a long moment. "May I ask why?"

"I'm one of the potential investors in the development going up, and I want to make sure my friends and I are doing the right thing."

The priest seemed to evaluate them and the request. She finally gestured. "This way. We'll talk in my office."

It was a tiny, cramped space filled with old furniture and a large number of open, half-packed boxes. Dark wood that matched the wood of the pews in the sanctuary made up the office's built-in bookcases. From the open spaces on the shelves and what Lily could see of the contents in the boxes, the books were being packed away.

The reverend moved some of the boxes to reveal the chairs hidden beneath. Bernadine and Lily took seats, and she went behind her desk to an old leather recliner. "So what would you like to know?"

"Are you okay with the sale?"

"No, but my bishop made a strong case for why he wouldn't be opposing it, so I'm packing up. Not much else I can do."

"How long before you have to leave?"

"Officially, the church will be padlocked in less than thirty days."

Lily could tell that she was deeply saddened by the news. "Where do you go from here?"

She shrugged. "Honestly, I don't know. The bishop has no other church for me, so I'll have to wait and see where the Spirit leads me next." She studied Bernadine for a moment before adding, "I don't think I've ever heard of a Black woman having the cash to invest at the level the city is asking from the developers."

"There are a few of us out here. I'm with a group of female investors made up of women of all races and creeds."

"The fact that you stopped by says a lot to me about your group's moral values."

"We try to do no harm."

The reverend nodded understandingly.

"I have one more request," Bernadine said to her. "And then we'll leave you in peace."

"Sure. What is it?"

Bernadine fished around in her tote for the picture of Zoey and handed it to the priest.

The reverend's eyes widened. "Where'd you get this?"

Lily and Bernadine sat straight up, and Bernadine said warily, "Please, tell us that you know her."

"I do," she responded softly. "Is she alive?"

"Alive and well."

There were tears standing in the reverend's eyes. "Oh, my goodness. Zoey. I was so worried when she and Bonnie stopped coming around. Where're they living?"

"How well did you know them?"

"I knew them very well. Bonnie played the organ here on Sundays, with Zoey sitting right beside her." She met their eyes and came to her own conclusion. "Bonnie's dead, isn't she?"

They nodded.

She solemnly crossed herself and finally looked up from Zoey's smiling face. "Bonnie had a gift. She made our decrepit old organ sound like Carnegie Hall. Even when she showed up here some Sunday mornings so cracked out she couldn't walk straight, she'd sit down on the bench, put her hands on the keys, and you'd swear it was the angels playing. How'd she pass away?"

Bernadine and Lily related all that they knew. When they described how and where Zoey was found, the lady priest cried softly. Finally gathering herself, she said, "I used to run a soup kitchen here, and one morning, a few years back, a young woman came in with her pale-as-chalk, big-eyed daughter. Bonnie wasn't high that day, but I could tell by the rotted teeth that she was on crack. It didn't matter—she and her child were hungry, and I was there to feed them."

She paused a moment, as if the memories were taking her back to that time. "She said she wanted to pay me back for the meal. I knew she didn't have any money, but when she asked if she could play the organ on Sunday as a way to say thanks, I said sure. I didn't think for a minute that she'd actually show up, but she did, and her skill blew us away."

"Was Zoey mute when you knew her?"

"Mute? That chatterbox? Of course not."

Lily said, "She is now. Hasn't spoken a word in the two years she's been with us."

She looked puzzled. "Was it the trauma of the rats?"

Bernadine shrugged. "The doctors think so. They can't find anything physically wrong."

"So where is she living?"

They gave her a thumbnail sketch of Henry Adams and Bernadine's foster program.

The priest asked with wonder, "You own a town?" She turned to Lily. "How rich is this woman, Lily?"

"If I told you, you wouldn't believe me."

Paula shook her head in amazement.

"Tell me a bit about your background, if I'm not being too nosy," Bernadine asked.

They learned that Paula was a native Oklahoman. When she mentioned her degrees in child psychology and that she'd run her own practice, Lily's heart began to beat with excitement. A quick look Bernadine's way showed her that the Boss Lady was experiencing the same rush.

"So you've no immediate job prospects?"

"None. Your town wouldn't need a woman of the cloth, would it?"

Lily and Bernadine shared a knowing smile.

Bernadine finally replied, "Presently, we don't have a church, but I can get one built. How big do you want it to be?"

Paula waved off the remark. "I'm just kidding."

"I'm not."

Paula's smile faded. "Excuse me?"

"You just said you're unemployed, right?"

"Ever been convicted of embezzlement?" Lily wanted to know, wearing a big smile.

"No."

"Ever been convicted of anything?"

"No," Paula said, glancing between the two visitors as if she wasn't real sure what was going on.

Bernadine declared, "Then at the conclusion of a positive background check, consider yourself hired."

She stared dumbstruck. "Just like that? Wait a minute."

Lily's eyes were dancing with laughter. "Welcome to the world of Bernadine Brown, Reverend Grant. Glad to have you aboard."

While Bernadine continued to reassure the priest that they were indeed serious about hiring her, Lily pulled out her phone and speed-dialed a three-way between Roni in New York and Reggie in Henry Adams to tell them who they'd found.

CHAPTER
4

True to her word, Tamar had left the keys to the trailer on the kitchen table. Once Trent and Gary were inside, Gary glanced around and whistled appreciatively.

"Wow. When you said trailer, I wasn't expecting anything this classy." He peeked in at the kitchen area, then walked to the rooms in the back. "There are three bedrooms," he called out excitedly.

"Yep. The girls won't have to share."

Gary came back to where Trent stood. "I like this. They'll like this."

"How are they handling the split between you and Colleen?"

"Leah seems okay, nothing really throws her, and to tell you the truth, she and her mother have never connected. Now, Tiff? She's having issues. Keeps asking me when Colleen's coming back. No matter how many times I tell her the truth, she doesn't want to believe me. Tells me that if I just apologize to Colleen for whatever it is I did to make her mad, she'll come back."

Trent shook his head sadly. "That's rough."

"Yep. Tried explaining that her mother is the one driving all this, but she won't believe that, either. Tiff's always been Colleen's favorite, and she's devastated, as well she should be."

"I've been divorced twice, and as much as I wanted kids, I'm glad we didn't have any."

"And now you're going to have what, three sons."

"Yep. Going from zero to sixty in a blink." Although Davis was grown and wouldn't need Trent's hand in his life, Devon and Amari would be his to parent for some time to come.

"That has to be a little weird."

"It is, but it's a good weird. I'm kind of excited, to tell you the truth."

"Me? I'm scared to death. I don't have a clue how to raise those girls."

"First, you might start by claiming them. They're no longer 'those girls,' they're 'your girls.'"

Gary nodded. "Point taken. Colleen's done all the parenting up until now. All she ever allowed me to do was stay out of the way."

"Now you are the way, and remember, there are plenty of females around here who'll help. Don't be afraid to reach out. Tamar is always looking for someone to give fits to."

Gary chuckled. "Man, she wore us out back in the day."

"Yes, she did. She's doing the same to Amari and Preston. They try and sneak by her, hoping she won't see them and give them something to do, but they've learned. She sees all."

They shared a smile.

Trent said, "How about we pick up some lunch at the Dog and take it over to the garage so I can show you the car Amari and I are going to be working on?"

"Sounds good."

Trent watched Gary take one last long look around the trailer's interior as if he was enjoying the prospect of moving in, then the two left to drive over to the Dog.

Over lunch they sat and talked about the old T-Bird Trent planned to restore and about life. "We have a fathers' support group here, too, now," Trent informed him. "You might want to come to a meeting and check us out."

"A support group?"

"Yeah," Trent replied before taking a bite out of the big burger known as Rocky's Deluxe. "We meet once a week. Keeps us from going insane while we raise these kids."

"I may need that."

"You will need that, trust me," Trent countered and told Gary where they met and when.

"I'll see if I can make the next meeting."

Later, after more reminiscing and talk of the future, Gary glanced down at his watch. "School lets out in a bit. I need to get back over to Franklin and pick up the girls. Last day for them at the school there."

"Hope things go well when they start here tomorrow."

"Me, too." Gary stood and said quietly, "Thanks, Trent. For everything."

"No problem. Let me know when you're ready to move. I'll help."

"Will do."

"Looking forward to kicking your butt in horseshoes when summer rolls back around, too."

"You wish," Gary replied with a grin. "I'll give you a call in the morning."

Gary departed, and Trent was left to ponder the town's newest resident. They'd been best friends growing up; close as brothers, folks would say, then separated by life and time. Now they were on the road to renewing their friendship. In a way, it mirrored Trent's relationship with Lily; the old and the new.

His reverie was broken by the arrival of Amari strolling in with Devon and Zoey.

"Hey, Dad."

"Hey, you." Trent turned his smile on Devon and Zoey. "Hey, you two, too."

All three kids grinned.

"How was the day?" he asked

"Can we have juice boxes first?" Amari asked.

"Sure can."

While Amari went to the old stand-up fridge Trent had resurrected from Tamar's barn, Trent gestured Zoey and Devon toward the old leather couch against the wall. They took seats. Amari passed out the juice and then pulled up one of the ancient lawn chairs that also served as seating. Trent could see Zoey's eyes darting around as she took in the orderly but still chaotic interior of his domain. He couldn't remember if she'd ever been inside, but the way she was looking around made him think she hadn't. In the center of the room, hidden beneath a large brown tarp, sat the car he and Amari were restoring. He watched as she studied that, too. Devon, on the other hand, looked very uncomfortable. Why, Trent didn't know.

"Was that Mr. Clark I saw leaving?" Amari asked, bringing Trent's attention back.

"Yeah."

"Preston says the Clarks may be moving here soon."

"He's right. In fact, the girls will start school here tomorrow."

Alarm filled Amari's eyes. "What! No! Why?"

"Because kids who live here go to school here. They'll be moving into one of the trailers on Tamar's land."

"How long are they staying?"

Trent shrugged. "Forever, maybe."

"No! I hate that girl."

"Hate's a pretty strong word, son."

"I know, but it's how I feel. Leah's okay, but what's her name? Tiffany Adele. She still sounds like a store in the mall, and she's mean."

"I understand, but cut her some slack if you can. She and her family are having a rough time right now."

Amari slumped down in his chair. "She's going to be meaner than ever then."

"Maybe, maybe not. Coming to a new school, she'll need some friends, though, probably."

"Better find her a pen pal, because I'm not it."

Devon piped up, "Zoey and I will be her friends, Mr. Trent. Won't we, Zoey?"

Zoey nodded enthusiastically around the plastic straw between her lips.

Amari responded with a roll of his eyes. "You're too young to even know what this is about."

Trent ignored his son's grousing and replied to Devon's offer, "Thanks, Dev. You, too, Zoey."

"You're welcome, Mr. Trent."

Amari shot Devon a withering look before asking, "Is this family trouble something a kid like me can be told about?"

"I suppose. Their parents are getting a divorce."

Amari paused. "Oh. That's rough."

"Which is why I'd appreciate it if you'd try and be nice to her when you see her in school tomorrow."

"Okay, but if she goes off on me, all bets are off."

"That's fair, but sometimes you have to keep offering the olive branch."

"Olive branch? What's that got to do with this?"

"Stands for peace."

"Anybody ever get smacked with one?"

Over on the couch, Devon and Zoey were signing back and forth, and it looked as if they were having a pretty heated argument. Bernadine had arranged American Sign Language classes for everyone who wanted to better communicate with Zoey. Reg, Roni, and Bernadine were very good, but Trent was a long way from mastering it. Devon, however, ruled. Trent asked Amari, "What's going on over there?"

Amari watched them for a moment. "Not sure, they're moving too fast, but whatever it is, Zo isn't feeling it. She's saying, 'No, you dummy!'" Amari laughed so hard he almost fell off his chair.

Trent grinned, too. "Devon," he called. "What's up? What are you and Zoey arguing about?"

Devon turned to Trent, "I told her it's time for us to go to her house now."

"And what is she saying?"

Zoey quickly held up her hand in a silencing motion and scooted off the couch. She walked over to Trent's cluttered desk, where she picked up a pad of sticky notes and a pen and took a moment to write something. Done, she handed it to Trent and waited while he read: *I want to stay here and work on cars!!*

He looked down at her determined face and matching folded arms. "Yep. When you grow up you are going to fit right in with these wild women around here. Has to be in the water."

"What's it say?" Amari asked.

Still looking down into the pleased brown eyes of Miss Zoey Raymond Garland, he handed the note to his son.

Amari read her words and crowed, "Go 'head, Zoey. Can she help, Dad?"

"I don't see why not."

Trent looked over at Devon. "Ever worked with your hands, Devon?"

"Just to preach the Word and to pray."

"Good grief," Amari mumbled under his breath.

"You might like working on cars."

"I can't get dirty."

"Why not?"

"I have on my suit," he pointed out, as if no other explanation was necessary.

Trent could see Amari watching him and waiting to see how he'd respond. "I don't think you'll get that dirty. Take off your coat, and you can work over here with me. Amari, you get Zoey."

Amari responded with, "Cool. Grab that bucket, Zoey, and then I'll get you some gear to put on. Safety is top dog around here."

It pleased Trent to hear Amari introducing Zoey to the work with such concern and care. Rocky's father had once owned the garage, and she had worked with him on everything from fancy sports cars to big rigs. He'd have to remember to tell her that Zoey appeared to be following in her footsteps.

Devon, however, was a whole different model. He was removing his jacket, but if his tight-set jaw was any indication, he wasn't liking it. That was okay with Trent. At least the boy was showing some emotion. Like Lily, Trent respected Devon's desire to spread the Gospel, but he also agreed that the kid needed to work on being a kid first.

Amari returned with Zoey, now decked out in gloves, safety glasses, and a long apron. Everything was way too big. If her interest in cars proved true, Trent would get her some gear that fit. "Looking good, Zoey."

She shot him a grin and held up her gloved hands.

Amari handed Devon an apron, gloves, and glasses, too. "Put 'em on."

Devon studied the pile of items in his hands, looked up miserably at Trent, and woodenly followed Amari's instructions.

"You'd think I was making you face a dragon, son."

"I don't want to do this, Mr. Trent."

"I get that part, but life is about trying new things, Devon."

"I don't like new things."

"I can see that."

Amari asked, "Can I take off the wrap now, Dad, please? Zoey and I are ready to get to work."

Trent nodded permission and watched Amari slowly draw back the canvas tarp to reveal the beat-up old car hidden beneath.

"This, Zoey," Amari announced with a flourish, "is a 1964 Thunderbird." As he went on to regale her with the T-Bird's manufacturing specs and history, Zoey glanced back and forth between him and the car.

"It might look a hoopty now," Amari continued, "but once we Julys get through with it, it'll be sweet and good as new. Right, Dad?"

"Absolutely."

Zoey's large eyes filled the goggles.

Devon, on the other hand, looked bored, or put-upon; Trent couldn't decide which, but that was okay, too.

The old relic belonged to Bing Shepard and hadn't run in decades. Trent had been trying for years to convince Bing it would be roadworthy again once it was restored. Bing remained skeptical but had given Trent permission to try. First thing they needed to do was remove all the old hardware, like the door handles, mirrors, bumpers, and hubcaps. That would be Amari and Zoey's job. Amari had worked with Trent on the restoration of Black Beauty, Trent's old high school ride, so he was confident that Amari could do his part without much oversight.

Trent's focus would be the engine. It would have to be taken out and replaced. "Devon, go inside and pop the hood."

Devon looked at him blankly.

Amari glanced up from the mirror he and Zoey were removing, put down his screwdriver, and said to Devon, "Come
here. I'll show you."

Devon walked around the car, and Amari opened the
door. "See that lever right there? Pull it."

But Devon took one look at all the dirt and dust covering
the seat in the car's dark interior and backed away.

Zoey blew out an exasperated breath, pushed past Devon,
and slid into the seat. Trent could barely see her little face
above the steering wheel, but he loved her fearlessness.

Amari bent down to show her the lever. Following his
quick instructions, she hit the lever and the hood released.

"Good job, Zoey." Trent raised the hood to its maximum
height and set the stick that would keep it open so he could
work.

Devon was staring down at his shoes.

"Okay, Devon. Come see."

He complied, albeit reluctantly.

Soon, the garage was filled with the sounds of the air
blasts from the pneumatic tools, the jazz from the CD player,
and Amari telling Zoey all about how he'd helped restore
Black Beauty.

While they all worked, Trent couldn't help but inwardly
smile at his two new helpers. Every time Trent handed Devon
something that was covered with grime and gunk to put in the
bucket he was manning, Devon handled it as if it were a snake
or something else he didn't want to touch. Zoey, on the other
hand, appeared to be having a ball. Trent had no idea how
she'd gotten the streaks of oil and dirt on her face just helping
with hardware removal, but she looked like a Lakota painted

up for war. Her skinny little arms didn't have a lot of strength, but she was putting all she had into the socket wrenches in her effort to remove some of the more stubborn screws.

Trent tried to engage Devon in conversation, but the boy didn't say much, so Trent didn't press.

They'd been at it for about an hour when Dr. Reg walked in. "Oh, wow!" he exclaimed as he took in the old Thunderbird. "My aunt had one of these." Only then did he see Zoey. "Wow," he said again with a big grin. "Zoey, look at you. You look like Mechanic Barbie."

Her face lit up like fireworks, and he laughed in reply. "Came to take you home."

Disappointment instantly replaced her joy, so Trent said, "Zo, you can come back anytime. Okay?"

As she removed her gloves and the rest of her safety attire, her lip was on the ground.

Reggie and Trent shared a grin, and Reg said, "Trent, can I talk to you outside for a minute."

"Sure. Hold on. Amari, would you get the Lava soap and help Zoey clean that grease off her hands and face?"

"Sure, Dad."

When Devon began to remove his apron, Trent asked, "What are you doing?"

"I'm going with Zoey."

"Nope. You get to hang with me and Amari until Lily comes home, remember? Take a break. I'll be right back."

Devon pouted, but Trent ignored him and stepped outside to have the talk with Reg.

Once they were there, Reg told him about the call he'd received from Lily.

Trent was amazed. "They actually found somebody who knew Zoey and her mom? That's great news."

"Sure is. The woman is a priest, and according to her, Zoey wasn't mute when she knew her."

"Do you think Zoey will remember her?"

He shrugged. "We'll have to wait and see, but Bernadine, being Bernadine, has hired the priest and is going to build her a church. At least we now know that Zoey did talk once upon a time."

Trent was very pleased with the news.

"I kind of like the idea of us getting a church and a real pastor."

"So do I." Trent had never been a very religious man, but he was convinced that a church would add another rock to the foundation they were trying to rebuild in Henry Adams.

Reg asked, "Think Devon's going to be upset?"

"We'll have to wait and see on that, too. Did Lily say whether they were on the way back or not?"

"No. But I can take Devon home with us now if you want."

"That's okay. He and I need to work on being dad and son, so he's going to hang with me and Amari."

"Good idea. I know how close he and Zo are, but they both need to widen their horizons."

"Like this interest she seems to have in cars. Who'd've ever thought."

"Certainly not me. Looks like we might have a car-fixing musical genius on our hands."

"Could be, but I'm serious about her helping out here if

she wants. She's been beaming the entire time. Good little worker, too."

"You sure she won't be in the way?"

"Positive."

"Okay. Let's see if she asks to come back. Devon's going to have a fit if she starts spending her time here."

"He's going to be here, too. So it works out."

Reg chuckled. "Okay."

They went back inside, and there stood Zoey alongside Amari, both with their heads under the raised hood of the Thunderbird. She was standing on her toes to give herself the height she needed to see.

Amari was saying. "Now this is the carburetor. That's the fuel pump. That's the battery."

Devon was seated on the leather couch, shooting daggers their way. He looked so mad, Trent had to swallow a laugh.

Reg walked over to where the two kids were, and said gently, "Hey, Zo. Time to head home."

She looked so disappointed, and signed, *Can I come back tomorrow?*

Her dad nodded. "Sure can."

She turned to Trent and signed, *Thank you, Mr. Trent.*

Trent knew the basics, so he signed back, *You're welcome.*

She waggled a good-bye to Devon, but he turned away. Zoey looked so crushed, Trent wanted to smack the little deacon upside the head. Instead he said, "Devon, I'm going to assume you didn't see Zoey sign good-bye, so here's your second chance."

The serious set of Trent's face apparently got Devon's attention because he turned to his supposed BFF and grumbled, "Bye."

Trent thought that was a pretty pitiful second try, but he let it go, for now.

Reg and Zoey departed, and before Trent could say a word to Devon about his behavior, Amari walked over to Devon and asked testily, "What's up with you dissing your girl that way? You know you hurt her feelings, right?"

Devon squirmed on the couch.

"That was wrong, Devon. She's your sister and your best friend. Do it again, and I'm telling Tamar."

Devon's eyes widened.

Trent's did, too.

Amari wasn't done. "You're about to be a July pretty soon, so start acting like it. You might be Mr. President with Ms. Lily, but here, you're just a kid with a clip-on tie who doesn't know a tire iron from a screwdriver."

That said, he looked to his dad. "Is it okay if I go over to the Dog and hang out with the OG until you get there?"

Trent was so stunned, he stammered, "Uh, sure. I'll text you when Devon and I are on the way."

"He eating with us, too?"

Trent nodded.

Amari said with feeling, "Bye, Devon."

Devon mumbled, "Bye, Amari."

And Amari left.

In the silence that followed, Devon, looking absolutely miserable, again raised his eyes to Trent. "I'm sorry."

"I appreciate that, son, but Zoey's the one you need to apologize to."

Devon dropped his gaze again.

Trent went over and sat down beside him. After a few moments of thinking about what he wanted to say, he began, "Devon, you've been dealing with a lot since your grandma died. You've come to a new place, you have new family and friends, and you're trying to find your way. I know that Zoey has been a big part of your life here, but you can't get mad at her for wanting to do stuff that you don't."

"I don't like working on cars."

"That's fine, but Zoey does."

"We're supposed to be friends."

"And what, friends only do what you want them to do?"

He didn't respond.

"You've spent the past two years being the best friend to Zoey anybody could be. You and Amari and Preston were there for her that day she got scared by Cletus at Ms. Marie's party. You've talked for her, you've helped her with her music, and you've been a great brother, but the two of you are growing up, and as you do, your interests will change. Just because you two share a love for music and church doesn't mean she can't like working on cars."

"Girls aren't supposed to work on cars."

"Better not let Ms. Rocky hear you say that. This used to be her garage."

His eyes went wide.

"Yep. Girls can do anything you can do, except maybe write their names in the snow."

He stared.

Trent shook his head. "Never mind. Have Amari explain that to you."

He folded his arms. "Amari is the devil."

"And who were you when you turned your back on Zoey a minute ago?"

Devon went still.

"Don't judge, lest you be judged," Trent cautioned.

"You know the Bible?"

"A bit, but knowing the Bible means nothing if you don't practice what it teaches."

Devon appeared to think that over and finally responded, "I like wearing my clip-on ties."

Trent didn't call him on changing the subject. "Amari and I can teach you how to tie a real tie."

"But I don't want to tie a real tie."

Trent's eyes were lit with amusement. "All I keep hearing from you is what you don't want to do. Is there anything in this world you do want to do?"

"Yes. Get a preaching license so I can be the Henry Adams preacher and marry you and Ms. Lily."

Trent threw up his hands. He was done. "Let's get cleaned up so we can go meet Amari at the Dog."

As Devon left to wash his hands, Trent shook his head in wonder. At one time, he'd thought raising Amari would be life's biggest challenge, but he had a feeling that the little deacon with the clip-on tie was going to give him a run for his money, too.

CHAPTER
5

G riffin July guided his big Harley up the quiet tree-lined street. All the houses looked like mini mansions, and the people walking their dogs and watering their pristine lawns paused to watch him ride by as if knowing he had no business there. He supposed that a half Black, half Lakota biker wearing worn leathers and a blue bandanna won off a Seminole cousin during a poker game last year didn't fit the mold of their wealthy neighbors, but in truth, he was on business—family business.

The house he was in search of turned out to be farther up the street and on the left. He swung the bike into the drive-way, cut the engine, and pocketed the key as he got off. There was no guarantee the lady of the house would remember him, but he was betting she would, even though they hadn't seen each other in over a decade.

The doorbell was answered by an older Black woman whose brown dress and white apron made him assume she was hired help. Her startled reaction upon finding him on the porch led him to believe the household didn't get many visitors like him, but Griffin was a July and therefore polite. "Good evening, I'm here to see Mrs. Carlyle."

"Your name?"

"Griffin July."

"Wait here, please."

She disappeared, and Griffin spent a few minutes checking out the expensive surroundings and wondering how a woman he'd known as a stripper named Melody Lane wound up playing lady of the manor in a wealthy suburban enclave like this one. Her brother Jimmy said she'd married a congressman; that too was surprising.

The maid returned. "I'm sorry, but Mrs. Carlyle says she doesn't know anyone by that name."

"Give her this. I'm sure it'll jog her memory." Reaching behind his head, he unhooked the brown leather chain with its distinctive red and black beads. It had been given to him by his grandfather when he'd completed his Spirit Quest. Griffin had been wearing it around his neck since he was twelve. During the two weeks he and Melody were together, it was the only thing he'd worn. The skeptical-looking maid took the chain and disappeared again.

When she returned, Melody was at her side. The look in her brown eyes could have frozen water. "What do you want?"

"An answer to a question. Can I come in?"

"No. Ask it and leave."

Brushing his eyes across the maid's face, he cautioned, "You might want to do this privately."

"Helen's been with me for years. I've nothing to hide."

Griffin nodded and studied her silently for a moment. She

was older, of course, but the wild pole dancer she'd once been lay totally concealed beneath the polished veneer of her high-end makeup and clothes. "Did we make a child? Specifically, a son?"

The question rocked her, but she pulled herself together. "Who told you?"

"That isn't important."

"I will not be blackmailed."

"Not here for that, just an answer." In reality, she'd given it, but he had another question. "Why didn't you let me know?"

"So you could do what, come back and marry me? After you rode off on that bike of yours, I knew I'd never see you again, and that didn't change when I found out I was pregnant."

"So you gave him up?"

"Of course. You expected an abortion?"

"No, but I would have wanted to know about the child. Babies are precious in my family."

She rolled her eyes. "How'd you find me?"

"Your brother, Jimmy."

"Cellmates?" she asked disdainfully.

"No. Went to visit him a few weeks ago, though. He said to tell you he'd be out in six months."

"Like I care. Why are you so interested in this baby all of a sudden?"

"Because I believe I know where he is."

Her eyes widened. "Don't you dare tell him where I am! I want no contact, not even a phone call, you hear me? Now get off my property!"

She turned to Helen. "Give him his necklace. If he's still on the porch in thirty seconds, call the police."

The terse Griffin took the chain, remounted the Harley, and roared out of Melody's life for the last time.

After grabbing dinner at the Dog, Trent drove the boys home. There were at present five homes in their small subdivision, but with the wealth of open prairie land surrounding it, many more could be added. The resurrection of Henry Adams was the talk of the county. The new infrastructure, cutting-edge technology, and souped-up new school had begun drawing tourists, something unheard of before Bernadine and her checkbook came calling. Trent's hometown was becoming a destination instead of a place to drive past on the way to or from the airport. He'd even gotten a few inquiries as to the costs of new housing lots from people wanting to move in, but all the land not owned by the residents was owned by Bernadine, and he didn't see her throwing open the gates to any and all comers anytime soon, if ever.

Trent and Amari lived between the Paynes and the Garlands. Lily and Devon lived directly across the street next door to Bernadine and her daughter, Crystal. Crystal and Eli were sitting on Bernadine's porch with a drawing pad each, and Trent gave them a wave. They waved in return, and he followed the boys up the steps to his front door.

Devon looked across the street at his house and asked plaintively, "When is Ms. Lily coming home?"

"Good question." Trent knew from his talk with Reg Garland that she was okay, but not hearing from her had him wanting to whine like Devon. Then his phone went off. The number on the caller ID made him smile. "Speak of the devil. This is her now."

When he glanced back up, the boys were still standing in front of him as if waiting to watch and hear what he and Lily had to say. "Go on inside. I'll be there in a minute."

They left.

"Hey, babe. How are you?"

Lily responded excitedly, "Did Reggie tell you about Reverend Grant?"

"Sure did. Bernadine's optimism paid off."

"Big-time."

"Does the reverend think she can help Zoey?"

"She doesn't know, but she's as concerned about our little diva as we are."

"Are you in the air on the way home?"

"No. We're still in Miami, helping the reverend get her move under way. The sooner she can tie up things here, the sooner she can get to Kansas, so Bernadine has her credit card out and is making things move at the speed of light. We'll fly back in the morning."

Trent put away his disappointment as she continued, "The reverend wants to have a last supper with her congregation on Sunday, and then she has to meet with her bishop to have an exit interview. She'll fly out midweek. How's my baby boy?"

Trent smiled. "Me? I'm fine."

She laughed. "Not you, crazy man. Devon."

The man inside Trent who loved her wanted to pout upon hearing her ask after Devon first, but the parent in him understood. "He's surviving."

"What's that mean?"

He told her about the car fixing and Devon's lack of enthusiasm.

Her laugh tinkled in his ear. "He definitely doesn't like getting dirty. Cleanest little boy I know. Probably from being raised by his grandmother. You and Amari weren't too hard on him, were you?"

"Of course not. I'll fill you in when I see you." Trent was done talking about Devon for now. "Missing you, Lily Flower."

"Missing you, too. See you tomorrow."

"Sounds good. Be safe."

"Love you, Trenton."

"Love you more. Going to give the phone to Devon now. Hang on."

Trent took the phone inside. When he handed it over, the smile he received in response let him know just how much Devon loved her. Whatever the future held, that love would get them through.

After the call, because Devon would be spending the night, Trent accompanied him across the street so he could grab his PJs and whatever else he might need.

"But why can't I sleep at Zoey's like I always do?" Devon protested with a pout while Trent stuck Lily's spare key into the lock and opened the door.

"Because you're trying new things. And don't say you don't like new things," Trent cautioned as Devon was opening his mouth to do just that.

He closed it firmly and glanced up solemnly. "I'll go get my things."

"I'll wait." As he trudged away Trent wondered if that woe-is-me face ever worked on Lily. Not that it mattered. Being dad to Amari had given Trent all the patience he'd ever need. Devon the sad-faced boy was no match for Amari I-steal-cars

Steele, so Trent wasn't the least bit moved to let Devon have his way.

Devon returned carrying a backpack and his Bible. Trent relocked the door and led him back across the street. Amari was coming out of the house. "Homework's done. Okay if I go hang with Preston?"

"Be home by eight."

"Okay." He gave Devon a nod, jumped off the porch, and ran next door.

Upstairs, Trent showed Devon into the guest room where he'd be sleeping and watched the boy slowly glance around at the furnishings, the curtains, and peer in through the door that led to the adjoining bathroom.

"This okay?" Trent asked.

"That's a big bed."

"Yep. It's a king. Sleeps good, though."

Devon walked over to it to take a closer look. He ran his hand over the soft blue chenille bedspread.

"Okay?" Trent asked quietly.

Devon nodded.

Trent supposed the idea of spending the night in a strange room would be challenging to a kid who'd never slept any-place other than home or at Zoey's. "Being in a new room can spook you sometimes. Think you'd like to have a nightlight handy, just in case?"

Devon nodded and then said genuinely, "Thank you for not making fun of me, Mr. Trent."

The sincerity made tears sting Trent's eyes. "No problem, man."

Devon then said, "I never had a dad."

"So what do you think so far?"

He shrugged. "Can I ask you a question?"

"Sure. Shoot."

"Why won't anybody let me be a preacher?"

Trent wondered if Lily had ever seen the seriousness below the boy's surface. He was what Tamar called an old soul. "Number one, you're only nine. And two, you don't know enough about life to do all the stuff preachers have to do."

"Like what?"

Trent thought it over for a moment. "Take marriage counseling. What would you tell a married couple considering divorce?"

"I'd tell them to read their Bible. If they just trust—"

Trent held up a hand. "They tried that. Not working for them. What about a marriage counselor? Do you know how to put them in touch with someone like that?" He added gently, "Do you even know what a marriage counselor does?"

"No, but the Bible instructs a woman to follow the advice and desires of her husband."

"What do you think Ms. Lily would do if you told her something like that?"

He shrugged. "I don't know."

"I do. We'd probably find you up on Jupiter somewhere."

He looked away.

"Devon, the Bible gives you wonderful rules to live by, but you have to have some life experience in order to truly understand and apply them, or to show someone else the way."

"My grandma said I was anointed."

"I know better than to argue with grandmas."

Devon tossed back, "And Jesus said, 'If any of you put a

stumbling block before one of these little ones who believe in me, it would be better for you if a large millstone were fastened around your neck and you were drowned in the depth of the sea.' Matthew, chapter eighteen, verse six."

The smug face made Trent again want to smack him upside his head, but instead, he replied coolly, " 'Honor they father and thy mother, so that your days may be long.' Exodus, chapter twenty."

Devon stiffened.

Trent gave him an understanding pat on the shoulder. "Bed at eight."

Trent didn't allow himself to smile until after he sat down on the couch. Once upon a time, Amari had thought himself smarter than the average bear, too, but just like Devon, Trent had set him straight. He hoped the checkmate in this mini challenge would make the little deacon think twice before trying to chastise somebody, especially an adult, with self-serving biblical quotes, but then again, who knew. Trent sensed a lot of simmering going on beneath Devon's calm exterior and wondered how long it would be before it bubbled to the surface. From the classes and information Bernadine had provided the foster parents that first summer, he'd learned that it sometimes took years for children to reveal their true personalities. Many were carrying so much pain inside that they were afraid to open themselves for fear of more. Devon had only been in the system for a few months before being found by Bernadine, and from all indications he'd been well loved by his late grandmother, thus escaping the traumas borne by Henry Adams's other children. However, being torn from the bosom of family and set down in a town filled with strangers had to have been traumatic, no matter how you cut it, especially for a boy his age.

As Trent picked up the remote to turn on the Thursday-night football game, he vowed to be patient, but couldn't help wonder who the real Devon Watkins might turn out to be.

The teams were just kicking off when Amari walked in. The dejected look on his face made Trent mute the sound. "What's up, big guy?"

Amari sat down in the leather chair across from Trent. "Preston has started looking for his birth parents."

Trent studied his son's face. "Really?"

"Yeah. He's got Leah helping him."

"Is that why you look so down, because he asked Leah and not you?"

"No. I don't mind that so much, but he said he didn't have time to help me find mine, too."

Trent now understood. During the preparation for last summer's August First parade, Amari had let Preston do all the heavy lifting while he'd basked in the glory until the adults put a stop to the imbalance. Trent didn't like seeing Amari so glum, but he was pleased that Preston was learning to tell Amari no. "That's really something you should do on your own, son."

"I guess. Which means I'll never know who my folks are, because no way can I use the computer like him."

"I didn't mean on your own, by yourself. I'd help."

Amari straightened. "Would you?"

"Of course. Tamar is convinced you have July blood and has been asking around the family."

"There are other Julys?"

"Yep. Cousins. Second cousins. Tamar has a brother named Thaddeus, and he has nine kids. There's also supposed to be Julys still living down on the Texas-Mexico border, where the original outlaw Julys hailed from."

"That's awesome."

Trent had a question. "So has Preston talked this over with the Paynes?"

"Not yet, but he plans to tonight."

Trent shook his head with amusement over where Preston had placed his foster parents on the pecking order, and wondered how Sheila and Barrett would react.

Amari's voice brought him back. "So when will Tamar know?"

Trent shrugged. "There's no telling, but in the meantime, how about you and I do some computer work on our own, and learn how to start this search?"

Amari beamed.

"And," Trent added, "if it's okay with you, I want to call over to the court and ask about what we need to do to make your adoption final."

The wattage on Amari's smile tripled. He launched himself at Trent and hugged him with all his might. Laughing, Trent held him close, savoring the boy's joy and his own. After a moment, he drew back and looked down into Amari's face. "Do I take that as a yes?"

"Oh, hell yes—I mean, heck yes."

Trent's laughter exploded. "You are something else."

"Just being me."

"You're growing up."

Amari settled himself on the arm of Trent's chair. "You think so?"

"Yep."

"Maybe because I got my own family, my own room, my own best friend, at least when Leah lets me borrow him."

"That turning into an issue for you?"

He shook his head. "I'm just playing. Leah being around Preston is helping him with stuff I can't."

"Like?"

"Which colleges he should try for. Stuff like that."

Amari was an expert at hiding his true feelings, and Trent sometimes had a hard time deciphering the truth. Now was one of those times. "You sure you're okay with the time Preston is spending with Leah?"

"Yes, and even if I wasn't, there's nothing I can do about it."

Trent noticed that he'd said "can" and not "could." That told him a lot.

Amari asked, "Do you think you'll still want to talk to me like this when you and Ms. Lily get married?"

That question told Trent a lot as well. "If you mean just the two of us, one on one, the answer is always. We'll still be talking when you have your own kids."

Amari met his eyes and nodded approvingly. "I like having our one-on-ones before I go to bed."

"So do I, son."

"Like being called son."

"Like being called dad."

They grinned.

Amari said, "This is getting mushy."

Trent chuckled. "I know. So how about we check out the game before you head up to bed."

He hit the sound on the remote, and father and son turned their attention to the TV.

Upstairs on the landing, and hidden by the shadows, the eavesdropping Devon listened for a moment longer, then tiptoed back to the guest room. In some ways, the conversation between Amari and Mr. Trent reminded him of his talks with his grandma. Her voice would be soft with love just like Mr. Trent's, and thinking about her brought tears to his eyes. He missed her so much it made his stomach hurt sometimes. He knew she was up in heaven, living in one of God's many mansions, but he wanted her back on earth because he was so scared that he'd forget her when he grew up.

As he got back into the giant bed and wiped at his tears, he could still see her face and hear her calling his name.

"Devon! Time to go."

"Yes, ma'am. Be right there."

Dressed in his suit and tie, he'd step out of his tiny bedroom, and at the sight of him, she'd always say proudly, "You are the handsomest preacher in the state of Mississippi."

He'd giggle, and she'd grin.

Having had their breakfast earlier, there was nothing left to do but for her to pick up her pocketbook and Bible and to take one last look at herself in her big blue hat in the small mirror on the wall. "Gotta look my best for the Bridegroom."

Once she was satisfied that she looked just right, they'd set off walking down the dirt road for the half-mile trip to the Good Will Missionary Church of God. She couldn't walk very fast due to the swelling in her legs from diabetes. Sometimes, if they were lucky, one of their neighbors would drive up and offer them a ride the rest of the way. Most Sundays, however, they walked, rain or shine, and on the rare occasion that she couldn't muster the strength to make the trip, Devon went alone.

In his memory's eye he could see the old abandoned cinder-block building that had served as the church, and the lush, overgrown greenness of the Mississippi countryside that surrounded it. He could hear the off-key singing of Ms. Myrtle, his grandma's best friend, as she led the hymns. If a raven could sing, it would probably sound like Ms. Myrtle, but she hadn't cared. What she lacked in tune, she made up for with enthusiasm and volume. His grandma said when Myrtle sang, not even the angels could sleep in on Sunday morning.

Devon missed Ms. Myrtle and the other ladies of the congregation. He even missed old man Lemon, who came to church every Sunday and slept in the back chair. As the memories filled him, Devon remembered the fun he had planting the garden in the spring and listening to the frogs and crickets at night through the window of his room.

But all that was gone now, along with his grandma, and tears stung his eyes again. The other Henry Adams kids might like having a new life and doing new things, but he didn't. He wanted the life he'd had before.

Down in Miami, Paula Grant plopped down heavily into her old chair, not out of sadness or frustration but out of sheer awe. Talk about miracles. Not only did she have a new job, but from the story told to her by Bernadine and Lily, it was going to be in a little piece of heaven. Yesterday evening, she'd had no prospects; now, it seemed as if she had more blessings than her arms could hold. In many ways, she felt as if she'd somehow stumbled into a parallel universe. How could what Bernadine described as *her* town possibly be true?

She turned to her ancient computer and googled Henry Adams. After spending an hour reading articles, watching cable news clips, and researching the Great Exodus of 1879, she was even more blown away. On one hand, she was deeply saddened by the finality of leaving Miami, on the other, she was so excited about what the future might hold, she felt like a little kid. Even though Paula had tried to protest, Bernadine had gone ahead and paid for movers, storage for her old Ford, and even encouraged her to think about the size and layout of the church Bernadine planned to build. Paula thought back on her years spent at Old Ab and the hardships she'd endured heading up a church and a congregation no other clergy wanted or even cared about. She'd worked countless hours and made endless sacrifices to keep the doors open and her people fed both physically and spiritually, and now, God was leading her to a ministry halfway across the country. That Zoey Raymond would be playing a part in Paula's new life was a surprising twist. When had the little one stopped speaking, and why? she wondered, but hoped she could help in some way. In the meantime, this chapter of her life was closing, with another poised to open.

She glanced at her watch. It was time to lock up and go home. As she turned out the light, she paused for a moment to say a prayer for the congregation she was leaving behind, and for guidance on the journey ahead. She also prayed to remain humble in the face of the astonishing wealth of Ms. Bernadine Brown.

CHAPTER
6

Lily and Bernadine flew into the Hays airport the following morning. Nathan met them and drove them back to the Power Plant so they could pick up their cars. Lily had made plans last week to take the day off, so she wasn't going back to the office. Bernadine knew to call her only if the world caught fire.

Once at home, Lily sent a text to Trent to let him know she was back, then opened a text message waiting for her from Marie. *Need to see you asap,* was all it said, so she took a quick shower, changed into fresh clothes, and drove out to see what Marie wanted.

The drive out to the Jefferson homestead took only a few minutes. Marie's ancestor, Chase Jefferson, had been a sergeant with the Tenth Cavalry before he was elected Henry Adams's sheriff. His wife, Cara Lee, was the town's first college-educated schoolteacher.

Lily parked and walked up the gravel path to the porch. Marie lived with her mother, Agnes, a contemporary and running buddy of Tamar July's. Staying with them temporarily was Genevieve Curry, who'd moved in after walking away from her marriage to Riley and his hog, Cletus, and who according to Trent had knocked Riley the hell out yesterday. Lily really wished she'd been at the Dog to see it.

Lily called through the screen door, and Marie came to let her in.

"Hey there."

Marie was tall and thin and wearing her signature cat-eyed glasses. Today's pair was aqua with rhinestones. Viewing them made Lily give her a smile. "You and those glasses."

Marie grinned.

The house's interior, with its old-fashioned doily-topped furniture, brought back memories of the years Lily had lived within its walls. After leaving for college, she'd sworn never to return to boring, slow-paced Henry Adams, but life had a way of changing things. "So what's up with the cryptic message?"

"Come on into the kitchen."

The stylish stainless-steel appliances, courtesy of Bernadine's improvement fund, were a marked contrast to the doilies and overstuffed sofas and chairs in the living room, or as Ms. Agnes preferred to call it, the front parlor.

Lily took a seat at the table.

"You want coffee?"

"Love some."

While Marie did the honors, Lily told her about her trip to Miami, the new reverend, and her connection to Zoey.

"Let's hope the reunion will make Zoey smile," Marie said, placing a steaming blue cup in front of Lily.

She took a seat on the other side of the table. "Speaking of reunions—read this."

Marie passed her an envelope. Lily curiously assessed it and then Marie before taking out the letter. It read:

Hello. My name is Brian French. I think I am your son. Please call.

There was a phone number listed.

Lily was confused. "Whose son is he claiming to be?"

"Mine."

Her mouth dropped. "Yours?"

"Gave him up for adoption. I was, what, eighteen, almost nineteen. Got pregnant my first year of college. The father refused to marry me, so I came home. You can probably imagine Mama's reaction."

Lily could. Ms. Agnes was all about appearances. The day Lily came to live with them, she'd been sternly warned not to bring dishonor on the Jefferson name, or she'd find herself living elsewhere. At the time, Lily had been the epitome of a good girl. She'd just lost her mother to cancer, and being chastised about her behavior before barely getting her foot in the door hadn't set well. All these many years later, it still didn't.

Marie was staring off as if she, too, was reviewing the past. When she finally turned back, she confessed with a sad whisper, "I never even held him."

That broke Lily's heart. "So are you going to call him?"

She shrugged. "Leo says I shouldn't."

"But what do you want to do?" she asked, emphasis on the *you*. Who cared what Leo thought?

"Not sure."

"Do you want to talk to him?"

"Of course, but what if he's bitter about my giving him up? What if his childhood was like Amari's or Crystal's?"

"What if it wasn't? What if he was raised by a wonderful family and just wants to connect with his birth mom? I'm thinking it took a whole lot of courage for him to reach out like this, especially not knowing whether you want the contact or not."

"But how on earth did he find me? The records were sealed."

"Times have changed. Many states are allowing adoptive kids to look at their files. The only way to know for sure is to call him."

Marie seemed to ponder that for a moment. "I haven't shown the note to Mama. She's liable to hit the ceiling. It's bad enough I'm seeing Bernadine's ex. Getting in touch with the child she insisted I couldn't raise is only going to make her go off again on what she calls my 'evil past.'"

Lily didn't respond. Out of respect, she'd always kept her feelings about Agnes Jefferson unspoken.

"I'm over sixty years old, and still scared of my mother. Pitiful." When Marie smiled, Lily met it with one of her own.

"I really want to call him, Lily."

"Then go for it. Who knows? This may turn out to be a blessing."

It was easy to see that Marie wanted it to be just that, but the thought of her mother's reaction had to be looming like a hawk over prey. The situation brought Preston's quest back to mind. Would his mom want contact?

Lily turned the envelope over and saw that although it bore a Tennessee postmark, there was no return address. The person who'd mailed it seemed as uncertain as Marie. "Have you talked to anyone else about this besides Leo?"

"Genevieve. And her advice was the same as yours."

"Great minds think alike." Another thing Lily kept to herself was how she felt about Marie possibly letting Leo influence her thinking on this. For as long as Lily had known her, Marie had always been in charge of Marie. Lily hoped she wasn't turning into one of those women who wouldn't cross a street without asking her man first.

"Thanks for listening, Lily."

"No problem, and if you need to talk it through some more, I'm your girl."

Marie nodded approvingly and after a few more seconds of silence asked, "So how's the wedding coming?"

Lily shrugged. "I don't know. Bernadine wants to throw the Wedding of the Ages, and I just want a quiet ceremony with a reception at the Dog."

"Then say that."

"I have. Many times."

"Not listening?"

"Seemingly."

"She's a tough lady."

Lily assessed Marie in an effort to try and determine if she'd meant that to be complimentary or not, but Marie was an excellent poker player and hid her emotions well. Lily changed the subject. "Sorry I haven't been out to see you. It's been crazy."

"I understand why you haven't. Has Bernadine asked you to choose?"

Lily went still. "No."

"And neither will I. I know how she feels about my being

with Leo, but we're all adults. You are still my godchild—always will be. I can even still be friends with Bernadine, if she'd let me."

"She's just concerned about you, that's all."

"So she says."

Lily heard the snipe. "Do I need to sit the two of you down and have a come-to-Jesus meeting? The last thing I need is another layer of drama before my wedding."

"Another layer?"

"Yes. Devon is insisting on being the preacher, and no matter how many times I tell him no, he keeps asking. I also have Bernadine trying to smother me with her checkbook. If I have to referee a catfight between two grown women, too, I swear I'm going to elope."

Marie smiled. "A Jesus meeting won't be necessary."

"You sure? Both of you are in my wedding because you mean the world to me."

"I know, but have your wedding. Emphasis on the *your*. You're the one getting married. No one else."

Lily knew she was right, but Bernadine wanted the nuptials to be a grand affair so badly.

"Go on back to work. I know you probably have a million and a half things to do."

"Nope, I have the day off, so I can sit awhile unless you have someplace to go."

"Nope. I'm waiting for Genevieve to get back so we can head over to the rec and set up for tonight's movie. You heard about her and Riley?"

"Yeah."

"Cliff is so mad at her, he can't see straight."

"Why?"

"Told Genevieve she's supposed to be a lady, not Muhammad Ali."

"Riley can bring out the Ali in a girl."

"Amen."

"How's her hand?"

"Broken in three places, but she's displaying the cast so proudly, you'd think she was Ali."

Lily smiled at that. "Where is she?"

"With Cliff. He said they needed to talk."

"I never knew he was so rigid."

"He used to be as big a knucklehead as Mal, but when he came back from 'Nam, he'd changed. Not sure why, but he loves the ground Gen walks on, so they'll work it out."

They spent a few more minutes chatting, and then Lily had to go. "Today's laundry day. I suppose I should get to it."

Marie walked her out. Before they parted, Lily gave her a strong hug. The visit had been a good one. "You should come over and have dinner with me and Trent and the boys."

"I'd like that. Leo invited, too?"

"Of course." It was a lie, but for Marie's sake she'd be nice to Leo even if it killed her.

They set the date, and Lily drove home.

With the laundry done and the house clean, she was wondering if she really wanted to tackle the windows, too. But before she could decide, her stomach protested, not having been fed since the quick breakfast in Miami at the crack of dawn, so she called Trent to see what he might be doing, and if they could meet for lunch.

"Just sitting down at the Dog," he said on the phone.

She loved the sound of his velvety voice against her ear. "Alone, I hope."

"Nope. Gary's with me so, if you're coming, behave."

"Aww, that's no fun."

"Crazy woman," he muttered affectionately.

"See you in a minute."

The hip-shaking sound of Wilson's Pickett's "Engine Number Nine" was rocking the house when Lily entered the diner. The music competed with the noise of what sounded like a hundred different conversations. The place was packed like it always was between eleven and two, and the mouthwatering smells of the food coming out of Rocky and Siz's kitchen filled the air.

Behind the counter Malachi was moving to the beat and counting a stack of paper money over the opened cash drawer. Looking up, he shot her a smile. "Hey, girl. My lady with you?"

"Nope. She still has herself chained to her desk. Me, I have the day off."

"Good for you, but your boss has to be the hardest-working person on the planet."

"Amen."

"Trent's over there on the left," he informed Lily just as she spotted him, so she left Mal bopping and counting, and threaded her way over to Trent.

She greeted him with a quick kiss on the lips. Slipping into the booth, she gave Gary a grin. The waitress arrived and set down the men's loaded-up plates.

"You all didn't wait for me?" Lily asked with mock offense.

Trent gave the waitress a nod of thanks and began covering his fries with ketchup. "Seven times out of ten, when you say you're on your way, you get distracted by the job and arrive a week later. I want lunch today."

She punched him playfully in the shoulder. "I have the day off, but at least I do work, unlike you."

He peered at her over the giant burger filling his hands and countered, "I work, too. As mayor, I officially welcomed my boy Gary back to town by helping him move today."

"Where to?"

"The empty trailer out on Tamar's land."

"Good. Welcome home, Gary."

He toasted her with his large chocolate shake.

"You got keys and everything, then."

Trent said, "We got keys, Lil. Otherwise we wouldn't have been able to get in."

"Thank you, Mr. State the Obvious."

"Why are you mad?"

"I'm not mad."

"Could've fooled me."

"Keep that up, and I will be," she countered coolly.

Gary chuckled.

They both glared.

He shook his head in amusement. "I feel like I'm in Mr. Peabody's Way Back machine and we're seventeen all over again. Think you can take me back to the year before I married Colleen?"

That broke the tension.

Lily stuck out her tongue.

To give Lily something else to think about besides her

hair-trigger temper, Trent leaned over and gifted her with a kiss that was so all that, everybody in the diner saw it and began cheering and whistling. When he finally let her up for air, she saw stars.

Gary's laughter made his shoulders shake. "And thus ends another fiery episode of the July and Fontaine Show. Stay tuned, boys and girls."

Trent raised his soda in reply.

Lily wanted to smack them both, but the room was still spinning. Holding Trent's mischief-filled eyes, she smiled and beckoned him closer. When he complied, she whispered in his ear, "You are so going to pay for that."

He whispered back, "Counting on it."

She chuckled, pushed him away, and looked around for the waitress to place her order.

As they enjoyed their meals, the three friends talked of old times. Soon the conversation drifted to who they'd run into, who was working where, and the classmates that had passed away. Some of the names were of people Lily hadn't thought of in years, but with each mention a seventeen-year-old face rose up clearly from her memory. Like Irene Parrish, who was on the Henry Adams girls' track team with Lily. "We really ought to have a reunion," she said over her salad.

"You willing to be the organizer?" Trent asked.

"I'd consider it. It would have to be after the wedding, though." She looked Gary's way. "What do you think about a reunion, Gary?"

"Might be fun. We've never had one that I can remember."

Trent replied, "Neither can I."

"Then let's put it away for now and talk about it after the first of the year."

Bernadine entered the dinner. She and Lily exchanged a wave over the sizable crowd and the sound of Al Green crying about how tired he was of being alone, blasting on the jukebox. Lily watched Bernadine and Malachi greet each other with a quick kiss before they slid into a booth.

"Bernadine's been good for him," Trent said.

Lily hadn't known he'd been watching them, too. "The only time she seems to relax is when he's around."

"She's made him grow up. That alone makes her gold in my eyes."

Lily understood. When they were in high school, Malachi July had been in his glory days as a wild man. Although Trent never talked about it, Lily knew how much it hurt him to be the son of a man seemingly bent upon self-destruction. She remembered many a Friday and Saturday night riding shotgun in Black Beauty with a worried Trent while they scoured the county's dives and truck stops, hoping to find his father before he killed someone driving drunk. Mal was a mess back then.

"I'm glad she came to town," Trent said as he turned and met Lily's eyes.

She agreed.

They spent the next few minutes discussing Gary's move and his plans for his girls. He explained to Lily, "Leah's being pretty supportive, but as I was telling Trent yesterday, Tiff is not happy."

"I know how she feels. Losing your mom doesn't make for happy times. Even though our circumstances are different, a loss is a loss. Do you want me to talk to her?"

"I'd like that. Warning you, though, she's got a lot of her mother in her. She may not want your help."

"I won't force myself on her if she's not comfortable."

As the cast of diners came and went around them and the ruby red jukebox continued to kick out the jams, Rocky appeared, carrying a tray. She stopped beside Lily. "When are you going to get me that list?"

Lily was supposed to have decided weeks ago on what food she wanted served at the reception.

"You're going to mess around and have everybody eating peanut butter and jelly on crackers."

Lily hung her head.

"Get with it, Fontaine," she scolded and moved on.

Gary quipped, "Rocky hasn't changed much, either."

Lily sighed dejectedly.

Back at home, Lily took a cup of tea out onto her deck and sat down at the wrought-iron patio table. She could still hear Rocky's admonishment ringing in her ear. *Get with it, Fontaine.* She supposed she should, but she didn't want to. First, she didn't want to take the time away from all the other stuff she was doing; who knew that town building would be such a rush? She loved her job, whether it be going over the blueprints for rebuilding Main Street, or arguing with the county over an out-of-date building code, or riding around in her hard hat and boots.

The second reason was that she didn't know the first thing about how to do it. When she married the first time, it had been a quick trip to the judge, and that was it. Although she wouldn't mind doing that again with Trent, Henry Adams was a small town, and no matter how much she protested to herself, it was understood that her friends and neighbors would want the day to be one to remember, and because of that there had to be at least a wedding dress and a reception dinner.

She let out a frustrated sigh. She needed to have someone else do the planning, which automatically meant Bernadine, but as she'd mused earlier, by the time the Boss Lady was done flashing her onyx card, there'd be glass slippers, seven dwarves, and lord only knew what else. There had to be a middle ground between glass slippers and a quick trip to the country courthouse, but she had no idea what it might be or how to go about finding a compromise that didn't take away from her life. Yes, it was her wedding, but she was far more excited about marrying Trent than she was about the ceremony. She glanced down at her finger, sporting the beautiful sparkler he'd given her in San Francisco, and once again she voted to just elope.

Lily heard Sheila Payne calling her through the screen of the front door, so she set down her tea and hurried inside.

"Hey, Sheila. Come on in. How are things?"

"Interesting, let's just call it that."

Lily directed her back out to the deck and offered her tea, but Sheila declined. Lily gestured her to a seat and waited to learn the purpose of her call.

"First, thank you for counseling Preston."

"About what?"

"Preston said you told him to talk to Barrett and me about his search for his birth family."

"Ah." She understood now. "I'm assuming he did?"

"Yes, but it's not sitting well with Barrett. He and Preston are back to circling each other like boxers in the ring."

"I'm so sorry."

"Barrett's just being a hard-ass. He doesn't understand why Preston would want to do this, and frankly, he's taking it personally, as if maybe Preston wants to leave us."

"Is that what you think?"

"Of course not. Preston made it very clear what he's about on this, and I told him I'd help in any way I could."

"Good for you."

"Even though Barrett's not on board, I wanted to thank you."

"You're welcome."

"Now my second reason for coming is to offer to host a bridal tea."

"A bridal tea?"

Sheila explained, "You don't impress me as a bridal shower kind of woman, but it might be nice to bring all the ladies together and have a tea, maybe on the weekend before Thanksgiving."

"Sheila, that is so sweet of you. You don't do weddings, too, do you?" she tossed out teasingly.

"I've arranged a few in my day."

Lily paused. "Really?"

"I may not know how to run a town or stand up to an adulterous husband, but I'm an expert at entertaining. I've overseen officers' dinners, Red Cross luncheons. I even put on a dinner for two hundred generals, various senators, and their wives, and did I mention the president and first lady were there as well?"

Lily almost fell off her chair.

"So do you want to have the tea?"

Lily searched Sheila's face as if seeing the woman for the first time. "Yes. Very much." She supposed the colonel knew about this side of his wife, but no one else did. This Sheila, speaking with confidence and humor, was not the Sheila she thought she knew. "You're not making all this up, are you, girl?"

"Of course not. Who'd lie about being able to plan a dinner? This may sound silly, but spearheading events gives me joy. Trying to decide on the right china pattern or whether to use damask or linen for the table keeps one's mind off your husband sleeping with another woman."

Lily didn't say a word.

"So do you want me to plan your wedding, too?"

"I would."

"Then how about I come over tonight, and we can make some decisions."

"Not tonight. It's Friday. Movie night at the rec, remember? We can get together in the morning, if that's okay."

"Of course. Sorry to be so eager. It's been a while since I've had anything like this to do. I'm excited."

Lily sensed the happiness. "Glad I could help, and I'll expect a bill for your services."

"You're not getting one, so forget that."

"Sheila—"

"No, this is my wedding gift to you, and my gift to myself. No bill."

Lily didn't argue, but planned on revisiting the matter at a later date.

Sheila got to her feet. "Thank you, Lily."

"You're welcome."

"I'll give you a call around nine."

"Sounds good, and Sheila?"

She stopped and turned back.

"Thanks," Lily whispered with emotion.

Sheila winked and exited.

After the departure, the first thing that came to Lily's mind was the biblical saying "Ask and ye shall receive." She wasn't sure the verse applied to things like weddings, but she sure wasn't going to complain. She also hoped Sheila knew what she was doing.

CHAPTER
7

The rec was nearly full by the time Lily and Trent arrived. Devon was with Zoey and the Garlands. Amari was seated down front with Preston and Leah, so she and Trent were on their version of a date. He spotted Gary and Tiffany Adele seated in the midst of the noisy crowd. Trent and Lily walked down the center aisle to join them.

"Hey, Gary. Tiffany."

Gary greeted them with a smile.

Tiffany spoke, then went back to looking angry.

"How are you, Tiff?" Lily asked. "School go okay today?"

"Yes."

"Your dad has my number—call me if you need anything."

"Thanks," Tiffany said, with no sincerity in her tone.

Gary sighed.

Lily didn't let it bother her; she was too busy scanning the crowd to see who was there. On the far right, Leo and Marie sat talking. Watching Marie smile at something Leo was saying did little to dispel her concerns, but she had to admit that her godmother did seem relaxed and at ease in his company. She saw Mal entering with Bernadine, and right behind them were Cliff and Genevieve. Cliff was decked out in a nice suit that was a perfect complement to her pretty green dress and pearls. "Genevieve is having people sign her cast," Lily told Trent with a laugh.

There was a small line of folks waiting to give their autographs. "Cliff doesn't look happy, though."

Trent directed his eyes up to the entrance. "No, he doesn't."

He could be seen standing by her side with a pained look on his face. While Trent explained to Gary the backstory on Genevieve's cast, Lily said ominously, "Uh-oh."

Riley and Eustasia came in. Riley had a white bandage the size of Iowa across his nose, and not even distance could hide the fact that his eyes were black and blue and swollen closed.

"He can't even see the movie," Lily said, turning to Trent in confusion. "Why's he here?"

"Probably to show Genevieve he's not intimidated. You know he's got more pride than sense. The way he looks, he should be in bed."

Gary stared with wonder. "Did she break his nose?"

"Yeah."

"Goodness."

As they continued to watch, the atmosphere by the door grew tense when Genevieve offered Riley the Sharpie so he could sign her cast. He puffed up like a bantam rooster. Genevieve, who was five inches taller, leaned down over him like an angry crane. As they began jawing at each other, Cliff took her arm to lead her away. Eustasia just stood there, looking confused.

"His lady friend looks like she's not sure where she is."

"Folks around here can have that effect on you," Trent drawled.

Cliff marched the tight-lipped Genevieve to a seat. To their credit, Eustasia and Riley didn't turn tail, but found seats as well.

The auditorium lights began to dim. As the interior faded to black and the opening music of *The Mummy: Tomb of the Dragon Emperor* sounded, everyone took their seats.

"Thank God," Lily declared.

Trent laughed.

During intermission, Lily ran into Bernadine at the concession stand. After they made their purchases of popcorn and sodas, they stopped to chat for a moment about the Riley and Genevieve drama.

"She's going to need a criminal lawyer if she keeps this up," Bernadine pointed out. Marie walked by, waving. They returned the wave with smiles and began the walk down the crowded hall back to the auditorium.

"I'm having her and Leo over to dinner."

"Okay," Bernadine replied in a neutral-sounding voice.

"She is my godmother, and I haven't spent a lot of time with her lately, but apparently I can't have her without him."

Bernadine must have correctly interpreted Lily's feelings on the matter because she said, "It'll be okay."

"He's just using her. Why, I don't know, but he's after something."

Bernadine looked around to see who might be hearing their conversation. "Lily, I don't want to talk about this."

"I know. Sorry. It's just—" She'd planned to let the matter

rest, but couldn't seem to stop. Keeping her voice down, she whispered fiercely, "He came here supposedly to get back with you, but when you kicked him to the curb, he's suddenly in love with Marie? I'm not feeling that."

Bernadine maneuvered her box of popcorn so she could stick her fingers in her ears, and began to chant, "La la, la la, la. I can't hear you."

Lily laughed. "Okay. I'm done."

"Good. Now tell me what's happening with the Clark family before we sit down. I saw him at your table during lunch."

Lily filled her in about the trailer.

"Mal told me about the big kiss."

"Back in high school, the man's kisses could stop an argument cold."

"Sounds like they still work."

Lily took a sip of her cola. "I don't want to talk about it."

Bernadine laughed. "I'm going back to my seat."

A grinning Lily did the same.

Lily and Trent didn't stay for the second feature, *Cabin in the Sky*. Instead, they walked home hand in hand. The temperature was warm for a late September night, and they were enjoying their kid-free interlude. The boys would be spending the night with their friends and weren't due home until noon, so the only issue that remained for them was: Trent's house or hers?

"In the spring, I think I'm going to put up a swing for us in the backyard," he said to her. "That way, after the boys are in bed we can sit under the stars and neck like we're at the drive-in."

Lily snorted. She loved him so much. "Sounds wonderful. I think the spot over by my roses would be the perfect place."

"Your roses? The swing's going up in my yard."

She stopped. "Why?"

"Because that's where we're going to be living, right?"

"Says who?"

They studied each other under the moonlight.

He spoke first. "Guess this is something we need to talk about."

"Duh," she replied with amusement.

"I just assumed."

"Wrong, pardner. We're living in my house. I don't want Devon to have to move again."

"And what about Amari?"

"Amari's flexible. You know he'll land on his feet."

He disagreed. "This is the first time in his life he's had his own room. He's not going to like packing up and starting over any more than Devon."

"But he'll be okay."

"That's not the point, Lil."

"What is the point?"

Trent wasn't feeling this, especially her seemingly flippant attitude toward his son's well-being. He realized his plans for the swing had inadvertently opened up a can of worms. He also realized that this was going to escalate into a full-fledged argument if they weren't careful, and by the flash in her eyes, she was halfway there. He chose his words carefully. "My point is that Amari needs to be given the same consideration you're giving Devon, that's all."

"Then what? Do we live in a brand-new place? I don't

think Bernadine's going to build us a new house just because we can't agree."

"And I don't expect her to, so the word is compromise."

"Which means your way, right?"

He paused and sighed. "No, Miss I Got a Temper."

"Don't start."

"Then cut out the snippiness."

She turned and marched off angrily down the road.

Trent shook his head. He loved her like he loved sunshine in spring, but Lily Fontaine was a trying woman, lord knew she was. He called out. "When you cool off, give me a call. I'll be at home."

She didn't look back.

By the time Lily got to her front steps, she realized she was about to waste one of the few nights she and Trent had been able to have alone. Yes, he'd been wrong to have assumed that she and Devon would be moving to his house, but she'd been equally wrong to throw a mini tantrum in response. Gary was right, they were still seventeen—particularly her—but Trent loved her enough to marry her, and that meant something, especially considering she'd been the cause of their breakup twenty years ago.

Another part of her snit was rooted in having been divorced and single most of her adult life. Letting someone else run the show, or at least attempt to, wasn't something she was accustomed to. It occurred to her that being married again was going to be more than a notion.

She looked over at him, standing on his porch in the dim moonlight. He'd parked himself against the banister and was watching her, arms folded, seemingly waiting. The nonchalant stance was a familiar one. He'd used it often back in high school, usually after she'd blown up and stomped off. It was almost as if he were saying, *When you stop being crazy, I'll still be here,* and he always had been. It only took her a moment to decide what to do. She turned and walked across the street.

When she reached the top of the steps, he didn't say a word. Instead, he simply opened his arms. She basked in the feel of him enfolding her and the tenderness of the soft kiss he placed against her brow. All she could think was, How could she not love a man who took her as she was, feet of clay and all? She leaned back and looked up into the shadow-shrouded planes of his strong face. "Sorry for going off."

"I appreciate that. Now my turn."

The darkness hid his expression, so she had no idea what he was about to say.

"My apologies for not considering that you might have an opinion on where we should live. It was thoughtless of me. And if you say, 'Yes, it was,' I'll understand."

"Yes, it was."

He laughed, and then pulled her closer, and they wrapped their arms tightly around each other.

She confessed, "And you were right about Amari. I was so focused on Devon not having to move, I didn't think about how Amari might be affected."

He took her by the hand and led her over to the old porch sofa. They cuddled close and basked in their togetherness, the darkness, and the star-studded silence of the sky. A cold wind blew in for a moment, and Lily shivered in response.

"Winter's coming," he said.

"I know, and I'm not looking forward to another winter on the plains."

"It has its own beauty."

"Not for a girl from Atlanta."

He gave her a squeeze. "Could be worse. If we were back in the early days, we'd have to worry about livestock, the pump freezing—did we lay in enough stalks and grass to keep warm all winter. Some of the Dusters spent that first winter living underground in dugouts. Some froze to death."

"And here we are fussing over two homes equipped with every gadget known to womankind and we can't decide which one to live in. Pitiful."

He looked down at her face. "How about we do this? I'll talk to Amari and see how he feels, and if he's okay with it, he and I will move in with you and Devon."

She looked up excitedly, threw her arms around him, and gave him a big, fat, melt-his-bones kiss.

"There's a caveat, though."

She waited.

"In the spring, I want to add more square footage to your house. You're going to need a room to escape all the testosterone, and Amari and I have been kicking around the idea of adding a gym, so now, we'll just build it onto your place, along with your new room."

The thought of adding a gym to her house made a voice inside Lily scream, *No!* loud and long, but she kept it to herself. "Anything else?"

"I know you like to cook, so if you want a larger kitchen, we can add that to the floor plan, too. What do you think?"

She thought it over and said, "Okay, now, let me get this straight."

He responded with muted laughter. "Uh-oh."

"No, I want to make sure I'm hearing you right. After you and Amari move in, I go from having my whole entire house to myself to just a room?"

He grinned. "Yep, and testosterone free."

She grinned back. "I'd have to be crazy to turn down a sweet deal like that, wouldn't I?"

"Yes, you would."

She wrapped her arms around him again and listened to his heartbeat. "Thank you for a wonderful compromise."

"I love you, woman. How many times do I have to tell you that?"

She hugged him tight. She then told him about hiring Sheila to plan the wedding.

He asked, "You think she really knows what she's doing?"

Lily shrugged. "How bad could it be?"

"At least it's not Amari."

She laughed and thought back on Amari's handling of the August First parade.

"Mal says Amari's been looking at hotels in Hawaii."

"I'm almost afraid to ask, but why?"

"I think he thinks he's going on the honeymoon."

"He'd better think again."

"You got that right."

After a few moments of silence, while they both thought about Amari and his over-the-topness, Trent looked down at her and said, "I like this new version of you."

"New version?"

"Yeah. Back in the day, you wouldn't've come over here so we could work this out. You'd've sashayed your sweet little behind into the house and simmered about it for a week."

She couldn't deny that. "True. We spent almost as much time arguing as we did cuddling."

He placed a kiss on the top of her head. "Thanks for hearing me out."

"I love you. How many times do I have to tell you that?"

She heard his amusement rumble in his chest.

He glanced down. "How about we build a big fire, pop some corn, and watch a movie?"

"I'd love that. What are we watching?"

"You choose."

"My favorite big-fire, popcorn movie is *Pretty Woman*."

"Oh, no." He laughed, shaking his head. "We're not watching *Pretty Woman*."

"Yes, we are, so I'm going to sashay my sweet little behind over to my house and get my movie while you start the fire."

"*Pretty Woman*?" he asked, mortified.

She smiled and purred, "And when the movie's done, I'm going to show you something even more fun than making popcorn."

He grinned. "Go get your movie."

"I'll be right back."

After hustling across the street, Lily walked into her dark house and turned on a lamp. She took a long look around at her quiet, well-furnished living room and imagined it being overrun by men bearing sports equipment, fishing rods, hunting rifles, and lots and lots of car parts. As she smiled, she reflected back on her talk with Trent. It felt good to get the day's moodiness off her chest. She'd had her say, and he'd had his. If they continued to be as open and honest with each other as they'd been tonight, she believed their marriage would flourish.

She grabbed the movie from her DVD stash and turned to leave. Before turning off the lamp she took one last wistful look around then plunged the space into darkness.

Over at the Garlands', Devon and Zoey were preparing for bed, but Devon was blue. His relationship with Zoey was changing, and he didn't know how to make it stop and go back to the way it had been before. He blamed a lot of it on Mr. Trent and Amari. If they hadn't let her work on that dirty old car, he and Zoey would be watching their favorite *Toy Story* DVD and having a good time. Instead, all she seemed interested in doing was taking her Barbie cars apart and putting them back together. Earlier, on the computer downstairs, she had Doc Reg go on the Lego website so she could show him the car kits she'd had her dad order. When she signed, *Aren't they awesome!* he'd nodded, but hadn't meant it. He didn't want her working on cars. Boys worked on cars. She was supposed to be his music director, and as soon as he convinced Ms. Lily to let him preach again, he was going to need her help. "I'm ready to go to bed, Zoey."

Dressed in her green Princess and the Frog pajamas, she glanced up, raised a finger to signal just a moment, and finished putting the doors and wheels back onto her pink Barbie SUV. The car was now in one piece again. Grinning, she held it up for him to see, but instead of smiling back, he groused, "Come on. I'm sleepy."

She gave him a tight-lipped glare, then scrambled to her feet to place the car back into the Barbie garage. She climbed into bed and made sure her big stuffed tiger, Tamar, was comfortable.

As always, Devon was sleeping on the big fat air mattress. He liked it because it reminded him of the one he used to sleep on when he and his grandma went to the summer night revivals. But his grandma was in heaven, and this wasn't a revival. "Can we turn out the light tonight? I don't like sleeping with the lights on anymore."

She signed: *I do, and plus, it's my room.*

He didn't like this new lippy part of her either, as his grandma used to call it. Because he didn't know how to handle all the new experiences life was throwing his way, he had no sympathy for her fear of the dark, and he was mad. At everybody. "Okay, you baby. Keep the lights on. I don't care. You and that stupid tiger."

Zoey signed furiously: *I am NOT a baby. Take it back, Devon Watkins, or I will kick your butt!*

He sneered, "Baby! Baby! Zoey is a baby! That stupid tiger is stupid, stupid, stupid, and so are you! I hope the rats come tonight and eat you up!"

Zoey jumped off the bed, launched herself at him, and the fight was on.

Devon had never been in a fight before, but from the fury-fueled punches Zoey got in before he could put his hands up to defend himself, she must have been in plenty. He kept crying out for her to stop, but her small angry fists continued to rain down on his now-turtled form.

Next thing he knew, Dr. Reg was pulling Zoey away, and

Devon tasted blood from his bleeding nose and his busted lip. Zoey was so mad her face was red, and her hair was plastered to her face with sweat. Dr. Reg stared at them both in amazement. He then leaned down and looked at Devon's busted lip and swelling eye. "What are you two doing fighting? You're supposed to be best friends."

Zoey started signing, and she was going so fast because she was still so mad, Dr. Reg had to hold up a hand. "Wait. Let me fix his lip and stop his nosebleed first." Before leaving the room, he warned them both, "No more fighting. Zoey, go sit on your bed."

She did, but if looks could kill, Devon would've been laid out in a casket.

When Lily's phone rang, she and Trent were watching the credits for *Pretty Woman* and getting ready to move their party upstairs. Looking at the caller ID, she said to Trent, "It's Reg."

The conversation only took a few seconds. Ending the call, she told Trent, "He's bringing Devon home."

Trent dropped his head.

"He and Zoey got into a fight. Guess she kicked his little behind. Reg says he has a busted lip and a black eye."

"What happened?"

"Apparently, Devon called her a baby for wanting to keep the lights on."

"He knows she's scared of the dark."

"Yes, he does, and I guess he really knows now." She shook her head. "Zoey never impressed me as a fighter."

"Growing up with a crack addict, she's probably got a lot more street in her than we think."

"True. Reverend Paula said Zoey was a chatterbox when she knew her and her mom."

"She say anything about her being the reigning heavy-weight champ?"

She laughed, and then sobered as she thought about their abbreviated evening. "Sorry we couldn't make a night of it. At least you got to see *Pretty Woman*."

"But not the pretty woman I wanted to see."

She kissed him. "You're so sweet."

"Devon owes me one."

"And me."

"There might be a lot more to him than we think, too."

Lily paused and thought about that. "Not sure who he'll turn out to be, though."

"Could be some anger beneath that clip-on tie."

"I'm sensing that, too. We'll talk about it. Let me go. See you in the morning." She gave him another quick kiss and hurried home.

As the silence of the house echoed around Trent, he thought about Lily having to go home, and all he could say was, "Damn."

Following Reg's instructions, Lily had Devon lie on the couch with a small ice bag on his lip and another on his eye. His face was a mini version of Riley's. "You're going to have a real shiner in the morning, buddy. You made Zoey pretty mad, teasing her that way. Why would you do that to your best friend? You know she's afraid of the dark and needs the light on."

"She's mean."

"Sounds to me like you were the one being mean, Devon."

"She's changed."

"People do as they get older."

"I don't want her to get older."

Lily stroked his brow. "I know, sport, but you can't stop it. You just have to go with it."

"She doesn't like me anymore."

"The way you've been acting, I can't much blame her, but you'll work it out. Friends always do."

"What if she doesn't want to be friends anymore?"

"I don't think that's going to happen. In a few days, or even in the morning after she calms down and starts missing you, your friendship will be okay, but don't tease her like that again, Devon. It's not right."

"Am I on punishment?"

"Nope. Zoey gave you all the punishment you need. She's on punishment, though, for fighting. According to Doc Reg, no movies for her at the rec next Friday night." And before he could gloat, she warned, "Smile, and you'll have no movies next weekend either, sir. And you will be apologizing to her."

She watched him swallow his glee. "We'll keep the ice pack on for a few more minutes, then get you in bed."

He nodded.

Later, Lily tucked him in and gave him a good-night kiss. "Get some sleep, sweetheart. If you start to hurt in the middle of the night, come and get me."

"Okay," he replied, sounding sad. "Night, Ms. Lily."

As he lay alone in his bed in the dark, Devon's eye hurt and his lip throbbed. The medicine Ms. Lily had given him for pain was making him sleepy. As he drifted off, his last thought was that he never wanted to be in another fight again. Ever.

* * *

After leaving Detroit, Griffin headed west. He spent one night with his mother, Judith, at her home on the Pine Ridge Reservation in South Dakota before riding west to Oklahoma, where his grandfather Thaddeus July lived.

It was dark when he pulled up in the dusty front yard. Thaddeus was seated in a chair on the broken-down porch. His emaciated, one-eyed hound, Donut, lay at his feet.

"Good to see you," his grandfather called as Griff strode toward the porch. "So?"

Weary and stiff from the road, Griff sat down on the top step and stripped off his leather jacket. The T-shirt beneath was damp with sweat, but the cool night air felt good. He dragged off the bandanna to free his hair. "I got my answer."

"Cub's yours, right?"

"Right."

"How's the mother?"

"Very rich and very pissed. Told me not to tell the boy where she lived and threatened to call the cops if it took me more than thirty seconds to leave her place."

"Real happy to see you, huh?"

"Yeah."

"So now what?"

"We call Great-Aunt Tamar and tell her what we know."

"Not we. You. She hasn't spoken to me friendly-like in ten years, and before that nearly thirty. It probably burned her fry bread to no end to have to call me and ask for help in finding out about Amari."

"She's had good reasons to be mad."

"I know, but she and I will be on our way to the Ancestors

soon, and Old Tamar's not going to be happy if we bring this feud with us to the other side."

It was the first time he'd ever expressed a desire to reconcile with his sister Tamar. Griff turned to look his grandfather in the face. "You're serious, aren't you?"

"I am."

Griff teased, "You been drinking?"

"No. Should've done this decades ago."

"Maybe Amari will be the bridge you two need."

"We'll see. You hungry?"

"As a bear."

"Come on inside. Saved you some dinner. How's that pretty Lakota mama of yours?"

"Still gorgeous."

"Good."

Inside, Griffin ate the chicken, beans, and fry bread on his plate and watched his grandfather making his way around the tiny kitchen. Like most of the men in the July family, Thaddeus was well over six feet tall, with dark skin. He'd always been a vibrant, hard-living man, but in the last few years, age had slowed him down considerably. "You take your meds today?"

Thaddeus shot Griffin an exasperated look. "Every time you all visit, that's the first thing out of your mouths."

"Well, did you?"

"Yes, I did. Now don't ask me again."

Griffin hid his smile and went back to his meal. Age may have slowed him down, but mentally Daddy T, as he was affectionately known to his legion of grandkids, was as sharp and irascible as ever. "So how're all the uncles, aunts, and cousins?"

Thaddeus took a seat at the table and filled Griffin in on the tales of one divorce, two college graduations, and three jailings for car theft for nineteen-year-old Diego, one of his younger cousins, which exasperated his grandfather to no end.

"Diego is named for one of the original outlaw Julys, Daddy T."

"And you're named for the outlaw Griffin Blake, but you're not out robbing banks."

"Car theft's in the blood, you know that."

"For some of us."

"And that some includes you, or did somebody else steal Great-Aunt Tamar's truck, Olivia, the last time we were in Kansas?"

He chuckled. "I can't lie. Wish I'd've been there that morning when she found the truck gone."

"And you wonder why she's mad at you."

"Just me being coyote."

"Uh-huh, be glad she didn't shoot you like one. So what about Trent's wedding? Are you going?"

"Yep, me and the whole clan. Talked to Mal a few weeks back."

"Tamar's not going to be happy."

"Nope, but weddings mean family, and since we are, we're going."

Griffin could just about imagine the chaos that would result. The Oklahoma Julys would descend on Henry Adams like locusts in the Bible. "Guess I'll go, too. Need to talk with Trent about Amari's future, and somebody's got to keep our side of the family in line."

"You going after custody of the cub?"

"No, but I'd like to be in his life."

"Me, too. By blood he's my great-grandson, not my sister's."

"You approach this with that attitude, and she will shoot you."

"I know, but we'll figure it. Family always prevails."

Griffin knew he was right, so he went back to his meal.

CHAPTER
8

True to her word, Sheila Payne stopped by early Saturday morning so that she and Lily could begin planning the wedding. Although Lily was still grateful for Sheila's offer, she remained a bit doubtful about the woman's true abilities to pull this off, but as they sat in the kitchen and discussed the ins and outs, Lily got the impression that the colonel's wife did indeed know what she was doing.

"Now about your gown," Sheila asked. "Are you doing the traditional white gown?"

Lily thought back on the catalogs she'd gotten from Bernadine. "I don't really want to. They seem so expensive."

"What about a nice new suit?"

Lily hadn't considered that as an option. "That's a great idea, Sheila."

"And it can be any color you decide. Although I'd stay away from black."

Lily contemplated the idea a bit more. "If I go with a suit, that means the men in the wedding party won't have to wear tuxedos either, correct?"

"Right. Nice suits will work for them as well."

Lily sighed with relief. "Trent will love that."

They then spent a few more minutes going over the food to be served for the reception. Sheila asked, "Do you want a cake?"

"I do, but not the traditional tiered thing. If Rocky and Siz don't mind, I'd like a variety. Maybe a red velvet, a German chocolate, and a coconut."

Sheila wrote that down. "I'll talk to Rocky and see what she thinks. Where do you want the ceremony to take place, and do you have a pastor in mind?"

"I'd like to use the school's kiva or the rec, and Bernadine has just hired a town priest. Her name's Paula Grant. I thought I'd ask her to do the honors."

"She's a priest?"

"Yes. Episcopalian, I believe. Not real familiar with that denomination."

"I am. Barrett and I are both Episcopalian. When will she be arriving?"

Lily made a mental note to get the information out to the community about the priest's arrival. "In a few days. She has some loose ends to tie up down in Miami."

Sheila seemed pleased. "That's wonderful. I'll speak with her about the service after she's settled in. Might be nice to welcome her with a dinner of some kind."

"Since you're now the Henry Adams VP of social affairs, that'll be up to you."

Sheila stared.

Lily explained, "Bernadine doesn't have the time to head up stuff like this, and I'm not making the time, so the job's yours. I'll check with Bernadine, but I'm pretty sure the title will come with a salary and a budget."

Her mouth dropped. "A salary?"

"It won't be a large one."

"I don't care. I've never had my own money, Lily. Oh, my. I married Barrett right out of college."

"Then let me be the first to welcome you to the World of Working Women."

Sheila looked so stunned, Lily laughed.

"Does that mean I get to plan next year's August First parade?" Sheila asked.

"If you think you can handle Preston and Amari, have at it by all means."

Sheila sat back in her chair and placed her hand over her heart as if it were racing.

"You okay?"

"I'm overwhelmed." She straightened, leaned forward, and looked Lily in the eyes. "Why are you giving this position to me?"

"One, because every town needs elegance, and if you can add that to Henry Adams, I know Bernadine will be grateful. And two, frankly, Sheila, we've all been waiting to find out who you are."

Her lips thinned. "Really?"

"Yeah, girl. It's been what, two years, and none of us really know you."

"My apologies," she said softly.

"You have nothing to apologize for. We just haven't seen the strength it must have taken to get Barrett to move here and become a foster parent. Everyone in town knows that man did not come here of his own free will."

Sheila smiled and nodded. "True. But I never thought about my convincing him taking any kind of strength."

"It had to. He's a hard-ass."

Sheila nodded again. "He is that, although Preston's helped soften some of the marine edges. After I went on retreat this summer, our marriage seemed to be better, too."

"Glad to hear it."

"The Dads group is helping as well." Sheila then asked, "Will I have an office?"

"Yes. That a problem?"

"No. I think it'll be wonderful having some place to go every morning." She paused for a moment as if thinking. "Are you sure about this, Lily?"

"Just as long as you don't go overboard and have us doing teas every three days, we're good."

Sheila laughed. "I won't, I promise."

"Good. I don't want to have to confiscate your white gloves."

There was a pause as Sheila went silent again. She finally turned her attention Lily's way and declared in a satisfied-sounding tone, "Guess I have a job."

"Guess you do."

Sheila's face beamed. Lily couldn't remember ever seeing her so pleased.

"It's going to take a while for me to digest all this," Sheila admitted. "So how about we go back to the wedding plans. That I can handle."

The conversation moved to the subject of how many invitations Lily might need sent out. To which Lily replied, "I assume everyone in town will want to come, and maybe the construction crews and their families, too. We're all pretty close around here."

"Okay. How about we plan on, say, a hundred? In reality the invitations should have gone out already."

"I know, but the only person coming from out of town for sure is my son, Davis. No sense in sending early invites to the people here. I've everyone's address on a spreadsheet. I'll print it out and get that to you on Monday."

Sheila took a look down at her notes. "Think I have enough to get started."

Lily felt relief wash over her like the blue waves of Hawaii. The wedding plans were finally under way, and Sheila hadn't mentioned anything about glass slippers, fairy coaches, or seven dwarves.

Lily walked her to the door.

Sheila paused before leaving to say, "You've no idea how much you've done for me today, Lily Fontaine."

"Feeling's mutual."

They shared the smile of women on the way to becoming friends, and Sheila departed.

Having enjoyed Sheila's visit, Lily turned from the door just as Devon came downstairs. He'd slept in, in response to his troubling evening. The ice packs from last night had kept his eye and lip from swelling too much, but the skin around his eye was bruised, and his bottom lip was split and fat. It was easy to see that he'd been in a fight. "How're you feeling?"

"My eye hurts. I think I need more medicine."

"I'll get you some after you have breakfast."

He sat down at the table, and after he poured cereal into his bowl and had his glass of juice close by, she said, "Want to talk to you about something. Mr. Trent and Amari are going to move in here with us after we get married. Think that's a good idea?"

He shrugged. "It's okay, I guess."

Lily tried to gauge his true feelings. "Do you think it's a bad idea?"

He shrugged again. "Why can't they live in their own house?"

"Because a married couple should be under the same roof."

"Oh."

Lily added, "It'll probably be a lot noisier around here, and maybe more commotion, but I think we'll get used to it. And we'll be a family."

"You and I are already a family."

"True, but we'll be a bigger family. And you'll be getting a brother and a dad."

Devon didn't reply. He ate his cereal instead.

Peering at his downcast eyes, she asked, "Don't you want a brother and a dad?"

"No."

"Why not?" she asked gently.

"I just want our family to be me and you, and maybe Davis."

"I see, but our new family will be fun."

"I don't want a new family. I just want us to stay the same."

"Life is always changing, Devon."

"I hate life!" he declared angrily and crossed his arms with emphasis.

Lily paused and studied him for a silent moment. "Devon?"

"I hate it," he echoed. "I don't like it when things change."

"But sweetheart—"

He pushed his bowl away. "I'm not hungry anymore. Can I have my medicine and be excused?"

Lily observed the angry face and found herself at a loss for words. "Can you tell me why you're so mad?"

"Because I want to be."

"Excuse me?"

"You asked me. I answered."

Lily cocked her head. She'd never met this mouthy little boy before. Holding on to her own rising temper, she said to him, "Usually people get mad for a reason. I'd really like to understand yours, and maybe we can fix whatever it is."

"Stop trying to make me do new things!"

She understood now, or at least she thought she did. "You're going to be doing new things for the rest of your life, baby boy. There's no way of getting around it."

"I don't care. I want to stay me."

"And who is that?"

"Devon Watkins, the anointed preacher," he threw back in a sullen tone. "God's going to punish you for not letting me preach the Word."

"Really?"

"Yes. You and everybody else are going to burn in the pit."

"Zoey, too?"

He shot her a dark look, but he didn't reply.

"There's a lady pastor coming to live here, and I think you're going to like her."

The look on his face said otherwise, but Lily chose to

ignore it. "She's also a counselor and has spent many years helping kids with their problems. I'm going to have you talk with her when she gets here. Maybe she can help you sort out some of these feelings you're having."

"I don't want to."

"Doesn't matter."

He shot her another look.

She shrugged and said, "It doesn't, and if you want to add me to your list of why you're mad, fine. My job is to love you and help you, and I take my job seriously."

He refolded his arms in a huff. "Then why won't you let me do what I want? My grandma let me do whatever I wanted."

"I don't believe that for a minute."

"She did," he countered, raising his voice. "And I don't like you anymore."

"I'm not liking you a whole lot either, so add that to your list. Now I'm going to get you your medicine, and you can take your little mad self back up to your room."

She gave him the pill. He washed it down with the last of his orange juice and stomped up the steps loud enough to be heard in Georgia.

Lily got up. "Devon!"

"What?" he demanded from the landing.

"Get back down here."

At first she thought he was going to give her more lip, but as she glared up at him from the bottom of the stairs, he must have seen the cool fire in her eyes, because he complied. He wasn't happy, but she didn't care. Her mother would have smacked her into next week for making such an exit. "Now," she said in a voice reminiscent of mamas everywhere, "you don't get to storm around here like some kid on TV. Walk back up those steps like you have some sense."

He had the decency to look ashamed and muttered, "Yes, ma'am."

This time he climbed the stairs with a lot less attitude.

"And don't even think about slamming your door," she warned, went back into the kitchen, and sat down. Lily put her head down on the table. Reverend Grant couldn't get to Henry Adams fast enough. Devon needed help, and so did she.

Across the street, Trent and Amari were discussing the move to Lily's, too.

"What do you think of the plan?" Trent asked him. "And you can be truthful, son."

Amari looked at his dad, seated across from him at their kitchen table. "Do I still get my own room?"

"Absolutely."

"And I can put my NASCAR posters back up on the walls?"

Trent nodded. "We'll build the gym over there, too."

Amari's face brightened. "She's okay with that?"

"Yep." Trent was certain Lily wasn't, but he'd made the biggest capitulation, so what could she say?

"One last question," Amari said. "No, two."

"Shoot."

"I've seen the inside of her refrigerator. Are we going to have to eat all that yogurt and stuff she buys? I'm used to meat."

Trent chuckled. "We'll still eat meat, don't worry. I'm not fond of the yogurt and stuff, either. What's your second question?"

"Do you think it'll be okay if I call her Mom? Never had a mom before."

Trent went still. He met his son's serious gaze and felt his own heart fill with emotion. He'd never had a mom either, and knew how that lack had saddened him while growing up. "I think she'll like that, Amari."

"Good. When do we pack?"

Amari's beaming face let Trent know that everything would be okay. He just hoped Devon was smiling, too.

He wasn't. Devon was up in his bedroom smoldering because every time he turned around, somebody was making him do something he didn't want to do. When Ms. Lily demanded that he come back down the steps, he'd started to refuse, but the look in her eyes said she wasn't playing, so he'd obeyed. His grandma had given him that look a few times, and it usually came with a whipping on the end, so he knew better than to keep acting up. However, he was still so mad he wanted to beat up something the way Zoey had done him. Since he didn't know how, he snatched a pencil out of his X-Men pencil holder and tried to break it in half. He wasn't strong enough, and that further inflamed his anger so he threw it across the room. Every pencil in the cylinder went flying after that. The crayons came next, followed by all the pieces of chalk. With furious tears streaming down his cheeks, he threw his bed pillows and kicked his Spider-Man slippers lying so innocently next to the bed. He snatched open his dresser drawers and grabbed handfuls of the nicely folded items inside and gave them the same treatment. All he wanted was his grandma and his other life back, but because that could never be, he threw himself onto his bed and cried until the medicine eased him back into sleep.

Trent was still basking in Amari's approval of the move when his phone rang. It was Barrett Payne, and he wanted to call an emergency meeting of the Dads. He wouldn't tell Trent why over the phone, but Trent agreed to make the calls to alert the others. They set the meet for noon at his garage, and after Trent hung up, he wondered, Now what?

The *what* turned out to be Preston's search for his biological parents.

"I don't like it," Barrett declared once they were all seated around Trent's garage.

"Why not?" Trent could see the other men watching Barrett closely.

"Because."

Reg sighed aloud. "Because why?"

"It's just going to blow up in his face, and I told him that."

Jack saluted him with the bottle of water he was sipping from. "That's real supportive, Dad."

Barrett glared.

Reg shook his head. "I'm with Jack. What were you thinking?"

Apparently offended, Barrett stood and declared, "If you're just going to criticize, I may as well leave."

Mal waved him off. "Oh, sit down. You're not going anywhere."

Barrett sat.

Trent hid his smile behind the draw he took from his can of soda.

Reg asked, "If you were adopted, wouldn't you want to know where you came from?"

"Not if I had a good adoptive family."

Jack shook his head as if he couldn't believe Barrett's stance.

"So in other words, you're taking Preston's quest personal?" Mal asked.

"No, of course not."

"Sounds like it to me," Jack countered.

"Me, too," Mal agreed sagely. "Let the kid do his thing. Whoever his folks turn out to be, I don't see Preston wanting to leave."

"Legally he can't anyway," Trent pointed out. "The biological parents have given up their rights."

"Then why even look?" Barrett countered. "Sheila and I provide him with everything he needs."

It was Trent's turn to shake his head. "Barrett, I hate to pile on, but sounds like you're taking this personal to me, too."

Barrett sat back against the old leather couch and firmly folded his arms across his chest. "So what am I supposed to do?"

"Try seeing things from Preston's perspective," Jack suggested. "He's a brilliant kid. Of course he's going to want to know about his biological past. Not everything's about you, Barrett."

That earned Jack a glare, which he shrugged off.

"How's your wife handling all this?" Mal said, bringing the conversation back.

"She's all for it, of course."

Reg raised his bottle. "To Sheila."

The look on Barrett's face said he didn't agree with the tribute, but no one in the garage called him on it.

Trent asked instead, "Would you rather Preston not know who he is?"

Barrett didn't respond.

Mal gave him a disgusted look. "Grow up, man. Like Jack said, this isn't about you. It's about your son. Whatever insecurities you have, deal with them."

"I'm not insecure. I'm a marine."

Jack said, "Which is probably the problem."

Barrett looked him up and down. "What do you know about the Corps, schoolteacher?" The sneer was plain.

"Oh, that's real mature," Jack tossed back. "But to answer your question. I don't know a damn thing about being a marine, but you don't know a damn thing about being a parent, so that makes us even."

Barrett got up and walked out.

Trent said, "Looks like the meeting's adjourned."

"Hallelujah," Mal declared sarcastically. "In the meantime, I vote we give Preston as much support as we can. Mr. Hard-Ass will get it together, but if we wait for him to come around, Preston'll be thirty-five."

They all agreed.

"One last thing before we break up," Trent said. "We're getting a new member. Name's Gary Clark." He went on to tell them a bit about Gary's situation, and about restoring the Clark homestead.

Jack said, "Hammers aren't my strong suit, but I'm in."

Reg was, too. "I'm not good at the hardware stuff either, but when somebody falls off the roof, I'm your man."

"Okay," Trent said. "Meet me out there tomorrow around one. Jack and Reg, I'll give you directions." He turned to Mal. "Dad, if you could talk to Clay and your crew and see if they'd be willing to pitch in, we should have enough manpower to put up new walls and a roof before the snow falls. We can finish the interior over the winter."

"Sounds good," Mal replied.

With that, the meeting adjourned.

Jack and Reg departed to enjoy the rest of the sunny afternoon, but Trent and his dad lingered in the garage.

"Amari and I'll be moving into Lily's place after the wedding," Trent informed Mal.

"Amari okay with that?"

"Yeah, just as long as he can put his posters up and not have to eat Lily's yogurt."

Mal chuckled.

"He also asked if he could call Lily Mom."

Mal nodded appreciatively. "Beneath all that street is a great young man. I'll bet Lily'll be honored."

"I think so, too. Oh, and listen to this. Devon and Zoey had a falling-out last night, and Devon came home looking like he'd gone ten rounds with Ali."

Mal looked up from his soda. "What?"

"Black eye. Busted lip."

"Zoey did that?"

Trent nodded.

Mal chuckled. "That girl's got a whole lot of layers under that little button nose."

Trent agreed. "We probably don't know the half of it."

"So what started it?"

Trent told him.

Mal sipped. "Lot of layers to the preacher man, too. He's been hiding it well, though."

Trent then related the tale of Devon's afternoon at the garage and his refusal to try new things.

"Zoey liked working on the cars?" Mal smiled. "Why am I not surprised."

"Devon just didn't want to get his suit dirty."

"Gotta toughen that boy up."

"I think so, too, but what do two country boys from Kansas like us know about child psychology?"

Mal shrugged. "True."

Trent scanned the tarp covering the old T-Bird. He really wanted to work on the car, but spending time with Lily held more power. "I'm heading over to Lily's. Where are you off to?"

"Back to the Dog to get ready for the Saturday-night rush."

"See you later."

They walked to their trucks and parted with a wave.

CHAPTER
9

On the drive back home, Trent mused on all the goings-on. Barrett. Preston. Zoey. Devon. The wedding. Gary. Gary's house. He had no idea when he'd become such a master multitasker, but figured it came from hanging around Bernadine and Fontaine. Lily's face floated across his mind. Lord, she was gorgeous. Focusing on her made all the rest of the stuff he was juggling fade away. Their upcoming marriage would be his third try at the brass ring. Although he'd considered himself in love when he tied the knot before, what he felt inside for her seemed to soar above and beyond. He knew her by heart, if he could call it that, just as she did him. And them being apart for so many years hadn't seemed to matter. At first, he'd been angered by her return to Henry Adams two summers ago, but once he got over himself and accepted her apology for hurting him so badly, they'd picked up seemingly right where they'd left off. Gary had been right to tease them about acting like teens again; they did have a tendency to get into it, but he and Lily had grown up. They'd been molded by their separated lives, and their present relationship was the better for it. Unlike Devon, Trent was more than happy to embrace the new, because the new had brought his Lily Flower back into his arms.

When he pulled into the garage, he checked his phone before going inside. A text message from Amari was waiting to inform him that he and Preston had ridden their bikes out to see Tamar and would be back in plenty of time for dinner. Trent smiled. In the face of all the other things swirling around town, none of it involved Amari for once, and he was happy about that as well.

Trent called Lily to make sure she was home, and as he came out of the house, he noticed Sheila on her knees in her front yard, planting bulbs. He wondered if Barrett was still pouting, but seeing Sheila reminded him that there was something he wanted to speak with her about.

She met his approach with a sunny smile. "Hey, Trent. Gorgeous day isn't it?"

"Sure is. What are you planting?"

"Apparently, deer food—the more tulips I plant, the more they eat. Last spring they ate everything."

"Tamar plants daffodils. Deer don't eat those."

She appeared surprised. "Really?"

"Yep. Call her. No sense in feeding the deer unless you want to fatten them up for hunting season."

She made an ugly face and cringed. "I despise venison."

He grinned. "Just wanted to come over and say thanks for taking on the wedding."

"You're welcome. I enjoy the planning. Since Lily has appointed me VP of social affairs, my first official event will be a dinner for the new priest when she arrives. As the mayor, your attendance is mandatory."

He replied with a skeptical-sounding "Okay. VP of social affairs. Congratulations."

"And I get an office, a budget, and a salary. Barrett's either going to be happy about my new job, or—" She paused and whispered, "I almost said 'shit bricks,' but that's not very lady-like, is it?"

Trent's stunned laughter broke the silence. "Who are you?" he asked. "And what have you done with Sheila Payne?"

"Mousy little woman? Weepy all the time?"

Trent stilled.

"Haven't seen her." She paused again as if thinking, then said, "This is all Lily's fault, you know. She told me that I had to have been a strong woman to convince Mr. Hard-Ass to move here and become a parent, but I'd never thought about it in those terms before."

"I'd have to agree with her."

"After I came home and thought about it, I had to agree with her, too. My talk with her this morning is one of the reasons I'm out here. Gardening helps me think things through. And do you know what I've decided?"

He was almost afraid to respond. "What?"

"I'm going to become that same strong woman. No more Sheila Payne doormat to the marines. I'm going to try and model myself after Lily and Bernadine and Tamar."

Uh-oh, said his inner self, but aloud he replied, "That sounds good, Sheila." He feigned a hasty glance down at his watch. "Oops. Gotta go. Lily's waiting. I just wanted to say thanks for the wedding and everything. Take care, and good luck with the new you."

"Thanks, Trent."

Still a bit stunned, he crossed the street to Lily's house.

He found her in the kitchen making the sloppy joes they'd be having for dinner. "You've created a monster, you know that, right?"

Wearing an apron over her T-shirt and jeans, she looked up, puzzled. "Monster? What are you talking about?" The smell of the onions and beef she was sautéing in a big shiny pot filled the house.

He gave her a quick kiss on her cheek. "Sheila Payne. I think Barrett may be driving her to drink. God, that smells good."

Spoon in hand, she turned his way and asked, "What?"

Laughing at the confusion on her face, he took a seat and related his conversation with Sheila.

When he finished, Lily went back to her cooking. "Could be worse. She could want to model herself after Eustasia Pennymaker and be in the market for a sow."

"True, but why does this give me a bad feeling?"

"Because you're a man, and it looks like another strong woman will be moving in. It'll be okay. The colonel's not going to be happy, though. How'd the Dads meeting go?"

"How'd you know we were meeting?"

"Is Dads Inc. a secret organization now?" she asked. "You know there aren't any secrets around here."

Resigned to that truth, he related the reason for the meeting and concluded by declaring, "Barrett's an idiot."

She sighed. "He and Preston seemed to be doing so well. Maybe it'll all work out. Me, I have problems of my own." She poured a can of pork and beans into the now done meat and onions and stirred as she told him about Devon's behavior.

His eyes widened.

"When I went up to check on him a little while ago, he'd trashed his room. Sat down with him and tried to get him to talk out what he's feeling, but it was like talking to this stove. He's cleaning up now."

"Frustrating, huh?"

"Extremely, but I'm going to keep pounding away at it. I'm not giving up on him."

"Do you want me to talk to him?"

She added barbecue sauce and a bit of brown sugar to the bubbling ingredients in the pot. "Yes, but let him finish first."

"What do you think is going on with him?"

She shrugged. "Says he hates life."

"Probably wants back what he had with his grand."

Lily nodded. "Understandable, but how do you explain to a little boy that life makes us go on?"

"Maybe the new reverend will help us figure out how to make that happen."

"Be nice, but as I said, I'm going to keep trying to reach him."

"How's his eye and lip?"

"Big."

"Zoey been by?"

"Nope."

They shared a look of concern. Trent tried to ease her worries. "Those two love each other so much, they won't be apart for long."

"I'm hoping on that, too."

Trent stood. "I'll go see what kind of progress he's made."

"Thanks. When he's done, I'm going to walk him over to Zoey's so he can apologize."

"I'll take him over."

"Really?"

"Yep. Sounds like a dad mission. Might give me a chance to talk to him, too."

"You're not bad at this dad stuff."

"Thanks. You're no slouch at being a mom, either. In fact, Amari wanted to know if he could call you Mom."

She stilled, and next he knew, she had tears in her eyes.

"Aw, girl. What's the matter? You know I hate it when you cry."

"Amari is so amazing. Of course he can."

"Come here."

She went to him, and he took her into his arms and held her tight. "One day," he whispered, "after we survive this child-raising business and they're both grown and gone, we're going to have Bernadine buy us an island to live on where no one can find us." He pulled back and looked down into her wet eyes. "And I'm going to show you every day what an amazing woman you are."

"Promise?"

"Scout's honor. I'll go up and get Devon."

"Thanks, Trenton."

"For you, girl, the world."

Trent went upstairs and knocked on Devon's door.

"Come in."

"Hey, Dev. How are you?"

"Fine." He was stretched out on his bed reading his Bible, and immediately focused his attention back on the pages. Trent's slow look around the room showed it to be as neat as he assumed it had been before the trashing, and he contrasted that to the chaos that reigned in Amari's bedroom. "Heard you and Ms. Lily got into a small spat this morning."

"What's a spat?"

"A little argument."

His lips thinned. "Yeah."

"She said you don't like her anymore."

"She won't let me do anything."

"Like what?"

He glanced Trent's way. "Be a preacher."

Trent sighed. "Did you worry your grandma this way whenever she told you no?"

He didn't respond for a long moment, then said, "No."

"Why not?"

"Because I knew better."

"So why should Ms. Lily saying no be any different?"

"Because my grandma never said I couldn't preach," he threw back.

"I see. You'll get to preach when you're older, Devon, but right now, your job is to learn how to be the best person you can be so that you can be ready. And your other job is to respect your mom. You don't raise your voice, you don't talk back, and you definitely don't tear up your room when she tells you something you don't like."

He looked down.

"Do we have an understanding, son?"

He whispered, "Yes, sir. Am I getting a spanking now?"

Trent stared in confusion. "Why would you think that?"

"Because when my grandma talked real soft like that, I usually got a spanking."

Trent understood. "I will never put my hands on you in anger, Devon, ever, okay?"

Devon nodded hastily.

"Now you and I are going to go see Zoey, and you're going to apologize for the stuff you said."

"But—"

"But what?"

He sighed. "Nothing."

"If you have something to say, now's the time, son."

He shook his head.

"You sure?"

"Yes, sir."

Downstairs in the kitchen, Lily was just putting the top on the sloppy joes when Trent and Devon walked in. She asked Devon, "Is your room picked up?"

"Yes, ma'am."

She looked to Trent, and he nodded in agreement, adding, "We're going over to see Zoey now."

"Okay."

Trent didn't pay any attention to Devon's hangdog face. "We'll be back in a few."

Reg met them at the door, ushered them in, and called up the steps for Zoey. While they waited for her to come down, Reg took a look at Devon's injuries. "Your eye's going be like this for a few more days, Devon. Is the pain medicine helping you sleep?"

"Yes."

"Good. Zoey!" he called again. "She's probably up there taking her bed apart. Caught her this morning trying to dismantle the dishwasher with a butter knife."

"What?"

"She wants me to take her to a hardware store to buy real tools like Mr. Trent's."

"Sorry," Trent said.

"No, I think this is pretty cool. Just have to keep an eye on her so she doesn't undo every screw in the house."

Trent hadn't any idea Zoey would take to tools the way she had, but he approved. "I'll get her some tools and some things she can take apart, like old clocks and radios."

"That would help a lot. Zoey!!"

She finally appeared, wearing a pair of winter gloves and swim goggles over her eyes. Trent supposed it was the closest she could find to genuine safety gear, and he wished Mal and Rocky were there to see her. "Looking good, Zoey."

She smiled back, but upon seeing Devon, turned away in a huff.

Devon cut her a simmering look in response, but Trent ignored it. "Devon, you have something you want to say to Zoey?"

"I forgive you, Zoey."

Trent stared as if the boy had suddenly grown three heads. "You forgive her?" he asked startled.

"Yes. I called her names, but she resorted to violence. The Bible says—"

Trent threw up a hand. "Hold it." He bent down and looked into Devon's eyes and said firmly, "Apologize to her now, or it'll be you and a paintbrush on Ms. Agnes's fence in two minutes."

Devon swallowed. "I'm sorry," he said belligerently.

Trent looked at Reg. The outdone Reg chuckled and shook his head.

Devon had his arms folded over his chest like a put-upon child king.

Trent wondered if he should have let Lily come over with Devon instead. Although he'd promised to never put his hands on the boy in anger, he wanted to smack him upside his little pea-shaped head. He calmed himself. "Devon. You're going to apologize again, and this time, sound like you mean it."

The second attempt was only marginally better.

Apparently, Zoey wasn't buying any of it. She signed, *Dad. Can I go back to my room?*

"Yeah, baby. Go on."

Before she departed, Trent told her, "Zo, one day next week, you, me, and your dad will go to Franklin and get you some real tools and safety gear. How's that sound?"

Her face brightened like the sun. She ran back and gave Trent the biggest hug she'd ever given him, and signed: *Thank you!*

"No problem, but until then, no more taking apart anything that doesn't have Barbie's name on it. Okay?"

She nodded.

"Promise?"

She nodded again enthusiastically. Smiling, she ran up the steps and disappeared.

Trent said to Reg, "Sorry this didn't go better."

Reg waved him off and said to Devon, "Obviously Devon believes this is all Zoey's fault. Right, Devon?"

Devon stared ahead stubbornly.

On the walk back to Lily's, Trent looked down at Devon and said, "So now you don't have a best friend. Not real smart, son. Not smart at all."

Devon told himself he didn't care, but inside, his heart ached.

And the day went downhill from there. First, Trent told on him the moment they got back, and Lily promptly put Devon on the first real punishment he'd ever received in his life. He tried quoting the Bible at her the way he sometimes did to his grandmother in order to shame her into lightening the sentence, but she wasn't his grandma. To prove it, he was denied access to his DVDs, television, and video games until further notice.

"You're going to need your mind clear to think of all the words you'll be putting into the three-page apology letter you're going to write to Zoey," she told him firmly.

His eyes went wide as dinner plates.

Second, Amari was there when they returned as well, and although he didn't say anything while Lily was laying down the law, Devon could see him shaking his head with disappointment. When she was done, Amari started in on his what-it-meant-to-be-a-July speech, but before he could get going good, Mr. Trent stopped him. "You're not in this, Amari."

It was the day's only saving grace.

After dinner, the sad-faced Devon helped Amari clear the table, then dejectedly climbed the stairs to his room. Once inside, he closed the door and threw himself across the bed. He would've much rather had a spanking.

On Sunday morning, he and Ms. Lily shared a silent breakfast and then left for the school auditorium. It would be the last Sunday of his preaching career, and he prayed Zoey would show up to play the piano. She didn't. In fact, the only people who did come were Mr. Trent, Amari, and Ms. Bernadine. He was very disappointed. "Where is everybody?" he asked Lily. Since late August, the crowds had been getting smaller and smaller.

She shrugged. "Do you know what a novelty is, sweetheart?"

Devon could see Amari and the others watching him. "No, ma'am."

After she explained what it meant, he asked, "So they weren't really coming to hear the Word?"

"Doesn't look like it."

"Can we go back home?" he asked her. "My eye hurts."

"Sure, sweetheart."

They walked back out to the car, and she drove him home.

CHAPTER
10

But later that afternoon plenty of people showed up to begin the work on Gary Clark's ancestral home, and Trent was pleased by all the support. Mal and his crew arrived first, along with a few of the local farmers and a large number of the area's construction workers. Next came Bernadine and Crystal, followed by Jack and Eli and Reg and Zoey. Lily parked and walked up with an unhappy-looking Devon, and on their heels came Amari, Preston, and Leah, who rode up on their bikes. Sheila came alone; Trent guessed Barrett was still pouting. When Gary finally arrived with an obviously angry Tiffany Adele, who was decked out in a dress and ballet slippers, Trent was ready to get the ball rolling.

However, before he could thank everyone for coming, Tamar and Ms. Agnes roared up in Olivia, and he had to wait for the dust to settle and for the latecomers to join them, too.

"Okay. Looks like everybody's here. First I want to thank you for coming. For those of you who don't know Gary Clark, that's him over there. He has two daughters. Leah, raise your hand, please."

She complied and smiled shyly.

"And Tiffany Adele."

She didn't raise her hand, but stood beside her dad smoldering instead, which of course drew the attention of Tamar, who walked over and stood beside her. All the kids shared a knowing look, and would've felt sorry for Tiffany if she hadn't been acting like such a brat.

Trent turned to Gary. "Do you have anything you want to say?"

He nodded. "I just want to say thanks. I'm real grateful for the support, and I know my girls are, too. You're giving us a home, and there is no greater gift."

"We're glad to do it," Trent responded. He opened his mouth to add more, but promptly closed it as he and everyone else watched Tamar march a mutinous-looking Tiffany Adele off to the side.

"Uh-oh," Amari said loud enough for them all to hear.

Crystal added with a laugh, "You got that right."

Knowing grins and chuckles greeted that; most of them had been in Tiff's ballet shoes at least once in their lives. It could be a very memorable and sometimes unpleasant place, but they knew Tamar would chew her out with love, so everyone turned their attention back to Trent as he began to divide all the volunteers into the crews that would be led by himself, Mal, Cliff, and Bing. Once each crew was clear as to its duties, the work began.

The balance of the day's efforts was spent emptying out the

interior rooms of their old, unusable furniture. They took out old sofas, chairs that had been converted into nests by mice and other small mammals, and mattresses that had also been turned into wildlife homes. Trent grinned, watching Zoey carrying out a warped and rotting dresser drawer almost as big as herself and tossing it into the pile. There'd be a bonfire later for all the old wood. Tiffany Adele had been turned into an assistant to Tamar and Ms. Agnes, and was helping to set out plates and cups on the long table where all the food would be placed. She didn't look happy. Neither did Devon, who kept trying to brush the dirt and dust off his suit pants and shoes while working along-side Mal, who kept chuckling and handing him more gunk-covered shingles to place in the industrial-sized Dumpster.

As the sun began to fade, Trent took a look around at the progress they'd made and the good time everyone seemed to be having—Tiff and Devon notwithstanding—and he decided it had been a productive day. When Tamar announced that the food was ready, it got even better.

Once the volunteers had washed up at the old pump behind the house, they feasted on hot dogs and hamburg-ers, ears of grilled corn, Ms. Agnes's famous potato salad, and Clay's spicy baked beans. There would be ice cream later during the bonfire, but from the happiness on all the faces, no one seemed to care about being made to wait.

Trent took his piled-high plate over to where Lily was seated in the grass and sat beside her.

"This was fun," she declared.

He agreed. "We got a lot done. Gives you an appetite, too. I could eat a horse."

She smiled, and as her eyes strayed toward the road that

ran by the Clark home, she went still. "Look who's shown up now that all the work's done."

The big black town car belonging to Leo Brown came to a stop, and out of its expensive cream-colored leather interior stepped Marie, Genevieve, sporting her signed cast, and then the man himself. His gray suit looked imported and screamed money loud enough to be heard in Denver.

Lily cracked sarcastically, "Doesn't look like he's dressed to haul wood."

"You're going to make yourself sick hating on that man," Trent noted amusedly.

Her eyes followed their approach onto the Clark property. "Can't help it."

Trent eyed Genevieve's hand. "Wonder how Riley's doing?"

"I wish I could have been a fly on the wall when she knocked him out at the Dog. She sure has changed."

"I'll bet Riley's saying the same thing." The memory of the way Riley slid beneath the booth and out of view made Trent chuckle. "He melted under that booth like a flattened Wile E. Coyote after one of his run-ins with the Road Runner."

Grinning, Lily crowed, "Beep beep."

He laughed and went back to his plate.

Devon was ready to go home. He was hot and tired, and his suit was a mess, but he knew he would have to sit through the bonfire first. He'd spent the day watching Zoey and being jealous of all the attention she was getting. Every time she walked by, carrying something out to the pile of wood, one of the adults would say, "Good job, Zo!" or "Looking good, Miss Z."

The Miss Z business had been started by Mr. Mal. He'd put himself on Devon's list, too, for making him get so dirty. Each time Devon bent over to brush the dirt off his pant legs, Mr. Mal would say, "That little bit of dirt won't kill you, boy. Here, come and get this." And he'd hand Devon something to carry even dirtier than the last thing he'd been given. Once again, Devon wasn't happy with his life or the people in it. He spotted Ms. Lily, sitting on the grass next to Mr. Trent. They looked happy. He wasn't sure how he felt about having Mr. Trent for a dad. He'd never had a man in his life before. The one time he'd asked his grandma about his mother and father, she responded with, "I'll tell you when you get older." Now that she'd passed on, he'd never know, but sometimes he did wonder who they were and where they might be. He'd hoped they'd come and get him after his grandma's death, but they hadn't. No one came to claim him.

"Hey, buckaroo. Why are you sitting over here all by yourself?"

Devon looked up into the kind eyes of Mr. Malachi. In response to the question, he offered a slow shrug. "Nobody likes me anymore."

"Heard you were having a hard time. Things any better?"

"Nope."

"Want to tell me about it? Sometimes having somebody to talk to takes the sting out of stuff, you know."

Devon thought that over for a moment and then said, "Okay."

So Devon talked about the fight with Zoey, his spat with Ms. Lily, and how he came to be on punishment. Through it all Mr. Mal listened. He didn't fuss, nor did he judge. Instead he said, "You know, Devon, life sucks sometimes."

Devon drew back, horrified.

"Sorry," Mal said with a chagrined grin. "But sometimes only your OG will tell it like it is."

Devon wasn't sure he really understood that, but he got the drift.

Mal explained further, "No matter how many times we think we got life licked, she throws us a curveball."

"Like Satchel Paige?"

Mal choked on his root beer. When he recovered, he peered closely. "What do you know about Satchel Paige?"

"Negro League. One of the best pitchers of his day, Black or White."

Mal's jaw dropped. "Who are you, and what have you done with our Devon?"

And for the first time that day, Devon smiled. "My grandma's daddy played with Mr. Paige and Mr. Gibson, and even Mr. Cool Papa Bell."

Mal blinked. He looked around as if he wanted to call someone for help but found Devon too fascinating to let out of his sight. "Your great-grandfather played Negro League ball?"

"Yes, sir. My grandma's family album had a bunch of old pictures and articles from the newspapers."

Mal sat back. "Well, I'll be. So you like baseball?"

"Yes, sir. Me and my grandma were Braves fans because of Mr. Henry Aaron."

Mal chuckled at the craziness of this interaction. "Why haven't you said anything?"

"Nobody asked."

That made perfect sense. "Tell you what. This weekend coming up, the playoffs start and your Braves are in the running. How about you and me watch together?"

Devon had no way of knowing that the way his eyes lit up made Mal realize he was going to love Devon just as much as he loved Amari.

Mal asked, "Would you like that?"

"Like a bullfrog loves flies."

"What?" Mal asked through his laugh. "Where'd you hear that?"

"My grandma used to say it all the time." He stilled, and the sadness in his eyes broke Mal's heart.

"Miss her a lot, I'll bet?"

Devon wiped at the tears filling his eyes. He didn't want Amari and Preston seeing him cry.

Mal asked softly, "Would you do me a favor?"

Devon nodded.

"I want you to tell me all about her while we watch the game. That okay with you, buckaroo?"

"Yes, sir."

Mal ruffled his hair.

Devon asked, "Do you call people buckaroo because of Mr. Herb Jeffries's movie *The Bronze Buckaroo*?"

Mal froze and stared. "How did you know that?"

Devon's answering grin made Mal wave him off. "Never mind. Bonfire's getting ready to start. Go get your ice cream before you give me a heart attack."

Grinning, Devon replied, "Yes, sir."

As Mal watched him go, he thought about Devon's struggles, and then peered through the growing shadows for Lily and Trent. They were across the yard, watching him. Feeling pretty good about himself, he walked over to join them.

Lily said, "We saw you with Devon. Did he let you talk to him?"

Mal replied nonchalantly, "Devon and I will be watching the baseball playoffs together this weekend."

"What?" Trent asked.

"Didn't know he liked baseball, did you?"

A perplexed Lily shook her head. "No. He's never said anything about that."

"According to him, it's because nobody ever asked."

Silence.

Mal chuckled. "That's how I felt." He met his son's eyes and boasted, "And this is what I meant about Dads Inc. needing my advanced wisdom. I'm liking this boy like a bullfrog likes flies."

Lily laughed.

Trent asked, "Dad, don't take this the wrong way, but like a bullfrog likes flies? Have you been drinking?"

"No offense taken, and the answer is no, but before this whole Devon thing is resolved, we may all need a drink."

That said, he walked off whistling music from *The Bronze Buckaroo*.

"What does he mean?" Lily asked.

"With Dad, who knows?"

Trent was about to add to that but saw some kind of commotion going on by the food table. Bernadine was yelling for Reg, and people began running toward her. Trent and Lily got up and took off at a run, too.

It was Ms. Agnes. She was lying on the ground, and the grim Reg was administering CPR. Due to the lateness of the day, visibility was limited, but quick-thinking truck owners ran to their vehicles, turned on their high beams, and drove up close. In the circle of light Lily saw the horrified Marie standing with Leo. Tamar pushed her way through the crowd. Marie immediately grabbed Tamar's hand in a grip that appeared tight as her heart had to be.

Bernadine closed her phone. "Sheriff said they'll be here in ten minutes at the most."

Everyone prayed it wouldn't be too late.

Reg managed to get Agnes's rhythm stabilized just as the ambulance roared up. Moments later the techs had her on a gurney and inside. Lights flashing, the ambulance sped off to the big hospital up in Hays, while Marie, Leo, Tamar, and Lily followed in Leo's fast-moving town car.

At the hospital they were ushered into a room set aside for families of loved ones undergoing emergency surgery, and the wait for news was excruciating. Marie appeared to have her emotions under control, but when Lily looked into her eyes, the bleakness mirrored there was soul-deep. It was well known that mother and daughter rarely agreed, but Marie loved Agnes very much—more than Agnes deserved, some might say, but the only thing that mattered to Lily was Marie's pain. The sight of it was breaking Lily's heart.

Marie stood and announced emotionlessly, "I need some air. Come and get me if anything happens."

Leo asked, "Do you want me to go with you?"

She shook her head and left the room.

Lily met his eyes for a moment and then glanced over at

Tamar, who was seated in a chair on the far side of the room. Her eyes were closed, and to a casual observer it appeared that she might be asleep, but upon closer inspection, you saw her lips moving, and if you listened hard you could hear her chanting nearly soundlessly in a tongue only her ancestors knew.

"What's she doing?" Leo asked quietly.

"Praying."

"In what language?"

"Seminole, I imagine, but I don't know that for sure."

"Can she hear us?"

Tamar opened her eyes. "Yes, Leo. I can hear you. Shut up, please."

He didn't say another word.

Forty minutes later the surgeon came in and introduced herself. Her name was Rita Sullivan, and she didn't have good news. "All we can do is make her comfortable. Her heart is just wore out. I'm sorry."

Marie bit her lip. "Can I see her?"

"Of course. She's awake. We have her on a couple of IVs, but it won't be long."

Lily's tears met Tamar's.

Tamar whispered, "Come on, you two. Let's go say our good-byes."

Leo stayed where he was. He knew without asking that Agnes would not want him at her bedside.

She was indeed awake. Seeing how fragile and small she looked lying in the hospital bed with the oxygen lines in her nose and the IVs in her thin brown arms sharpened their pain.

Marie didn't bother wiping away her tears as she bent

over the bed and stroked her mother's silver hair. "How you doing, Mama?"

"Not so good, baby," she rasped out. "Not so good. Need to tell you something."

"It can wait, you rest."

"I'm going to get all the rest I'll need in a few minutes, so just listen."

Tamar smiled. "You tell her, girl."

Agnes looked to her old friend. "Going to miss you, Tamar."

"I'll miss you more."

Tamar moved closer and placed a soft kiss on the forehead of her BFF. "I expect you to meet me at the Gates when it's my turn, Agnes Marie."

"I will. And maybe we can find a good man up there. Do you think?"

Tamar chuckled through her grief. "I hope so. We didn't do too good this time around, did we?"

Agnes quieted, as if she'd drifted back in time, then said finally, "No, we didn't."

She settled her eyes on Marie and said softly, "And that's what I've been trying to tell you. All these years I've lied to you, Marie."

"About what?"

"Your father. Your birth. He wasn't killed in Korea. I made up that story."

Marie stared. "Then who was he?"

"A boy I met while I was at Spelman. He wouldn't marry me, so—"

"You took out your anger on me because my mistake reminded you of yours?" Marie asked incredulously. She turned on Tamar. "Did you know about this?"

"She's my best friend, and it wasn't my place."

Lily couldn't believe her ears. How much more would Marie have to suffer?

"How could you?" Marie threw back at Agnes in a voice thick with tears. "All the name-calling and the anger and derision, when you'd done exactly the same thing? Why couldn't you have helped me?"

"We Jeffersons don't have bastard children."

"Yes, we do!"

The monitors began beeping.

Agnes looked up at her only child and whispered with her last dying breath, "Get rid of that Leo. All he wants is our land."

The nurses rushed in, but Agnes Marie Jefferson was gone.

The memorial service was held outside on the open plains behind the Jefferson home. It was a raw, cold day. Dressed in mourning black, Marie greeted everyone and thanked them for coming. Agnes had requested cremation, and that her ashes be sprinkled over her land, so those who'd come formed a large shivering circle. In the center stood Tamar. She raised the vase holding the cremains high in the air as if offering up a final tribute and then said, "Agnes Marie, we loved you, and we'll miss you."

Everyone nodded in solemn agreement.

The ashes were spread, tears flowed, and when it was over, they all went into the house for the traditional repast.

That evening, after everyone had gone, Lily was in the

kitchen washing up the last of the dishes. The tired-looking Marie entered and said, "Thanks for helping."

"No problem. You go on back out there and sit down. I'll finish up."

Instead, Marie took a seat at the kitchen table. "Leo wanted to stay, but I sent him home."

"He's been very supportive."

"Yes, he has, but I wanted to be by myself tonight. Genevieve is going to stay with Tamar. I think Tamar's grief is even rawer than mine."

"They've been friends a long time."

"Before I was born." Marie added wistfully, "I keep expecting Mama to walk in the door."

Lily put the last of the dishes in the drain, dried her hands, and took a seat at the table. "She'll be missed."

"I can't believe the last words out of her mouth were to tell me what to do, though," Marie noted in a voice tinged with humor and disbelief. "She was something."

"Yes, she was."

"My life's my own now."

"Yes, it is. Any idea what you might do?"

"Finish my grieving and then contact my son."

Lily nodded. "Good girl."

"And then figure out a way to forgive Tamar for not telling me the truth."

"It wasn't her place, Marie," Lily said gently. "No sense in being angry at her."

"My head knows that, but my heart—it still hurts, and I want to scream. All those years Mama spent berating me and looking down her nose. Why couldn't she have just told me the truth? Life for us would have been so much better."

Lily had no answer, but she hoped Marie would someday find it within herself to forgive Agnes for what she'd done.

Marie glanced up at the clock on the wall. "It's late, Lily. You should probably head home."

"Anything else you need me to do before I go?"

"No, you've been a rock these past few days."

"Just trying to be here for you like you were for me when Mom died."

They shared a tight, emotion-filled hug, and Lily whispered, "So sorry for your loss."

"Thanks. I love you."

"Love you, too."

Lily drove home through her tears.

CHAPTER
11

As the plane lifted into the air, Reverend Paula Grant gazed out the window at the receding sight of Miami. Watching her old life fade from view was bittersweet.

Two plane changes later, she entered the Hays airport. She knew someone from Henry Adams would be meeting her, but she assumed it would be Ms. Brown, or her assistant Lily Fontaine. Instead there was a well-dressed young man in a suit holding a card with her name on it, and Paula felt very special indeed. He introduced himself as Nathan Nelson, helped retrieve her suitcases from the belt at the baggage claim, and escorted her out to a large black town car. After politely ushering her inside and closing the door, he got behind the steering wheel and drove them away.

It didn't take her long to learn that Nathan was a conversationalist. She heard about his wife, Lou, and the baby they were expecting around the Christmas holidays, and that if the child was a boy, he would be named Ethan after Lou's wife's great-grandfather. She learned that he was a native of Kansas and that being the driver for Ms. Brown was the best job he'd ever had.

"She makes me feel like I'm real important, you know."

Enjoying the smooth ride, Paula totally got that.

"She's been encouraging me to get my GED. Nobody in my family ever graduated high school. You'd think a lady with all her money would look down on poor folks like me and Lou, but not Ms. Brown. She's been real concerned about the baby. Even got me and Lou some health insurance so we could see a real good doc. Lou says she's like a fairy godmother. You're going to like her."

One of Paula's guiding tenets was to treat the lowly just like the mighty. She was glad to have further proof that Ms. Brown subscribed to that tenet as well.

During the ride, Paula looked out at the passing landscape. She hadn't seen such wide open spaces since leaving Oklahoma two decades ago, and the thought brought back bittersweet memories. Like Nathan's family, no one in hers had ever graduated from high school either until she came along. It hadn't won her any accolades, though. If anything, her thirst for knowledge had driven a death stake into her relationships with the kin she'd left behind. She'd been born to an unwed teen mother in one of Oklahoma's all-Black townships, where due to the ignorance brought on by poverty, the remnants of segregation, and a world without dreams, no one could fathom why Paula took her education so seriously. Uppity thoughts, her aunt Della had called them, and there was no place for that when all you were destined for was a job in the laundry or kitchen of the local prison, if you were lucky. Thinking back on those painful years, Paula was glad she'd gotten out, because from the moment the scholarship she earned took her to college, she'd never gone hungry physically or spiritually ever again.

Nathan interrupted her musings. "You here to hear little Devon preach?"

The question caught Paula off guard. "No. Little Devon?"

"Ms. Fontaine's foster son. He's been preaching up a storm this summer."

"Really?"

"Yep. My granny says he reminds her of somebody called Rev. Ike."

Paula chuckled. Ms. Brown hadn't mentioned the town already having a preacher.

Nathan continued, "At first, so many people came out to hear him there weren't enough seats. It was kind of fun watching him bouncing around on the stage and shouting 'hallelujah,' but then folks started noticing that he did the same thing week after week, and they stopped coming."

She found this very interesting. "So why did you call him little Devon?"

"Because he's eight, maybe nine years old."

She blinked with surprise. "Really?"

"Yep. Nice kid, though."

For the remainder of the ride, Paula pondered an eight-year-old Rev. Ike and what role she'd really been hired to play.

Nathan left the highway and took to a back road that cut through more wide open spaces. Finally he said, "We're here, Reverend. This is the Power Plant, where Ms. Brown and Ms. Fontaine have their offices."

"The Power Plant?"

"Yes, ma'am. It's called that because of all the power Ms. Brown has around here. It's a joke."

"Ah."

Paula peered out her window at the shape and flowing lines of the flat-topped red building. It looked like it should have been in Manhattan or on the cover of *Architectural Digest*, not the plains of Kansas.

Nathan came around to open her door, then retrieved her bags. "I'll walk you in."

"That isn't necessary."

"Ms. Brown said I was to bring you to her office, and that's what I'm going to do."

Paula surrendered to the rock-star treatment and followed Nathan to the building and inside.

Bernadine was on the phone when they arrived at her office door. A smile creased her face when she saw Paula. She excused herself from the person on the other end of the phone for a moment to say, "Welcome to Henry Adams, Reverend. How was the flight?"

"Long."

"I'll bet. I have to finish this conference call, but Lily will show you around and take you out to where you'll be staying. I'll hook up with you later."

"That's fine."

Ms. Brown turned back to her call, and Nathan left Paula in Lily's capable hands.

"Are you hungry?"

"Starving."

"Then let's get you something to eat first."

They walked out to Lily's car, and a few minutes later she

pulled up in front of the Dog. Paula peered at the sign. "The Dog and Cow?"

Lily smiled, explained the name and the owner's intent, and added, "He used to be the veterinarian here, and was doing a lot of drinking back when he opened the place. He's in recovery now, though."

Paula had no idea what she expected the former alcoholic owner of the diner to look like, but it certainly wasn't the handsome dark-skinned man who introduced himself as Malachi July.

"Welcome aboard, Reverend. Lunch is on the house."

"Why, thank you." It was easy to see the man was a flirt from the mischief in his eyes. He led them to a booth near the windows and left them to their menus. Paula looked around. It was late afternoon, and the place was almost empty. The music was thumping Rufus with Chaka Khan singing "Tell Me Something Good," however, and that surprised her as well. The waitress took their order, and after she departed, Paula asked, "Does Zoey know I'm coming?"

"No. We thought we'd wait to see how you want to play it. Her adoptive mom, Roni, flew in from New York last night so she could be here."

"Does the mom work there?"

"For the moment."

When Paula heard who the mom actually was, she stared in stunned silence. Finally, finding her voice, she said, "Zoey's been adopted by Roni Moore? THE Roni Moore?"

"Yep."

"Oh, my goodness."

"Would you like to meet her after we eat?"

"I would. I have all her albums."

"She loves Zoey like she loves breathing. She and her husband, Reg, couldn't be better parents."

Paula was blown away.

After a lunch that definitely hit the spot—who knew a place with such a strange name would serve such awesome burgers—Paula and Lily left the diner and headed for the school to meet up with Roni and Reg.

Once there, Lily made the introductions, and Paula had to stop herself from staring at the music legend by mentally reminding herself why they were there.

Reg asked, "Do you think she'll remember you?"

Paula shrugged. "Only way to find out is to bring us together."

So, while Lily, Paula, and Reg waited in the hall, Roni quietly stepped into the classroom. A moment later she returned hand in hand with the skipping Zoey. Upon seeing Paula, Zoey stopped and looked at her quizzically.

"Hey, Zo-Zo."

Zoey's mouth dropped open, her eyes went wide, and she began taking in deep, quick breaths, as if her excitement made it difficult to breathe.

Paula held out her arms and asked softly, "Can I get a hug?"

Tears were already streaming down both faces as Zoey ran to Paula and was scooped up and held tight.

"Oh, baby girl. I have missed you."

Lily and Roni were crying as well. Reg wiped at his eyes.

An emotional Paula gave Zoey a solemn kiss on the cheek and held on to her as Zoey sobbed with a rawness that pierced everyone's heart.

Paula asked the adults, "Is there an empty room we can use? I'd like to speak to her alone, if that's okay."

The wariness on the faces of Zoey's parents was plain and somewhat expected, so Paula sought to reassure them. "Just for a minute."

Zoey's nonstop weeping made them finally nod, and a tearful Roni whispered, "This is breaking my heart."

Paula's, too.

They were led to the school's clinic and left alone.

Paula sat on the nearest chair, the still-crying Zoey curled up in her lap. "Hey, it's okay," she whispered as she rocked the sobbing child. "It's okay."

Seeing a box of tissue on the counter, Paula pulled a few free and handed some to Zoey. After a while, they both wiped at their tears and blew their noses. Paula took a moment to ponder what tack to take. She'd been thinking about Zoey's muteness almost nonstop since meeting Bernadine and Lily, and she was pretty certain she knew the cause. With the sniffling Zoey now curled in against her like a lost child, Paula held her close and said quietly, "Ms. Brown told me about Bonnie. I'm so sorry for your loss. It had to be scary when you were alone."

Zoey's eyes welled up again, and she nodded.

Paula placed a kiss on the top of her head and gently tightened her hold. "Ms. Brown also said that your new parents love you very much. Do you love them?"

The dark eyes looked up at Paula's, and she nodded her head again.

"Honey, did Bonnie tell you not to talk to anyone before she went to heaven?"

The nod this time was short and tight.

"She'd be real proud of you, you know. From what I'm hearing, you haven't said a word for almost two years. I'm guessing it's been real hard not being able to tell your new parents how you feel, or how great they are."

And for the first time since her mother's passing, Zoey used her voice to croak, "Yes."

Above her head a smiling Paula silently praised God. "Well, I think if Bonnie was here now, she'd say it's okay to start doing just that. In her own way, your mama was trying to protect you." Paula looked down into her eyes. "Does your throat hurt when you try and talk?"

Zoey nodded.

"More than likely it's from not using it for such a long time."

Zoey croaked and then coughed as if her voice was stuck in her unused vocal cords. She whispered, "Daddy Reg is a doctor. Maybe he can give me some medicine."

Paula smiled. "I'll bet he can."

"Will they be mad?"

Paula searched the seriousness in her eyes. "That you're talking? No, doll. Not if they love you as much as I keep hearing they do. Your mom, Roni, will probably cry and let you eat Cheerios and bananas for the rest of your life. You do still like Cheerios and bananas, right?"

Smiling shyly, Zoey nodded, then her eyes turned serious again. "I was scared they'd get mad and send me back if I said I could really talk." Tears filled her eyes again.

Paula gently eased her closer. "It's okay. I'll explain. It'll be all right. I promise." Changing her tone, she added, "And check this out. I'm going to be living here, too. Ms. Brown is going to build me a church, so I'll get to pester you every day, just like in Miami."

Zoey's face lit up like this was the best news she'd heard all day, and she threw herself against Paula and hugged her as tightly as her skinny little arms could muster.

Paula hugged her back. "I like the sound of that, too. Now how about we go talk to your parents? I know they're probably worried."

Zoey looked up and whispered in her froggy voice, "I'm glad you came, Reverend Paula."

"So am I."

Hand in hand, they left the office, and Paula silently gave thanks to the Almighty for bringing them back together again in this remarkable little town called Henry Adams.

Later, while sitting in Bernadine's office, Paula explained to Bernadine and Lily the whys of Zoey's muteness. "I had this talk with Reg and Roni earlier, and they wanted me to share it with you. As for our Zoey. One of the first things drilled into children on the streets is to keep your mouth shut. You don't talk to the police, the lady from the welfare office, or the social workers. If you've ever been around kids, you know that given half a chance, they'll tell all your business."

Lily smiled. She liked the reverend's plain way of talking.

Paula explained further, "If you're a parent on the street, you don't want anyone to know where your drugs are stashed, or where you sleep at night, or that your kid doesn't attend school. If a child lets slip something that parent doesn't want her worker or the police to know, she might be locked up or declared unfit and lose her children to the state. Zoey was all Bonnie had."

Lily thought the muteness all made perfect sense now.

"The night Zoey was found by the police, she did exactly what her mom had schooled her to do. Around people of authority, keep your mouth shut."

Bernadine whispered, "She had to have been scared to death around the police and the doctors and the social workers."

"Yes, but in a way the muteness became her shield, something she could hide behind so she wouldn't have to answer a bunch of questions about herself or her mother."

Lily asked, "But why did she hold on to it? She's been adjusting well. It's easy to see how much she's loved around here."

"She was scared that if she told the truth, you all might be mad and send her back to foster care. Remember, she's only eight years old. Stuff's hard to figure out when you're little."

"She had just turned seven when she came to live with us."

Bernadine shook her head sadly. "So simple, yet so complicated."

Paula agreed. "But for me, having grown up dirt-poor in Oklahoma, totally understandable. Saying anything to the social workers, teachers, or anyone else about what was going on at home got you a serious whipping."

Lily said, "But now you're our miracle worker."

Paula chuckled. "Oh, lord. I just want Zoey to be okay."

Bernadine said, "Roni and Reg are going to fly her to Manhattan in the morning and have a specialist check out her throat and vocal cords and see what kind of therapy she may have to do to get her pipes working again. I can't wait to hear what that child has to say."

"Remember you said that," Paula said sagely and with a smile. "The Zoey I knew could talk up a hurricane."

"Reverend, thank you," Bernadine said in a tone that conveyed genuine emotion. "We are so grateful. I'll build you a cathedral if you want, for all you've done."

"No cathedrals, please, but a place to lay my head would be nice. It's been a long day."

Lily stood. "Come on. I'll run you out to your trailer."

Because the three emergency trailers were being used by Rocky, the Clarks, and Jack and Eli, whose new home in the subdivision was almost ready for occupation, Bernadine had Lily purchase another trailer for the reverend.

"We'll talk about building you something more permanent in the spring."

Paula opened her mouth to explain that she didn't need anything built, but before she could find the words, Bernadine looked her in the eyes. "Just say, 'Okay, Bernadine.'"

In an amused tone, Paula replied, "Okay, Bernadine."

"Good. I'll see you tomorrow."

On the ride out to the trailer with Lily, Paula stared at the blackness of the countryside. "I haven't seen darkness this thick since leaving Oklahoma."

"What part are you from?"

"Okfuskee County. Outside Boley."

"Family still there?"

"Yep."

"They're pretty proud of you, I'll bet."

"You'd lose your money."

Paula could feel Lily's questioning eyes, but she didn't offer anything further. There'd been enough revelations for one day.

Lily stayed at the trailer with Paula just long enough to get Paula settled in. They spent a few moments making arrangements to get her into town in the morning to meet more of the residents and back over to the Power Plant to sign some paperwork.

Finally alone, the tired Paula took a slow walk through her new home. Growing up, she'd lived in a trailer, but as she was finding with all things Bernadine, this one bore about as much resemblance to the one back home as an elephant to a Cuban cigar.

Now, as she lay in the dark in her stylishly furnished bedroom, she thought back on her day, the people she'd met so far, and Zoey. What the little one must have gone through. Under the same circumstances Paula thought she'd've stayed mute, too. That Zoey had been adopted by the Garlands was a good thing. It was her hope that all the love and understanding they'd showered on her would somehow make up for what she'd endured after Bonnie's death. A yawn seized her and reminded her how long a day it had been. She took a moment to say her prayers before turning over and slipping effortlessly into sleep.

When Lily got home, she went over to Trent's to pick up Devon. She'd called earlier to let Trent know how the meet between Zoey and the reverend had turned out, and he'd been ecstatic upon hearing the results. He'd also promised to tell the boys, so as she walked home with Devon, she asked, "Did Mr. Trent give you the good news about Zoey?"

"Yes."

"Isn't it wonderful?"

"She's just a faker," he said belligerently.

She sighed. Considering his recent behavior, she supposed his reaction was to have been expected, but she'd been hoping for the best. His moment of bonding with Mal over baseball had given her hope, too. "She had her reasons, Devon, and she was scared."

Devon didn't seem to care. "She ought to get a spanking for lying."

Lily shook her head. "What happened to the kindhearted, caring Devon that used to live with me? I really miss him."

But he didn't respond.

12

The next few days were bittersweet ones for the residents of Henry Adams. The bitter parts were tied to the memory of Ms. Agnes and her passing. The sweet to the news about Zoey. Word about her spread like a late July grassfire, and Lily thought it a good thing that Zoey and the Garlands were in Manhattan, because all the interest might have been too much for the town's favorite little girl. Everywhere Lily went, she was asked to explain the story, and each time she did, the questioners would shake their heads sadly and say, "Poor baby girl."

Everyone also wanted to meet Reverend Grant, and the task of making that a reality fell to the new VP of social affairs.

On Friday evening, when Lily and Trent, accompanied by Amari and Devon, arrived at the rec where the welcome reception was being held, they were pleased by both the size of the crowd and the tasteful but festive way the big meeting room had been decorated. The town's residents were present, of course, as were some local dignitaries from neighboring communities. Also in attendance were a few men decked out in clerical collars. None of their faces were familiar, but Lily assumed they were area pastors who'd come to check out Paula. The only people who appeared to be missing were Tamar and Marie. Neither of them had been seen since the funeral, as far as she knew. She had talked to Marie the day after the memorial about coming to dinner on Sunday, but her godmother had asked for a rain check, her way of saying she needed space. Respecting that, Lily hadn't called since.

Lily was about to suggest they get in the line with all the other people wanting to shake Paula's hand when Sheila Payne rushed up.

"Good, you're here. Trent, I need you to say a few words of welcome."

And before they could blink, she whisked him away.

"Ms. Payne looks real happy," Amari said.

Lily had to agree. "Yes, she does."

"Preston says she really likes her new job."

Lily was glad to know that. She'd yet to talk to Sheila about how the colonel felt, but decided she'd find out soon enough. Lily spotted Bernadine and received a thumbs-up, which Lily assumed meant the Boss Lady approved of the affair. Lily threw the sign back at her and grinned. Bernadine had also been skeptical about Sheila's abilities, but everything looked lovely, from the fresh flowers on the buffet table to the fancy tablecloth and gold-rimmed china.

Lily glanced down to ask Devon how he liked the affair so far and saw him shooting daggers Paula's way. She sighed sadly and looked up to find Amari watching her with concerned eyes.

He said softly, "Don't worry, Mom. It'll work out. You'll see."

She was so moved by his caring spirit and calling her Mom, she felt the sting of tears. She wanted to give him a big fat hug and a kiss, but rather than embarrass him in front of a room filled with people, she replied simply, "Thank you, Amari. I really appreciate that."

"You're welcome." He shot Devon such a pointed look that Devon lowered his eyes to his shoestrings. Seemingly satisfied that he'd put his soon-to-be younger brother in his place, Amari added, "Now let's get in line so we can meet Reverend Paula. I'm ready to eat."

A buoyant Lily let him lead the way.

Trent's speech was short, and when he was done, it was the reverend's turn.

She looked out over the assemblage and said, "I'm very honored to be in Henry Adams, and I'm looking forward to my new life here with you."

That her remarks were short, too, seemed to endear her to the crowd, because she left the mic under thunderous applause. Once she did, the reception line Lily and the boys were standing in began to move once more.

When their turn came, Lily made the introductions. The lady priest shook Amari's hand, who promptly said, "Your red boots are off the chain."

She laughed and looked down at her red-and-silver cowboy boots. "I think they're pretty cool, too. Thanks."

Amari added, "And thanks for helping Zoey."

"You're welcome, but I think it was more the Spirit. I was just the vessel."

Amari studied her for a moment. "I had to do a Spirit Quest this summer, so I actually understand what you mean." He looked at Lily with such an expression of astonishment, she laughed.

"You'll have to tell me about this quest," Paula said, smiling.

"Right now?"

"No"—she laughed—"but how about in a few days?"

He nodded.

She then peered at Devon. "How are you, Devon?"

"Fine," he tossed back curtly.

Lily held on to her temper and said evenly, "Your attitude's not real becoming, Devon."

Paula didn't seem to be put off by his mood. "Devon, I'd like to talk to you in a few days, too, if you have the time. I want to hear all about your preaching."

Lip poked out, arms crossed tightly over his suit, he nodded.

Lily rolled her eyes and prayed for strength. "Come on, guys. Let's move along. Thanks, Reverend Paula."

"No problem."

Once they were out of earshot, Amari asked Devon, "Do you know how embarrassing you are?"

Devon didn't reply.

Lily agreed with Amari but didn't add her two cents because she was too mad. She was also afraid that if she opened her mouth all hell would roll out, and only a bad parent cussed out a child, especially during a reception for the new reverend.

Across the room, Trent stood patiently listening to the low-voiced, judgmental concerns of Cecil Donovan about

Paula Grant. Donovan was the new pastor of a small Black church in Franklin, and to hear him tell it, Paula and her Episcopalians were the epitome of what was wrong with religion. Not only did they accept gays and lesbians into their congregations, they allowed them into the ranks of clergy as well.

Donovan was eating from a stack of shrimp piled high on his plate. As he daintily held on to the tails before taking a bite, his manicured fingers glistened. His expensive suit could have come from Leo's closet.

"And did you know that they not only allow women in the pulpit, they just consecrated an openly gay woman as a bishop in California? If that isn't blasphemy, I don't know what is," he added, and pointed a shrimp at Trent for emphasis.

Trent glanced around and spotted Lily and the boys in the reception line, speaking with the subject of Donovan's disdain. He'd planned on them all meeting the new reverend as a family, but before he could get with them, he'd been waylaid by Donovan.

Donovan went on speaking as if he were passing along secrets from Russia. "The Bible clearly specifies a woman's place in society. The men run things, and women serve. In the book of—"

Tired of this, Trent interrupted him. "Excuse me, Pastor Donovan. I'm not sure how long you've been in Franklin?"

"About six weeks."

"Then you may not know that Henry Adams is owned by that lady over there." He pointed out Bernadine. "Her name's Bernadine Brown. Any problems you have with the hiring of Reverend Grant should be taken up with her. I'm sure she'd be real interested in hearing your theories on why women shouldn't be running things."

Donovan choked on his shrimp.

Trent gave him a few hard whacks across the back that were definitely more forceful than necessary, but he was trying to help him out in his distress.

Once the man recovered, Trent said, "You make sure you speak with Ms. Brown, okay?" Offering the pastor a terse nod of farewell, Trent went in search of his family.

Because it was Friday evening, the celebration was topped off with a showing of *Night at the Museum* for the kids, and for the adults, *The Preacher's Wife*, the Whitney and Denzel version, because of its religious overtones.

When the movies were over, Trent drove them home. Lily and the boys got out of the car, but Trent had one more thing to do. He hadn't seen Tamar since Agnes's funeral.

"Tell her I send my love," Lily said to him.

"Will do. Be back later."

Once there, he parked and headed up the walk. Tamar was seated on the porch in the dark, just as he'd expected. They both loved the night.

"What brings you out here so late?" she asked.

He sat down on the top step just like he used to when he was young. "Came to check on my favorite old lady. So how are you?"

"Grieving."

The one word told him much. He'd been worried about her since Agnes's death, but hadn't visited because he wanted to give her her space.

Tamar said quietly, "I'm the last of my kind. The last living resident of Henry Adams who actually knew Aunt Teresa and her brothers, and I'm not sure I'm liking it."

He turned toward her in an effort to try and make out her facial expression in the darkness. "Why?"

"Thinking about my own mortality, I guess."

"The death of a friend will do that sometimes."

For a while they just sat and listened to the wind in the grass and watched the moon overhead go in and out of the clouds.

Tamar finally said, "I miss Agnes. I spent so many years wanting to strangle her for one thing or another, I never thought I'd feel such loss when she was gone, but I do."

Trent smiled softly. "She could get you going."

"And then some. I'm going to be joining her and the rest of them eventually. You prepared for that?"

She always did ask hard questions. "No."

"You have your family now. You'll be okay."

"No, I won't be. Not without you."

"Yeah, you will."

Her words made him worry. "Have the doctors told you something Dad and I should know?"

"No."

"Would you tell me if they had?"

"No."

He shook his head. Twenty years ago, she'd been diagnosed with stage-three ovarian cancer. They'd almost lost her. He prayed she wasn't girding herself to take up the battle again.

"And when my time comes, no heroics. Just let me slip away."

To him she'd been mother, grandmother, and friend. Hearing this was hard, but he forced himself to respond. "Okay."

There was another long moment of silence before she said wistfully, "You and I spent a lot of nights out here on this porch."

"Something about the night always spoke to me. Still does."

"Me, too. Not Mal, though. He doesn't like the darkness; too many demons in it for him." She went quiet again for a few moments, and he wondered if she was thinking about the past or the future. "You make sure you and Amari take care of Malachi after I'm gone."

"We will."

"Good," she whispered. "I've had a good long life. If the spirit took me with the morning's sunrise, I'd have no regrets. You've filled my heart, Trent. Thank you."

Fighting to keep a tight rein on his emotions, he turned again to where she sat shrouded by the shadows. "You're welcome."

"Amari has been a blessing, too. Never met a child so grateful for family."

"He is special."

"That he is. Hungry for the old stories, like you were. Comes out to see me almost every day and just sits and listens. Asks a million and a half questions, though."

Trent smiled. Amari was a question machine. "He loves you a lot."

"And I love him back. Convinced he's a July."

"Be nice if we could prove it, but either way, Wednesday I want you to come with me to the courthouse so we can make his adoption official."

"I'll be there."

When Trent was young, the night wind moving through the grass and trees always sounded like people whispering. Tamar explained it as being the nocturnal gathering of the July ancestors talking to each other and walking the land to make sure their living descendants were well. It was an image he still clung to decades later, and in silence he could hear them now. Off in the distance an owl hooted from somewhere down near the small stream that ran behind Tamar's land. The memories of growing up here were ones he'd cherish until he joined the nightly gatherings of his clan. "You know, you're not the last link. Whether you want to acknowledge him or not, your brother Thad is still alive and living in Oklahoma."

She snorted. "Don't remind me."

"When are you two going to declare a truce?"

"On the day I sprout wings. That coyote stole Olivia, took her tires, and left her sitting on the side of the road twenty miles away!"

"I know, but that was years ago, Tamar, and it only took us a few hours to find her."

"Doesn't change things."

Trent always got the impression that the feud between them went back farther than the Olivia prank, but he'd no clue what might have started it. "I'm going to invite him and his side to the wedding."

"No, you're not."

"Yeah, I am. They're family. Already had Mal call Thad."

"You're really ruining my evening."

"Sorry."

"They're just going to steal our cars again, you know that, right?"

"We'll see if we can't work something out with them before they arrive."

"Good luck."

He was certain he'd need it, but he set aside the potential antics of the Oklahoma branch of the family for now. She was his main concern.

But apparently she was done visiting for the night. "Trent, it's late. You go on home now and let this old lady continue her pity party and try not to think about her brother coming to town. I'll be back raising hell in a day or so."

"You sure?"

"Who else is going to whip Miss Tiffany Adele into shape?"

Trent laughed. Getting to his feet, he walked over to her and placed a gentle kiss on her forehead. "Call me if you need anything."

"I will."

"Love you, Tamar," he whispered.

"Love you more, baby boy."

Trent got back in his truck and drove away. He knew death would take her eventually, but he wasn't ready, and doubted he'd ever be. His world had always included Tamar, and he couldn't imagine it without her.

Saturday morning, Paula was having coffee at the small table in her new kitchen when the melodic notes of a flute drifted like a breeze through her open screen door. With every rise and fall of the intricately fingered music the talent of the flutist was apparent. At first the measures were slow and filled with such mournful tones, the instrument seemed to weep. Paula heard pain, grief, longing. The emotion made her want to hold the flutist close to her heart and help bear the burden of such deep sadness. But even in pain there is sometimes beauty, and in this case that beauty was the musician's pure skill. Each note was distinctive and filled with both vibrancy and life. Whoever was playing had the technique of a virtuoso.

As the music continued, Paula's curiosity got the better of her, so she got to her feet. She'd met her nearest neighbors, the Clarks, Jack and Eli, and the Pam Grier clone, Ms. Rocky Dancer, but had yet to meet the mayor's grandmother. She wondered if the music was coming from her house.

Outside, the music was now rising as sweet and as bright as the morning's sunlight. Paula gauged the direction from where it was flowing and set out.

It was Rocky. She was seated on the metal steps of her trailer. Upon noticing Paula, she slowly removed the silver flute from her lips. "Morning, Reverend."

"Good morning. You play beautifully."

"Thanks. Do you need something?"

Paula shook her head. "Just wanted to see where the music was coming from."

Rocky looked slightly embarrassed. "I don't play much anymore, but woke up this morning with the urge inside. Trent used to play once upon a time, too, but I'll bet he doesn't even know where his flute is."

"Feel free to start my morning with your playing whenever you like. I felt like I was at a concert." She wanted to ask about the pain she'd heard threaded into the music but didn't know Rocky well enough to inquire without coming off as nosy or rude, or both.

"How long have you been a reverend?"

"Going on fifteen years."

"And before that?"

"I had a child psychology practice in Atlanta."

"Ah," she voiced quietly. "Are you going to help out our kids?"

"If they need it, and will let me."

"Oh, they need it, believe me, and so do many of the adults."

A few yards away, Jack and Eli James exited their trailer. Eli waved, and Jack called out, "Morning, Reverend. Hey, Rock."

Rocky waved. Paula did, too, but she noticed the way Rocky's eyes followed them as they walked to their car and drove away. "Are they good neighbors?"

The question seemed to drag Rocky's attention back to the present. "Yeah, they are. Have you ever been married?"

Paula was caught off guard by the abrupt off-topic question. "No. You?"

"Once for a hot minute, and I swore off men big-time after the divorce."

"But now?"

Rocky smiled. "How do you know there is a but now?"

"I've been in the psychology business and the God business long enough to know that there's always a but now. So?"

For a moment Rocky appeared to be gathering what she wanted to say. "There's a guy, and he's a really nice guy, and I could probably fall for him forever and forever, amen."

"Then what's the problem? He isn't married, is he?"

"No. The problem is me. Scared of getting my heart broken again."

"Does he impress you as being a heartbreaker?"

"Not at all."

"Do you think he could make you happy?"

She shrugged. "I don't know. He's a widower, and I don't want to be the woman he's picking up on the rebound."

"Ah, I see."

"Not sure if he's really serious about me, or just looking for somebody to replace his wife."

"Have you talked with him about this?"

"No. I'm trying not to talk to him at all."

The amusement in her eyes made Paula laugh. "Don't block your blessings, girl."

"I know, but easier said than done."

"Has he asked you out?"

"All day, every day."

"If you keep hiding, how will you ever learn the truth? Life's too short not to embrace the things that could bring us joy."

"I know that, too, but it's easier to keep saying no. That way I don't get hurt."

"No pain, no gain, though, right?"

Rocky cocked her head. "Since when do reverends say 'No pain, no gain'?"

Paula chuckled. "Would you prefer 'No guts, no glory'?"

"I think you're going to fit in well here."

"I'm hoping to. And I think you should go out with this mystery man of yours and see where it leads. Nothing worse than being old and gray and filled with what-ifs. Life has sorrow, but it can potentially hold solace and love as well, and if this man can bring you those things . . . ?" She left the question open-ended. She'd heard the longing in Rocky's music. Solace and love were needed. "Just something to consider."

"Okay."

They were interrupted by the sound of a car's horn. They turned and saw an old but shiny green pickup truck bumping across the grass in their direction. Rocky asked, "Have you met Tamar?"

"No, I haven't."

"Then today's your lucky day."

The woman who exited the truck was tall, dark-skinned, and bore an amazing resemblance to the July men Paula had already met. The black-and-red caftan flowing around her like an African robe was shot through with silver swirls that matched the color of her flowing hair. In her ears were large silver hoops, and a multitude of bracelets graced her wrists. She was a beautiful woman. She was also wearing combat boots that hadn't been new in probably decades.

Rocky made the introductions.

"Pleased to meet you," Tamar said. "I came to see if you'd like to do a little bit of running with me today. There's also some people I want you to meet and a few places you need to see if you're going to be living here."

Paula had no plans for the day. "I'd like that."

Rocky said to Tamar, "You've been scarce since the funeral. We've been worried about you. You okay?"

Tamar nodded. "I'm getting there. I heard you playing a little while ago, so I came to make sure you were okay. I know today's Deborah's birthday."

Apparently Tamar had heard the pain, too, Paula mused, and she wondered who Deborah might be.

In response to Tamar's words, a mask slid down over Rocky's features. "I'm okay" was all she would say.

Tamar didn't press for more, but said gently, "Just checking." She then turned to Paula. "Reverend, you ready to roll?"

"Let me grab my purse. Be right back."

A few minutes later Paula was in the passenger seat. As Tamar turned the key in the ignition and the truck rumbled to life, Rocky grinned and called, "Reverend, make sure you got on your seat belt."

Tamar leaned her head out her window and called back with a laugh, "Hater!"

A confused Paula had no idea what Rocky meant, but when Tamar drove out to the dirt road and the truck began traveling at a speed faster than light, Paula understood, held on for dear life, and prayed.

CHAPTER
13

L ily had a decision to make. Devon was supposed to be spending the afternoon and some of the evening watching the baseball playoffs with Mal, but Devon was still on punishment and technically couldn't watch TV. He also hadn't as of yet produced the three-page letter of apology he was supposed to write to Zoey, and Lily knew she'd erred in not setting a deadline for it to be done. She wanted to encourage the bonding Mal was trying to forge with his soon-to-be grandson, but on the other hand, she didn't want to say yes, Devon could go, and have him think he'd gotten around her edict. She'd talked to Trent about her dilemma last night when he returned from checking on Tamar, and he'd agreed with her on both sides of the issue. In the end, though, he left the final decision up to her, saying he'd support her either way.

Devon came down to breakfast a short while later, and to her surprise handed her three sheets of lined paper. "It's my apology to Zoey."

She read what he'd written. On all three pages, front and

back, he'd written, *I'm sorry Zoey*. And that was it. He'd written the words in cursive, and his small handwriting filled the pages. When she met his eyes, she couldn't tell what he was thinking. In the past few weeks he'd learned to mask himself pretty well. However, this was not what she'd asked him to do, and they both knew it.

"So can I go watch baseball with Mr. Mal now?" he asked.

Lily was admittedly tired of being a hard-ass. She decided to relent, but only up to a point. "Yes, but once you come home, you're back on lockdown until Zoey gets back from New York and you can give this to her."

That drew a pout that he quickly covered up.

"And I expect you to be more charitable to her and everyone else in the future. You weren't very nice to the reverend yesterday."

He didn't respond to that but did say, "Thank you for letting me watch baseball, Ms. Lily."

The tone lacked the sincerity she was accustomed to hearing from him. As his foster mom, that saddened her. She wanted her baby boy back, but it appeared as if that child and those days were gone, so she had to go with what she had. She picked up her phone and punched up Mal's number before handing the phone to Devon. "When Mr. Mal answers, ask him what time he'll be by to pick you up."

She took a moment to unload the dishwasher while the two made their arrangements and heard Devon say, "Okay. Thank you, Mr. Mal."

Devon handed the phone back to Lily. "He said noon."

"Then we'll have you ready."

Meanwhile, Trent and Amari were at the garage working

on Bing's old T-Bird. The original engine was shot, and while Trent worked on replacing it, Amari handed him the tools he needed like a nurse assisting a surgeon.

"Let me have the caliper."

Amari handed it over. "Are you and Mom going to adopt Devon, too?"

"She and I haven't talked about it, but I'm pretty sure we will. Why?"

"He's such a dork."

Trent looked up. "That's kind of harsh."

"Sometimes the truth is."

Trent resumed his task. "Suppose I'd applied that standard to you?"

"I'm not a dork."

"No, but you were a car thief, and cursed like the proverbial sailor. Not exactly a poster child for exemplary behavior."

Amari met Trent's eyes sheepishly. "Oh."

Trent paused for a moment to let that sink in before saying, "Devon's going through some things right now, and as his family we have to be there for him, regardless of how we feel about his personality."

"But he's never going to be a July."

"When you had the whole town hauled into court, I had misgivings about you, too."

Amari looked away.

Trent softened his tone. "You have a big heart, Amari. Use it to help your brother. He may not know it at the moment, but he needs you, okay?"

"If you say so," Amari replied grudgingly.

"Hand me that socket wrench. We're supposed to meet up

with him and Dad at noon to watch the games. And so you'll know, on Wednesday you'll be missing school so we can go see the judge and sign the papers finalizing your adoption."

Trent saw the elation on Amari's face but was pretty sure missing school was a part of it.

"Will we have to go before that old mean Judge O'Hara?"

"No. He's retired. We'll be going before Judge Davis."

O'Hara had been the judge originally assigned to the case involving Amari, Crystal, Preston, and Mal's stolen Ford. When O'Hara tripped and fell and had to be carried out of the courtroom on a stretcher, Judge Amy Davis replaced him and settled the mess to everyone's satisfaction.

"I wonder if she'll remember me."

Trent chuckled. "I'm sure she will, son. You're the most memorable kid anybody around here has ever met."

Amari beamed.

Trent held his hand out for the next tool. Amari passed it to him, and Trent asked about something else he had on his mind. "How're Brain and the colonel doing?"

Amari shrugged. "Better, I guess. Preston said they're back to playing chess, and that the colonel's been calmer about the whole birth parent search, but Mrs. Payne has been at her new office a lot. Brain thinks the colonel's lonely."

Trent found that surprising. "Really?"

"He says the colonel asks her every morning what time she's coming home, and every morning she tells him, 'At the end of the day.' She told Brain that her answer is the same answer the colonel used to give her when he was working with the marines."

"Sounds like payback."

"Pretty much."

Trent wondered how often the two friends discussed his relationship with Lily and decided that maybe he'd rather not know. "Okay, let's test these pistons."

Paula had gone through a number of the many prayers she knew by the time Tamar brought the truck named Olivia to a halt beside an open field. In the warp-speed journey to wherever they were now, they'd made so many twists and turns, some on two wheels, that Paula prayed yet again that her heart would survive the trip back to the trailer. Rocky had been right: tightly buckled seat belts were a necessity.

Tamar glanced over. "You okay, Reverend?"

"I think I may have wet my pants on that last two-wheel turn, but other than that, I'm good."

Tamar's eyes were gleaming. "I like you."

Paula was glad to hear that. She wasn't sure she could walk at the moment, but Tamar's approval meant a great deal. "Can I ask you something?"

"Sure."

"Who is Deborah? Rocky's music this morning was almost heartbreaking."

"Deborah was her mom. She committed suicide when Rocky was nine."

Paula understood now.

"Come. I want to show you this."

Paula exited the truck and followed Tamar out into the field.

"This is our cemetery. The county plans to bulldoze it next summer."

Stricken by the news, Paula asked, "Are you trying to stop them?"

"Bernadine's lawyers are fighting back with everything they have, but this is county land, so we're not holding out much hope. Ideally, they'd let us inter the remains elsewhere, but the Health Department is saying the remains may be too old, there may be the danger of disease, etcetera, etcetera."

Paula shook her head sadly.

"We'll see what happens."

For the next hour, Paula accompanied Tamar through the overgrown field and listened as she told the stories of the Henry Adams and July ancestors buried there. Paula found the tales of the July outlaws particularly interesting, especially the men Tamar called the Terrible Twins.

"My grandfather Neil and his twin brother, Two Shafts, had different mothers but the same father, and they were born on the same day. Shafts's mother was Comanche."

"So in a way they were twins. Why was he called Two Shafts?"

"During an archery competition when he was young he hit the bull's-eye with two arrows. He was so accurate, the second arrow split the first one right down the middle."

Paula was impressed. "Does he have descendants in town, too?"

"Never married. Said he didn't want to father children who could not be free to be Comanche. He suffered a lot after being taken from his parents and sent to one of the so-called civilizing schools. The people in charge cut off the braids of the male children, put the hair in the center of the field, and made the kids watch as it was burned. He never forgot that. He was living alone in the mountains of Arizona when he died in 1910. His July brothers brought the body here and buried him."

"How did they know he'd passed on? Did someone write to them?"

"No. Tamar, my great-great-grandmother, came to Neil and my aunt Teresa in their dreams and told them. She is known to walk in the dreams of her kin. Even today."

Paula wondered if this Tamar was all there.

As if sensing Paula's skepticism, Tamar pinned her with her hawklike gaze. "You'll find many wonders here, Reverend. All I ask is that you keep an open mind."

The frozen Paula nodded quickly.

That proved to be valuable advice later on that morning when Tamar drove her to meet Marie Jefferson and Genevieve Curry, and Paula heard the jaw-dropping story of Cletus the hog, his role in the destruction of Genevieve's home, and the death of a man named Morton Prell.

After Mal drove over and picked up Devon, Sheila Payne paid Lily a visit.

"I have a few invitation mock-ups I want you to choose from."

Once they were seated in the kitchen, Sheila rifled through her stylish new black satchel and handed Lily the invitations. There were three different versions, and they were all nice— not too frilly or pretentious.

"Crystal designed them," Sheila revealed.

That made Lily appreciate them even more. She decided on the one she liked best, and Sheila agreed. "That one was my choice, too. Crystal did an outstanding job."

"Yes, she did. I'll have to thank her."

"She wanted to do them for free, but I made her charge me. I thought she should be paid for the beautiful work. She can also add the design to her portfolio for the art schools she's going to be applying to, and let them know the invitations were commissioned."

"Good idea."

They spent a few more minutes talking about the invitations, and then Sheila asked, "Have you been looking for a suit?"

Lily couldn't lie. "I haven't had the time."

Sheila didn't fuss, but the look on her face spoke volumes.

"Okay, okay. I'll start looking."

"Promise?"

"Yes."

"And get something gorgeous—not just any suit that will do."

"Yes, Sheila," Lily said in mock surrender. "You're not supposed to know me that well."

Sheila shot her a smile and glanced at her notes. "I've talked with Rocky about the food, and Reverend Grant said she'd be honored to perform the ceremony."

"I owe her a thank-you, too."

"Lastly, Bernadine has instructed me to tell you that she will be paying for the honeymoon."

Lily stilled and waited for the proverbial other shoe to drop. "Where is she sending us?"

"That is a surprise," she replied. "But she says the weather will be warm, the reservation is set for a week, and she will be handling the flight plans."

Lily shook her head at Bernadine's behind-the-back maneuvering.

"I'm also instructed to warn you that should you refuse her wedding gift, you will have to meet her in a cage match."

Lily howled with laughter.

A smiling Sheila stuck her notes back into her bag.

With the business completed, they had some coffee and kicked back. Lily asked, "So how's the colonel?"

Sheila paused over her cup. "A bit confused, I believe."

"By what?"

"Everything. My job. Preston and his search. The idea of having to cook dinner for himself."

"But you're only working part-time. Why is he cooking dinner? Is he helping out?"

"Nope. He's cooking because a few days last week, I didn't get home until after seven."

"Why not?"

"Because I chose not to. I sat in my office and caught up on some of my reading, looked over china patterns on the Internet. Mostly I just relaxed. This being a working woman is a wonderful thing."

Lily saw the mischief in Sheila's eyes. "You know you're wrong, right?"

"No, I'm not. I've catered to him since the day we met. This job's helping me grow up and making him do the same."

"What about Preston?"

"He's my cheerleader. He told me when I want to stay late, I'm not to worry about him eating because he cooked for himself a lot in foster care. He makes a mean grilled cheese sandwich."

That made Lily smile. "He should also know that I'll feed him any time he wants."

"I believe he knows that, but I'll make sure."

"Good."

"Would you do me another favor?"

"I can certainly try."

"Have Trent and the other dads see if they can't come up with something for Barrett to do with his time. There has to be a way for him to give back to the community that doesn't involve ordering people around."

"Any suggestions?"

"Not yet, but Barrett's a good man. The problem is, the marines have spoiled him, and so have I. It may take a while to undo all that damage."

"I'll run your idea by Trent."

"Thanks."

After Sheila's departure, Lily picked up her phone. She hadn't talked to her son, Davis, in over a week, and she wanted to check in. The call went through, but instead of it being answered by his familiar and sunny "Hey, Mom," she heard instead a female voice ask angrily, "Who is this!"

Taken aback, Lily looked at the display on the phone and, upon determining she hadn't misdialed, replied, "This is Lily Fontaine, and you are?"

Silence.

"Put my son on the phone."

The next voice belonged to Davis, and he sounded quite contrite. "Hey, Mom. Sorry about that."

"Who was that—" She stopped herself before saying "heifer" and replaced it with "woman."

"Her name's Jessica. She's kinda tripping."

"Kinda?"

"Um, look. Glad you called. I may not be able to make the wedding."

She was sure she'd misheard him. "Excuse me?"

He sighed. "Jessica wants me to meet her parents Thanksgiving weekend."

"Did you tell her you have a prior commitment?"

"Yeah, but—"

"She doesn't care?"

Silence.

"Put her on the phone."

He chuckled. "Oh, no. Not doing that."

"I understand, but let me ask you this. How long has she been walking around with your balls in her purse? She can't be that fine."

"Mom!" He sounded appalled.

"Just asking. I'll talk to you later, Davis. Oh, and tell Jessica I can't wait to meet her." Lily ended the call.

Hoping the steam pouring out of her ears would dissipate soon, she bounced her head on the table in frustration. First Devon and now this. If Jessica made Davis miss the wedding, she'd be trading in her wedding suit for prison stripes, because she was going to hurt somebody.

CHAPTER
14

Devon was enjoying watching the Braves play baseball. He liked that Mr. Mal had provided hot dogs, popcorn, and soda, and that for the first time Devon knew more about a subject than Amari. Amari didn't know a thing about baseball, but Mr. Trent, Mr. Mal, and Mr. Cliff kept praising Devon for his knowledge while Amari steamed.

But watching the game made him think about how much fun it had been sitting in front of the little television back home with his grandma. Devon wanted to go back to Mississippi. There he could be himself instead of whomever the folks in Henry Adams were trying to make him become. He was pretty sure if he could get there, his grandma's best friend, Ms. Myrtle, would take him in. Better yet, she might even know how to get in touch with his parents. He'd enjoyed being in Henry Adams with Ms. Lily, but he was ready to go home now.

However, there were two major obstacles. He didn't have a way to get there, nor did he have any money. Both problems would have to be overcome if he were to be successful, so he decided to wait for a sign and go from there.

Mr. Mal lived in a small apartment connected to the Dog. In order to get to the bathroom, it was necessary to walk through his bedroom. During the seventh-inning stretch, Devon excused himself so he could make a quick trip to the bathroom. On his way back, he spotted Mr. Mal's wallet sitting on top of his dresser. Devon looked around to make sure no one else was coming. He knew stealing was wrong, it said so in the Ten Commandments, but the wallet was lying there calling him, so he went over and opened it. There was a ten-dollar bill inside. Shaking nervously, he stuffed the money in his pocket, put the wallet back where he'd found it, and left the room. He settled himself back in his chair and glued his eyes on the game.

The Braves won.

Mal asked, "Did you enjoy yourself, Devon?"

"Sure did, Mr. Mal."

Devon could see Amari mimicking him, but he ignored it because real soon Amari and his teasing would be just a memory, if his plans worked out successfully.

"How about we ask Lily if you can come over tomorrow after we finish up out at the Clark place, and watch the start of the American League series?"

"I'd like that."

"Good." The men all smiled. Devon felt the pang of guilt about the theft rise inside, but he ignored it the way he had Amari, or at least tried to. "Thank you for inviting me."

Mal ruffled his hair. "Anytime, buckaroo. And Amari, you need to bone up on the game."

"I'll pass. Baseball puts me to sleep. Give me real sports like football or the NBA."

Minutes later everyone said their good-byes, and Mr. Trent drove Devon and Amari home.

Later that day, emboldened by his successful theft from Mr. Mal, Devon targeted Lily. While she was downstairs watching TV with Mr. Trent, he tiptoed into her bedroom and found her purse. Her wallet held two twenties. He pocketed them and slipped back into his room. Fifty dollars was a lot of money. He was pretty sure it would be enough to catch the bus and go home, but he needed to hide it until it was time to leave. His grandma always hid things beneath her mattress, so Devon did the same. Nobody would look there. In the meantime, he had to find out about the bus. He and his grandma always took the bus with the dog on the side when they went out of town. Although he'd yet to see a bus in Henry Adams, he knew there had to be one somewhere.

Downstairs in the living room Lily was seated on the sofa with Trent, and she was fussing about Davis. "How can you not come to your mama's wedding?"

"You didn't curse at the girl, did you?"

Lily touched her chest and asked innocently, *"Moi?* Curse?"

"Oui, vous, Miss I Got a Temper."

"No. Davis wouldn't put her on the phone."

"Smart man."

"Not smart enough to keep that crazy girl from screening his calls. I asked him how long she'd been carrying his balls in her purse."

"You didn't."

"Yes, I did. I'm his mother. I'm allowed."

He chuckled. "You're a mess, you know that, right?"

She folded her arms and sat back against the couch in a huff. "I just want my son at our wedding. Is that too much to ask?"

He put his arm around her and eased her close. He kissed her angry brow. "No, darlin', it's not, so let's give him some time and space to work things out. He'll show up, don't worry."

"But he's always been so sensible about his girlfriends. What's he doing with a jealous controlling hoochie like this Jessica?"

"Every man takes a walk on the wild side at least once in his life."

"Did you?"

"Yes. Subject closed."

Lily asked innocently again, "Who was she?"

"Not telling you, so let it go."

"You didn't catch anything, did you?"

He looked at her and laughed uproariously. "Come here, you."

Next thing she knew she was being kissed, slowly, thoroughly, and completely. This version was even more world-rocking than the one last week at the Dog. And when he pulled back slowly and asked as he traced her lips with a slow finger, "Any more questions, Fontaine?" all she could do was whisper, "No."

Grinning, he gave her another potent kiss, pulled her close, and they resumed watching the Stevie Wonder concert on PBS.

* * *

On Sunday Henry Adams awakened to rain. The wind blew, the temperature plummeted, and folks knew to start paying closer attention to the forecasts on the Weather Channel again because winter was coming. The scheduled work on the Clark home was canceled due to the inclement day, so after calling everyone to notify them of that fact, Trent called Lily to invite her and Devon over for breakfast.

Amari met them at the door and let them in.

Lily said, "Morning, Amari. Smells good in here."

Amari nodded a greeting at Devon, who didn't return the gesture.

"Dad's in the kitchen."

Lily said, "Okay. I'll go and see if he needs help. Devon, hang out with Amari for a minute."

Amari looked like he'd prefer another option, but said to Devon, "Come on. I'm watching SportsCenter."

Devon took a seat on the sofa. While Amari reclaimed his chair, Devon looked at what was on the TV and asked, "Why are you watching with the sound down?"

"I've got the closed captioning on. It helps me with my reading."

"Oh, that's right. I forgot you can't read."

Amari shot him a look. "I can read. I just need to get better."

"I want the sound turned up."

"Then go home. This is my house."

"You're stupid."

"And you're a dork. Chill out before I have Zoey kick your butt again."

Devon crossed his arms and pouted. "Stupid."

"You say that again, and I'm telling."

"Stupid! Stupid! Stupid!"

In the kitchen Lily was setting the table while Trent finished up the eggs and bacon in the skillets on the stove. "Thanks for talking me down last night about Davis."

"No problem."

She walked up behind him and wrapped her arms around his waist before placing her cheek gently against his strong back. "Can you teach me to be calm like you?"

He turned around. "I can teach you anything you like."

She grinned. "You are so good for me."

"I know."

"Modest, too."

"Another one of the July family traits."

She snorted, and then, looking up into his eyes, said, "I love you very much."

"After all we've been through, you'd better."

She punched him, and he bent down and gave her a kiss.

Amari's voice interrupted. "Hey. Hey. Hey. Cut that out. Kid in the room."

They broke the kiss and grinned his way.

Trent asked. "You need something?"

"Yes. Somebody to check Devon."

"What's he doing?" Lily asked.

"Dogging me about not being able to read well. If he calls me stupid one more time, I'll be on fence duty because I'm going to knock him out."

Lily threw up her hands and sighed.

Trent gave her the spatula. "I'll talk to him."

And he did, very sternly, and made him apologize.

After Trent left the room, a satisfied Amari went back to the TV.

But even though it was Sunday morning, the devil was riding Devon. He looked around for a piece of paper and something to write with. He found a pad of sticky notes by the cordless phone near the door. Using the pen next to it, he wrote the longest word he could think of, *blasphemy*, and walked back into the room. "Can you read this?"

Smoldering, Amari turned to Devon, looked at the word, and slowly got to his feet.

Devon sneered, "You can't, can you?"

Amari snatched the paper out of his hand, balled it up, and threw it in Devon's face as hard as he could. The fear that leapt into Devon's eyes gave Amari a little bit of satisfaction, but not enough, so he stormed up the steps to his bedroom and slammed the door.

Needless to say, it was not a very good morning for anyone, except maybe Devon. Now that he knew for sure that he wouldn't be spanked, he planned to make everybody around him miserable until either they sent him home or he found the bus that would take him there.

However, he forgot about another long word, *consequences*. When he and Ms. Lily returned home, she refreshed his memory by informing him that not only would he be writing a three-page letter of apology to Amari, which had to be a real letter this time, he was also on punishment for the rest of his life. As she left his bedroom, she said, "You'll be twenty-five before you see television in this house again."

The punishment also negated his afternoon of baseball watching with Mr. Mal. That really stung, and made parts of

Devon rethink his whole devil persona thing. But the pain-filled, hurting parts of himself thought about the hidden fifty dollars that would be taking him home and decided Ms. Lily and everyone else could kiss his butt.

Trent rapped quietly on Amari's door.

"Come in."

He was stretched out on his bed with his arms folded behind his head, staring up at the ceiling.

"How are you, champ?"

Amari swung his head in his direction. "I'm still mad, but I'm okay."

"I came to commend you on your restraint."

"I wanted to pop him so bad."

"I know, but you didn't. That took maturity."

"Maturity's overrated."

Trent smiled with affection. "Sometimes it is, but you did good, son."

"What was that stupid word anyway?"

"Blasphemy."

"What's it mean?"

"Being disrespectful to God."

"From the Bible, right?"

"Mostly."

Amari sighed and looked up again. "I should've known." A few moments of silence passed before he asked, "Do we have to add him to the family?"

"He and Lily are a package deal."

"How about we keep her and trade him to the Clippers for a draft pick and a player to be named later, like in the NBA?"

Trent chuckled.

Amari's voice grew thick as he whispered, "He really hurt my feelings, Dad."

Trent walked over and sat down on the edge of the bed. The pain in Amari's eyes tore at his heart. He placed a hand on his son's shoulder. "I know."

"Being here is making me lose my edge."

"You think so?"

"I know so. I never felt like this on the street. People dis you, you cuss them out, you punch them out, you move on. I'm not down with having feelings."

"They help mold us."

"If you say so."

"Knowing that Lily probably put her foot up his little behind makes me feel better."

"I suppose. I just want to clock him, just once. Now I see why Zoey went off. How's she doing, by the way? Do you know?"

"They're supposed to be back in a few days. Reg told me on the phone yesterday that she has to baby her voice for now and not use it too much."

"Good. Can't wait for them to get back and hear what she sounds like."

Trent was pleased to see his mood lighten. "How about we go to the garage, work on the T-Bird, and turn on the game? New England's playing."

"Can we get burgers and fries from the Dog?"

"You bet."

"Then sign me up."

Trent ruffled his hair and headed to the door.

"Dad?"

Trent turned back. "Yeah?"

"Thanks for coming up to check on me. You made me feel better."

"It's all part of the job, son. See you downstairs in a few." Trent closed the door behind him and walked back to the staircase with a smile.

At her wit's end, Lily put in a call to Paula. After a few minutes of relaying her concerns about Devon and his behavior, Paula agreed to talk with him. "But I can't do it today. I'm having dinner this evening in Franklin with Pastor Donovan and his wife. How about Monday, right after school?"

Lily was disappointed that she couldn't come immediately, but there was nothing she could do about it, so she said, "Okay. That's fine."

After ending the call, she went up to his room.

He was stretched out on his bed.

He looked over at her and then away.

Lily ignored that and asked with all the confusion she felt inside, "Why are you being so mean all of a sudden, Devon? This isn't like you."

"I want to go back to Mississippi. I don't like Kansas anymore."

"There's nobody to take care of you there, honey."

"Ms. Myrtle will."

"Who's Ms. Myrtle?"

"My grandma's best friend."

"I see."

"I know she'll let me live with her. I just have to ask her.

I bet she knows where my parents are, too. They've probably been looking for me."

Lily shook her head sadly. No one had stepped up to claim him after his grandmother's death, but how do you explain that to a child so that he'd understand and not become more heartbroken? As for his parents, there was no information in his file about them. In fact, he didn't even have a birth certificate, something no one down in Mississippi had been able to explain when she called the Human Services Agency about the missing document after Devon's initial arrival in Kansas. He looked so unhappy. She was trying to be a patient and loving parent, but he was testing her big-time. "Dinner will be later."

Downstairs, she stood in front of the patio door and looked out at the pouring rain. Her mood matched the dank gray day.

Paula was feeling pretty gray herself. She'd agreed to have dinner with the Donovans knowing full well the man was going to test her faith and patience, but she'd agreed to the invitation anyway. Bad move. The afternoon began in his church. He introduced her to the five-person congregation, and the service began. The Anglican/Episcopal service that Paula presided over in her home church on Sunday mornings took ninety minutes, tops, and that was with the sermon. Pastor Donovan's sermon alone was ninety minutes long, and most of it was devoted to the proper way to worship God. As he proceeded to attack her church's doctrine and denounce its spirit of openness as godless and misguided, she forced herself to remember that she was a woman of God and therefore should feel no malice. In reality, she wanted to turn over his pulpit and walk out. She'd never been so openly and blatantly insulted in her entire life.

After the service, as he drove Paula and his silent wife through the pouring rain back to their home for dinner, he asked, "How'd you like my sermon, Reverend?"

She responded from the backseat. "It was certainly filled with lots of fervor."

"I felt moved this evening. Sometimes the Spirit takes over and speaks through me, and when it does, and you're on the wrong side of the Lord, too bad if you get your feelings hurt. The truth has to be voiced."

Paula silently prayed for patience and tolerance, even though Donovan seemed to have neither. One of the things he'd pointed out during the sermon as a failing of her denomination was that Episcopalians didn't bring Bibles to church. "Pastor Donovan, do you know why we don't bring our Bibles to church?"

He grinned at her in the mirror. "No, but I bet you think you have a legitimate reason."

"I'll let you decide that. Sixty percent of our liturgy every Sunday is taken from the Bible. That's more than any other Christian denomination."

She saw his wife give him a hasty glance of surprise.

Paula continued. "We recite the Psalms, have readings from both the Old and New Testaments, and, depending upon the priest, the sermon is usually tied to the Gospel reading of the day. So when you take all of that into consideration, we don't really need to bring our Bibles, because most of our service is the Bible."

Silence.

Paula knew that up in heaven God was shaking His head, but she saw this as a teaching moment, and she really felt the need to get this man's attention. She'd ask forgiveness when she said her prayers at bedtime. "As for your disdain for our embracing our gay and lesbian brothers and sisters . . . We practice *via media*."

"What is that, some kind of Internet mess?" he asked impatiently.

Paula kept her voice even and kind. "No, it's Latin for 'middle way.' We don't presume to know how God feels about certain issues, but you and I both know that the one thing Jesus stressed was love thy neighbor. Period. So that's what we practice and preach."

"But you have Episcopal churches that don't believe gays belong in the church, either."

"True, and as a family we're working on that. If you look at it from a historical perspective, Black people were considered unfit for the church at one time, too."

With that, she had nothing else to say. Apparently, Pastor Donovan didn't either, because he remained silent for the rest of the ride.

CHAPTER
15

O n Monday morning everyone went back to work and to school, and no one was happier than Lily. Devon had made her insane with his uncharacteristic behavior, but once she entered the Power Plant, she felt the stress lift. As she recounted the details of the volatile weekend to a concerned-looking Bernadine, though, it returned.

"You've talked to him?"

"Talked, prodded, hugged, punished. You name it, I've tried it."

"What's Paula saying?"

"She's going to talk to him after school. I feel as if bringing her in on this means I've given up."

"No, it just means you know that you've done all you can do. Maybe a professional like Paula will see something in Devon that we haven't and know how to fix it."

Lily sighed. "I'm going to my office. Maybe work will help me take my mind off all this."

Mid-morning she got a call from Marie, who asked, "Are you busy?"

Lily prayed this wasn't another crisis. "No," she responded in a voice she hoped sounded cheerful. "What can I do for you?"

"I want you to drive me up to Hays this afternoon."

She wanted to scream about having another chore put on her plate, but kept her voice even. "To the airport?"

"No, my son's flying in for a conference. He wants me to meet him at his hotel."

Lily's mood brightened. "That's great news, Marie."

"Yes, it is," she said happily. "After last week I could use some good news."

"Amen. What time does he get in?"

"Around two. He wants me to meet him around three."

"I'll pick you up at one. Is that okay?"

"Perfect."

"Is Leo going with us?"

"No. He's at a meeting in Franklin, and even if he wasn't, I'd rather you go with me."

That warmed Lily's heart. "Okay. I'll see you later."

Turning back to her computer screen, she said, "Finally, some good news."

Lily let Bernadine know she was leaving for the afternoon, and when she got in her car, she checked her wallet to make sure she had some money just in case she needed cash during the day. Her wallet was empty. She thought that over for a moment and swore she'd had forty bucks and tried to remember where she'd put it. She glanced at her watch. There was no time to run to the bank in Franklin, but she did have time to swing by the ATM inside the Dog.

The place was filled with the late lunch crowd, and ironically, the O'Jays were wailing "For the Love of Money" via the speakers when she ran in. Smiling, she stuck her card in the machine's slot just as Mal walked to the cash register.

She told him, "This machine is a godsend. I misplaced some money, and this beats driving over to Franklin."

"Must be contagious. Misplaced ten dollars myself sometime this weekend."

"We must be getting old."

"Speak for yourself," he countered with a grin.

The ATM burped out two twenties. Lily stuck them in her wallet and waved good-bye to Mal.

On the drive to Hays, Marie had on her poker face as she rode shotgun, but Lily sensed the nervousness beneath the calm exterior. Conversation had been sparse. Lily didn't want to talk about Devon or Davis not coming to the wedding and add her own personal drama to whatever Marie was feeling inside. "So how did your son sound when you talked to him?"

"A little guarded, but that's probably to be expected."

"He'll be here just overnight?"

"Yes."

"Did he say where home was?"

"Memphis."

"Wow."

"Not sure how he ended up down there, but that might be something we can talk about."

"Are you nervous?"

Marie grinned. "I can barely sit still."

Lily totally understood. "We're almost there."

When they arrived at the hotel, Lily drove to the door with the intention of letting Marie go in alone. "I brought some work," she explained. "I'll sit in the coffee shop or somewhere until you're ready to head back. Just hit me up on my phone."

"Oh, no. You're coming with me. I'm not meeting him alone."

"Marie?"

"Park, missy, and let's go in. I don't want to be late."

So Lily parked, and they both went inside.

He was waiting in the lobby. He was tall, brown-skinned, and a bit out of shape. He wore his age well, though. "Ms. Jefferson?"

"Yes, I'm Marie."

He seemed to be as nervous as she was. "I'm Brian French."

Marie opened her arms for a hug, but he cleared his throat as if embarrassed and offered her his hand to shake instead.

Lily saw Marie's embarrassment as she shook his hand. "This is my goddaughter, Lily. She drove me down."

He nodded her way. "Pleased to meet you."

"As am I," Lily replied and shook his extended hand, too.

He glanced around the lobby, and after spotting a quiet corner, gestured them toward the burgundy chairs positioned there. "How about we have a seat?"

They sat, and an awkward silence followed.

Marie took the plunge and said, "So you live in Memphis?"

"I do."

"Married? Children?"

"Married, yes. My wife and I have two girls, thirteen and fourteen."

"Do you have pictures?" she asked eagerly.

The way he paused and then glanced away gave Lily a bad feeling.

"Um, look," he said to Marie. "Honestly, I don't want to have a relationship with you. I was adopted by a great couple, and my life's been good."

Marie drew back as if she'd been slapped. "Then why am I here?"

"Curious about who you were, I guess. Most adopted kids are. I also wanted to know if there are any health issues in your family that may impact me or the girls in the future."

Marie looked so stiff and brittle, Lily was afraid she'd crack into a thousand pieces.

"No," she whispered. "We usually live a long time."

He searched her face and seemed to see how his statement had impacted her. "My apologies if I've hurt you."

Marie shrugged. "No problem. I appreciate the honesty. Is there anything else?"

"No, ma'am."

"Then you have a wonderful rest of your life." She stood up. "Nice meeting you. Let's go, Lily."

Lily could see that he felt terrible about how this had turned out, but she wasn't concerned about him. "Nice meeting you," she said.

"Same here."

Lily and Marie left without another word.

In the car, Marie stared out the window.

Lily said, "Marie?"

"Just get us home, honey."

So she did, while tears streamed silently down their cheeks.

When they finally reached Henry Adams, Lily stopped the car in front of Marie's house. "Do you want me to come in with you and sit awhile?"

"No. I've wasted enough of your time today."

"You didn't waste my day."

"I feel like a fool."

"You shouldn't."

"I thought he wanted me in his life."

"That's a perfectly normal response, but he should have told you what he wanted on the phone."

Marie didn't respond.

"You sure you don't want company?"

"Positive."

Tight-lipped, Lily nodded.

Marie leaned over and gave her a hug that was so filled with emotion, Lily began to cry again.

"I'll see you later," Marie promised and got out of the car.

Lily watched her slowly climb the steps to the porch. Genevieve, sporting the cast on her hand, met her at the door and opened it. They spoke for a few seconds. Lily saw Genevieve gather Marie into her arms and hold her tight as the door closed them in.

Driving back to town, Lily thought back on the disastrous meeting. The parts of her that loved Marie thought French had been selfish to reach out just for curiosity's sake and not consider she might be expecting more than a handshake.

Marie hadn't given him up by choice, nor even been allowed to hold him after his birth. As a mother herself, Lily couldn't imagine having been forced to give away her son without so much as a kiss good-bye. She sighed sadly. How much more heartache could one woman bear?

She called Trent to tell him about the rotten day. He was sympathetic and heard her out, but then rocked her with the news that Devon had been caught stealing at school. "What?" she yelled. Fighting to stay calm, she listened for a few more seconds, then said, "Okay. I'm on my way." She slammed her fist against the steering wheel and drove to the school.

In hindsight, Devon realized he should never have gone anywhere near Crystal's tote bag, but Mr. James sent him to the art room to get some markers, and the bag had been lying there. Devon knew that Crystal had a job as a waitress at the Dog, and he'd been so greedily focused on how much money might be inside, he'd had no idea that she was in the adjoining storeroom, taking inventory. He'd grinned upon finding two five-dollar bills in her wallet and had just slipped them both into his pants pocket when he heard her yell from behind him, "What the hell are you doing in my bag! I know you're not stealing from me, Devon Watkins."

He'd jumped in panic and spun around, and there she was, bearing down on him with murder in her eyes. Shaking, he somehow managed to say, "But Amari made me do it."

She smacked him across the top of his head. "Give me my money, little boy, before I beat you to death!"

She smacked him again, hard. "And that's for lying on Amari. He didn't send you in here, and you know it. Have you lost your damned mind!" She stuck out her hand, palm up, and glared.

Devon's shakes increased tenfold, so he had difficulty getting his hand into his pocket to retrieve the bills and give them back.

"Hurry up!" she demanded.

Once he placed the money in her hand, she latched on to his upper arm and propelled him forward. "Let's go!"

She marched him from the room, which is how he came to be sitting in Mr. James's office with the angry Mr. Trent and Ms. Lily standing over him at that moment.

In truth, Lily was past angry. "Stealing, Devon? How could you?"

When he didn't respond, Crystal reached out and smacked him upside his head. "Do you hear her talking to you, boy!"

"Crystal!" Lily cried.

Crys looked at her and said respectfully, "Ms. Lily, he knows you aren't going to spank him, and that's the problem. I'm not his parent. I can smack the taste out of him, so you better answer her, Devon," she warned him, leaning down to make sure he got it.

Looking on, Trent wanted to cheer. He didn't know if that made him a bad parent, but Devon was out of control, and if it took peer pressure from the Henry Adams big sister to make him straighten up, he was all for it. Otherwise Lily was liable to strangle the boy with her bare hands.

Devon got the message. Eyes downcast, he muttered, "I'm saving money to take the bus back to Mississippi so I can live with Ms. Myrtle."

"You dummy!" Crystal snapped. "You can't buy a ticket to Mississippi with ten dollars."

"I can with the fifty dollars I have in my room!"

Uh-oh.

Lily cocked her head. "Where'd you get fifty dollars?"

Belatedly realizing he'd volunteered too much information, he shot Crystal a look of fury, but she simply folded her arms angrily.

"You may as well answer her, son," Trent advised him. "You're already in this mess up to your tie."

Devon saw that Mr. James was standing quietly with his arms folded. Devon hoped he'd rescue him, but there appeared to be no salvation there either, so he mumbled, "I got it from Mr. Mal."

"Mal gave you fifty dollars," Lily replied skeptically.

Devon squirmed.

Trent took out his phone. "Let me call him."

"No!" Then he admitted quietly, "He didn't give it to me. I stole it."

"The entire fifty?" Lily asked.

More squirming. "No. Just ten. I took the other forty out of your purse."

Lily's eyes went so wide, Trent thought they'd explode. He shook his head and announced to Devon, "You just earned yourself a fence painting, Mr. Watkins. I'll be by to pick you up in the morning at six. Be ready."

Lily fumed, "I thought I had misplaced that money. Mal thought he had, too. Wait until I tell him his baseball buddy is the one responsible. Come on, Devon. We're going home."

And with that, the three-day crime spree perpetrated by the now very contrite Devon Watkins was over.

As promised, Trent picked Devon up just as the sun was rising and drove him out to the Jefferson place.

"But I'm going to get paint on my suit," Devon protested as Trent parked.

Trent cut the engine and glanced over. "I know you didn't think wearing that would get you out of this. You took money from your family, Devon. Suit or no suit, you have to pay the piper. Now let's get out."

Devon grudgingly complied, and the awful day began.

Even though Trent showed him how to use the brush and how to make the strokes, Devon had never painted anything in his life, and when he began working alone, it showed. He had white streaks and splotches all over him by the time the first twenty minutes ticked off the clock. At one point during his ordeal he took a misstep and wound up with his foot in the paint tray, and there he stood with paint all over his shoes, socks, and pant legs. He hated it. He could see Mr. Trent sitting on Ms. Marie's porch step, drinking coffee and watching. Devon hated him, too.

To make matters worse, when it came time for him to stop working so that he wouldn't be late for school, it took him so long to clean up the brushes and put everything back into the Jefferson barn that there wasn't time for him to go home and change clothes. He had to wear the paint-stained suit to school. The moment he entered the classroom, all the kids looked up. They knew what he'd been doing and why. No one said anything, but he caught their looks of amusement as they returned to their assignments. Pouting and angry, Devon took his seat.

At the end of the school day, Mr. Trent appeared to take him back out to the fence. Devon decided he'd never steal anything again.

On the drive, Devon asked, "When do I get to do my homework?"

"After your two hours of work. You'll put in two hours before and after school until the fence is done."

"But that may take a year."

"The way you paint, you're probably right, but you should have thought about the consequences before you began helping yourself to other folks' money."

Trent parked and glanced over at his son. "You know you're breaking Ms. Lily's heart, right?"

Devon dropped his eyes.

"And mine, too, son."

Devon looked up with water-filled eyes.

"You're a better person inside than this, Devon, and you and everyone else knows it. I can't believe you'd steal from the people who love you so much. This has to stop. All the anger you're throwing around can't be making you feel good inside, either. Am I right?"

"No, it isn't."

"Then come on, help us out so we can help you. What will make this stop?"

Devon looked up out of tear-filled eyes and whispered, "I just want to go home, Dad. That's all."

An emotional Trent pulled Devon across the seat and held him like a father holds his son. Devon wept as if his heart was breaking, and Trent let him cry.

"Lily and I will see what we can do about a visit," he said thickly. "I promise."

When the crisis passed, Trent rifled through the glove box, found the small box of tissues inside, and gave some to Devon.

Devon wiped his eyes and blew his nose. "Please don't tell Amari I was crying."

"I won't."

"Do I still have to paint?"

"Yeah."

"Okay," he said with soft resignation, and got out. Before he walked away, however, he told Trent, "Thank you."

Trent smiled. "No. Thank you."

Devon looked confused. "For what?"

"Calling me Dad."

Devon assessed him silently for a moment more. "You're welcome."

Kids having to paint the Jeffersons' half-mile fence as a punishment for serious misdeeds was a Henry Adams tradition started by Tamar and Ms. Agnes, who'd been at their wit's end trying to exercise parental control over the teenage Malachi and his running buddies Cliff and Marie. Once they grew up, the tradition was passed down to Trent's generation, but with no children coming up behind them, it passed into legend. However, thanks to Amari and Preston it had been resurrected, and now it was Devon's turn. If the previous results proved true, he'd never want to be sentenced to paint duty ever again.

Devon agreed. Painting was hard, and from the looks of him and his clothes it was difficult to determine whether he was working on the fence or painting himself. He looked up with sorrowful eyes at Mr. Trent sitting on the porch with Ms. Marie and Ms. Genevieve, but knew they weren't going to commute his sentence, so he went back to stroking the white-wash on the picket fence.

He'd just finished his fifth slat when Mr. Reg in his white truck drove up and parked. While Devon watched, Zoey, wearing her signature green everything, opened the door and hopped down to the road. Mr. Reg waved at him and walked off toward the porch, but Zoey came over to where he stood with the dripping paintbrush.

She slowly scanned his paint-stained self, and the first words out of her mouth were "You look a hot mess."

He wanted to smile but said instead, "Go away."

To his dismay, she did. Distraught, he watched her walk to the porch where the adults were sitting. His new dad was right; being mad wasn't making him feel good inside. He went back to work.

Up on the porch, Trent saw Zoey approaching the porch. "Hey, Zo. Welcome home."

"Hi, Mr. Trent. Hi, Ms. Marie and Ms. Genny."

"And you're talking," Genevieve gushed. "This is wonderful."

"With a southern drawl," Reg pointed out.

Zoey put her hands on her hips and tossed back in a humor-filled voice, "It's 'cause I'm from Florida, Daddy Reg."

"I know, baby girl. Just teasing. How about you tell Trent and the ladies why you had me drive you out here."

"I came to help Devon paint."

Trent glanced over at Reg, who shrugged, so Trent said

to Zoey, "That's real nice of you, Zoey, but he has to do it by himself."

"Amari and Preston didn't paint by themselves."

Trent studied her. She had a look in her eyes that was reminiscent of every other strong female person in Henry Adams, and he knew he was in trouble.

Reg came to his rescue. "I tried to tell her it was because they were both in hot water at the same time."

Marie added, "And tradition says you mess up, you paint. Devon stole money, baby girl."

"No disrespect, but tradition needs to get a clue."

Trent looked around to see if Crystal was nearby and somehow had her hand up Zoey's back, using Zoey as a ventriloquist's dummy.

"He'a little kid. It's going to take him a year to do that all by himself. And he doesn't know what he's doing. Have you seen his suit? I know he's been doing dumb stuff, but he's my brother, and I'm going to help."

Trent tried again. "Zoey, it's tradition."

She crossed her arms and waited.

Genevieve said, "You know, he is probably the youngest one we've had out there. How old were you the first time, Trent?"

He gave her a quelling look. "Twelve."

"And you were pretty tall even then. Marie, we were thirteen. I remember because we got caught wearing that tawdry red lipstick at school."

Marie asked, "So you're throwing in with Zoey?"

"Yes. He is a little guy. Maybe we need to have an age limit."

Trent sighed. He pulled a brush out of the bag at his feet and handed it to Zoey. "You're a good sister, Zoey."

"Thanks, Mr. Trent."

Back down by the fence, the paint-covered Devon was still wielding his brush alone when another big pickup pulled up. This one he'd never seen before. It was silver and red and looked brand-new, so he stopped to see who it might belong to. Out stepped Reverend Paula. She was wearing jeans and a matching denim jacket over a black shirt and her pastor's collar. On her feet was a pair of navy blue cowboy boots that had small gold stars stamped into the leather.

Devon decided to ignore her by pretending to be too busy painting to notice her, but she walked over anyway.

"Hey, Devon."

"Hey," he replied grudgingly.

"Heard you were out here. Thought you might like some help."

"It's not allowed."

"Really?" She looked speculatively over at the adults up on the porch. "Be right back."

Devon wondered who she thought she was. They weren't going to let her help. No way.

Way!

Not only did Zoey return with paintbrush in hand, so did the reverend. Devon was so surprised he was speechless for a second or two.

Zoey said, "Close your mouth and get to work. We don't want to be out here all day."

Grinning, he turned to Paula, who echoed, "What she said."

For the next hour the three of them painted and talked. Zoey did most of it. Her voice was lower toned than Devon had been expecting, and her way with words reminded him a lot of Crystal.

Paula knew that Zoey's sassy southern way of speaking stemmed from her having been raised by an addict mother on the streets of Miami. It did Paula's heart good to have Zoey chattering away beside her, because it reminded her of Old Ab.

Devon's voice broke into her thoughts. "Reverend Paula, why are you helping me?"

She paused in her painting. "I don't know. Your mom told me a little bit about what's been going on, and I just thought you might need a friend."

"I'm sorry I stole the money."

"I know you are. Your mom says you miss Mississippi so much you want to go back."

"I do. I want to talk to Ms. Myrtle, and then go and see my grandma's grave. I didn't get to see her in the hospital after she got sick. Only after she died at the funeral parlor."

Paula was surprised by that. "Why?"

"Everybody said I was too little to go to the hospital."

"So you didn't get to say good-bye?"

He whispered, "No, ma'am."

Paula draped an arm over his paint-stained shoulder and hugged him close.

Zoey looked at her friend and declared sagely, "Then I think we should ask Ms. Bernadine if Ms. Katie can fly you to Mississippi in the jet."

Paula took in the serious set of Zoey's features and agreed wholeheartedly.

*   *   *

Later that evening, the adults in Devon's life had a meeting of the minds. Trent related Devon's emotional admission in the truck, and Paula added what he'd revealed to her about the death of his grandmother, and his being denied an opportunity to say good-bye. After a few more minutes of discussion, it was agreed that Devon, Lily, and Trent would be taken to Mississippi in the jet. Their hopes were that the visit would help the little preacher's broken heart and assist him in moving on with life.

Lily came into Devon's room that evening and found him in bed, reading his Bible. "Hey, you."

"Hey, Ms. Lily."

"Time to go to sleep. You have paint duty again in the morning."

"Mr. Trent told me thank you for calling him Dad."

"He told me. He liked that a lot."

Lily came over and sat down on the edge of the bed. "On Saturday we're going to fly down to Mississippi."

His eyes widened. "For real?"

"For real."

"And I can talk to Ms. Myrtle?"

"Yes, you can."

"Do you think she knows where my parents are?"

That he was still focused on trying to leave her and the love she had for him behind made her sad, even though she knew he'd be flying back to Kansas with her and Trent, regardless of the outcome of the trip. "I'm not sure, honey, but we can ask. We'll also go by the cemetery and put some flowers on your grandma's grave."

"I'd like that."

She studied him for a few long moments. "I'm still mad about what you did, but I do love you, Devon, and always will."

"I'm sorry I stole the money."

"I know you are. How about you give me a hug."

So he did, and she hugged him back fiercely. Placing a kiss on his forehead, she said, "Good night, Devon."

"Good night, Ms. Lily."

chapter 16

Now that Devon seemed to be coming around, and with Zoey home and talking up a storm, the next few days in Henry Adams were fairly drama free, or as drama free as a day in Henry Adams could be.

Lily went to work, and later met Sheila at the Dog for lunch to talk about the wedding plans. She hadn't heard from her son, Davis, since the Jessica incident, but she was okay with that for the moment—the less drama in her life, the better. Trent spent some of his time helping Gary Clark move the remainder of his family's possessions from the large home now in foreclosure in Franklin to the cozy, well-furnished double-wide trailer. Preston's search for his biological parents continued, and after school, Amari and Zoey worked on the old T-Bird, while Devon and Reverend Paula continued to paint the fence. As for Crystal, she was content with life because no one was stealing her hard-earned money.

On Wednesday, Trent and Amari put on their suits and

drove to the county courthouse for the finalization of the adoption. Amari was so excited he hadn't been able to eat breakfast. They met up with Mal and Tamar in the lobby and took seats to await their turn before the judge.

The bailiff came for them less than twenty minutes later and led them inside. Judge Amy Davis was seated behind the bench. She looked out at them and said with a smile, "Welcome."

"Good morning, Judge Davis," Trent said. Mal and Tamar echoed his greeting.

"And Amari, how are you?" she asked.

"Fine, Your Honor. Yourself?"

"I'm well. Glad to have you back in my courtroom for such a wonderful reason."

Amari beamed.

"The July family is to be commended for their commitment to this very special young man. Because of your dedication and love, he will make us all proud one day. I wish the country had more families like yours for the ton of foster children needing what you all are giving to him."

She then set her attention back on Amari. "Do you have anything you want to say before I make my declaration?"

"I do, Your Honor."

"The floor's yours."

He turned to his family. "I want to say thanks. If it weren't for you all, I'd still be in the D hustling, stealing cars, not knowing when I'm going to eat or where I'm going to sleep. I never knew family could be so awesome. Like Judge Amy said, I'm going to make you proud one day, and I love you. That's all I have to say."

Trent thought his heart would burst. He saw pride in Tamar's eyes and satisfaction in Mal's.

Judge Davis nodded approvingly. "Then by the power invested in me by the state of Kansas, I am approving the petition brought before me today by Mr. Trenton July to legally adopt Amari Steele, who from this moment on shall be known as Amari July."

She brought her gavel down, and Amari jumped for joy. "All right!!"

Trent, Mal, and Tamar thought it was pretty all right, too, and there were hugs all around.

Trent had to sign some papers at the clerk's office, but once that was done, Amari Flash Steele left the courthouse as Amari July.

That night they got together for a special dinner at Tamar's. The menu featured some of Amari's favorite foods, like big fat burgers from the Dog, and fries with tons of ketchup, and Tamar's homemade butter pecan ice cream. Just when he thought the day couldn't get any better, she brought out the old family Bible. It was an heirloom Amari had seen before. While they waited and looked on, she took a seat at the now-cleared dining room table and opened the weathered leather book to the pages in the back. "Come closer, Amari."

He went over and stood by her side.

"This is the family Bible. Mayor Olivia July purchased it back in 1890, and it holds the sunrise and sunset dates of every July in our line. Time to add you. I want you to write your old name and the day you were born, here."

Using the pen she handed him, he did that.

"And now, your new name and today's date, right here."

Trent's pride rose again as he watched his son write, "Amari July, Oct. 6," and the year.

When he was done, Tamar said with affection in her voice, "Welcome to the family, Amari July."

He gave her a long tight hug and whispered emotionally, "This is even better than court. Thank you, Tamar. I love you."

"I love you more."

Later that night, up in Amari's bedroom, he and Trent had their one-on-one. Trent was sitting on the edge of the bed, and Amari was sitting up in his pajamas. "I had an awesome day, Dad."

"I'm glad."

"Can't wait to tell Preston."

Trent studied him for a moment and tried to figure out how best to say what he wanted to convey. "I want you to go easy on the bragging at school tomorrow, Amari."

"But why? I'm official now."

"But Preston isn't, and Devon and Crystal aren't, either."

"Oh, I didn't think about that." Then he asked, "Why is growing up so complicated sometimes?"

"Wish I knew."

"Okay," Amari replied. "I'll keep it down tomorrow. I don't want to hurt their feelings."

"Good. Anything else we need to talk about before lights out? How're you getting along with Tiffany at school?"

"That is one angry girl. Me and Preston try and stay away from her mostly. Leah's still okay, though."

Trent stood. "Okay. Just checking." He looked down at the

amazing young man who was now legally his kin. "I'm glad to have you in my life, son."

"Same here."

"Get some sleep, and I'll see you in the morning."

"Night, Dad."

"Night, Amari."

As Trent left the room, the room went dark, and he closed the door behind him.

Dads Inc. met the next morning for breakfast at the Dog. All the members showed up, including Mal and the newest town dad, Gary Clark. The colonel had been keeping a low profile since the emergency meeting he'd called over the weekend, and Trent was curious to hear how he'd been doing.

As the meeting started with Reg gleefully relating how he felt about Zoey's voice, Rocky brought over their orders on a large tray. While she passed the plates around, she eyed Jack. He eyed her. She finished and walked away.

Everyone grinned.

They began eating, and Reg continued his story. "I think Zoey must be making up for lost time, because she starts talking the moment her feet hit the floor in the morning until she goes to bed at night. And it's nonstop. I love it, of course, but she's been wearing me out."

Trent had to agree. She'd worn him out at the garage earlier in the week. Trent knew it was bad when Amari turned to her and said, "Zoey, you have to stop talking, please. You're making my ears hurt."

"She's been pretty chatty in class, too," Jack related. "I hate to squelch it after all she's been through, but I can't let

her distract the other kids. Pretty sassy, too. Never disrespectful though, Reg, but she's like Crystal's Mini-Me."

"If she starts to cross the line, let me know."

Trent and Lily had discussed Sheila's request that the Dads
find something for the colonel to do, but he wasn't sure what
it might be. "So, Barrett, what's going on with you?"

He grumbled and played with the eggs on his plate. "The
wife's working, as you all probably know, and my household
is in chaos. Breakfast isn't on time anymore. Dinner, either.
She can never give me a specific time when she's coming
home."

"Sounds like you're not happy," Mal said.

"I'm not. She's turned into someone I don't know, and she
has the nerve to be snippy."

Jack dropped his head to hide his grin.

Trent, seeing his opening, said over his coffee cup, "Maybe
it's time for you to find something to do, so you're not just sitting around waiting for her to come home."

Barrett eyed him. "Never thought about that."

"There has to be something you'd like to do."

He could see Barrett considering the idea. Trent was
pleased that the man hadn't dismissed the thought out of
hand. He turned to Gary, who'd been eating, and so far
silent. "What about you, Gary? Come up with anything for
yourself yet?"

"Nope, not yet, but I'm working on it."

A short, swarthy man no one knew walked over to the
table. "Excuse me. Who's Malachi July?"

Mal eyed him suspiciously. "Why?"

"I have some papers for him, and for . . ." He pulled a

slip of paper from the breast pocket of his suit coat and read, "Trenton July, Dr. Reginald Garland, Colonel Barrett Payne."

Barrett said, "That's the four of us."

The guy dropped a legal-looking envelope down on the table in front of each man in question, and announced, "You've all been served. Have a great day, gentlemen."

The Dads stared, surprised, first at him as he walked hastily toward the exit, and then down at the envelopes.

Mal opened his first and read it. "I'll be damned. Riley is suing Genevieve for assault. I've been subpoenaed as a witness."

The others had, too.

Trent put his summons in his shirt pocket. "So much for a quiet day."

Mal drawled, "You got that right."

When Trent told Lily about the summons, she glanced up at him from behind her desk and said, "Genevieve should plead temporary insanity. After she tells her story, there isn't a jury in the world that'll convict her. Riley has a lot of damn nerve, considering what he put her through. He ought to be grateful she's letting him live."

Her hell and brimstone personality always made Trent laugh. "True."

"When do you have to go to court?"

"First week of November."

"I'll give her a call and see if she needs legal help." She shifted gears. "How'd the meeting go this morning? Was the colonel receptive to Sheila's idea?"

"He was, probably because I didn't tell him it was her idea. He says she's getting snippy."

"Go, Sheila."

He laughed. "What's on your schedule today?"

"The Boss Lady and I are meeting with Paula to talk about using the auditorium for her services until we get her church built, then finish going over those final blueprints you gave me for the Main Street build, and start lining up suppliers. And then meet with Sheila for like the fiftieth time this week to check off all the RSVPs that have come in for the reception." She paused to take an exaggerated breath. "And then—"

He threw up a hand to stop her. "Enough. I'm exhausted just listening to you."

"Have to keep the cradle rocking. Oh, and Paula called and said she and Devon finished the fence."

"Good thing. Weather Channel's calling for snow flurries by the end of the week. Having to paint while it's snowing is rough."

She cocked her head. "You've done that?"

"Yep, remember the time Gary's mom sentenced us for spiking the punch during his sixteenth birthday party?"

From the blank confused look on her face, he guessed she didn't. "Must have been before you got here or right after, but anyway, five of us were charged. It snowed overnight, and the following morning it was so cold, the paint wouldn't roll. Wind was blowing. We froze our butts, but his mom and Tamar refused to give us a break. Made us stay out there the entire two hours before school."

"How long did it take the five of you to finish?"

"Only a couple of days, but thawing out took at least a week."

"And you all never spiked the punch again."

"Let's just say we made sure we never got caught again."

"Gotcha."

Her smile was one of the many thousands of things Trent loved about her. It made her eyes soften and sparkle, and brought warmth to the hurt places inside that men kept hidden away. "Do you think all this drama will lie low long enough for us to get married?"

She gave him that smile again. "I told you months ago eloping was the way to go. There's no telling what may be going on around here by the time the wedding date rolls around."

He agreed. "I'm just wanting to get away to wherever Bernadine is sending us on the honeymoon, so it can be just you and me. Uninterrupted. No kids. No drama."

"I second that."

In the silence that followed, they fed themselves on what they read in each other's gaze.

Lily said quietly, "You're making a girl want to run away with you, so go to work, Trenton July."

"No, let's talk about this for a minute. The kids are in school. Both houses are empty."

Her laughter rang out. "Get thee from my office, devil man."

"We could get a carry-out, meet up at my house around noon, and who knows, maybe we'll take the rest of the afternoon off."

"You are so the serpent."

"That's my name, don't wear it out." Trent could see the wheels turning in her steel trap of a brain, though, as she mined the possibilities.

She confessed, "That's really a good idea."

"I'm just saying."

When mischief beamed from her eyes, he knew she'd come to a decision.

"Noon. Your place. Can't wait."

"See you in a few." Trent strolled out.

He'd just settled into his office chair and booted up his computer when Tamar walked in. "Good morning," he said affectionately. "How are you?"

She took a seat. "Doing good. Stopped by to show you something."

She reached into the pocket of the old quilted blue coat she usually wore once the weather began edging closer to winter. She'd also traded in the summer caftans for the jeans and sweatshirts that were standard wear at the change of the season. She handed him a piece of paper that had on it a list of terms and math values that appeared to be the results of some sort of medical tests. He stilled and asked warily, "What is this?" He prayed it had nothing to do with the conversation they'd had a few days ago about her health.

"Blood work."

"Whose?"

"Amari's."

Trent, thinking the blood work was hers, was now relieved but confused.

She explained. "Doc Garland suggested comparing Amari's DNA to the DNA of a known male July relative might help answer the question of whether Amari is family or not."

"You actually spoke to your brother? You didn't say anything about this when we talked that night."

"Do you want to hear this or not?"

He nodded affirmatively but didn't say another word.

"Doc said the tests would be more accurate if we used a direct male link to the Julys. So since Mal wasn't fathered by a July, we had to use my brother."

"So what did the test show?"

"Ninety-eight percent chance that Amari is blood. Doc said the DNA markers lined up just like they're supposed to."

"Wow. So now what?"

She shrugged. "I've got everyone in the family looking into any member who may have been in Michigan the year Amari was born, but so far nobody's stepped forward."

"Maybe whoever his father is doesn't want to be found."

"That may be, but he should step up anyway for Amari's sake. It's not like the mystery July is going to get custody."

"No, he's not. So the test means that Amari was fathered by a male July."

"That's the impression I got when Reg explained it to me, but I was so confused at one point, who knows. You should probably talk to him when you get the chance."

"I will."

She rose to her feet. "Okay, I'm on my way to the rec center. If you need me, that's where I'll be."

He studied her for a moment. "Tamar, how are you, really?"

"Better than I was the night on the porch, and that's all I can ask."

He nodded. "See you later."

And she was gone.

CHAPTER
17

Friday evening after school, Lily, Devon, and Trent boarded Bernadine's jet for the flight to Mississippi. They touched down late that afternoon at a small private airport outside Jackson and were met there by the car service Bernadine had hired to handle their transportation needs during their stay. The driver was a tall, barrel-shaped man named Harvey Miller who according to the dispatcher was a native of the area and very familiar with the back roads they'd need to negotiate in order to get to Devon's birthplace of Ibo.

"Not many folks in Ibo anymore," Harvey said. "Only ones left are the ones who can't leave."

"How far away is it?" Trent asked.

"Forty minutes, give or take."

So they sat back and let Harvey drive them to Devon's home.

Devon peered out his window at the familiarness of the land and felt all the stuff that had been roiling inside him for the past few weeks melt away like magic. He was home. And

if he had his way, he'd never leave Mississippi again. He knew
that Ms. Lily and his new dad would be sad when Ms. Myrtle
agreed to take him in, and he'd certainly miss them, but Ms.
Bernadine would find them another little boy. He couldn't
wait to see his old house and room. He'd probably have to live
in Ms. Myrtle's tiny place, but he'd be able to walk down the
road and look in the windows of the house he'd shared with
his grandma whenever he wanted. She'd probably let him be
the preacher again at the church, too, and that made him feel
even better. He'd never have to change, because she'd let him
be himself, and that's who he wanted to be.

Ms. Lily's voice interrupted his thoughts. "How are you
doing, Devon?"

"Fine."

She gave him a smile that looked a little sad. "Good."

"Don't worry, Ms. Lily, Ms. Bernadine will find you another little boy."

She didn't reply, but he saw her share a look with Mr.
Trent that he couldn't interpret. He didn't mind, though. As
soon as they found Ms. Myrtle, he wouldn't have to worry
about his life ever again.

While Devon continued to build upon his fantasy, Lily
and Trent watched the beautiful Mississippi landscape roll
by. Although Lily had spent most of her adult life in Atlanta,
after being in Kansas for the past few years, she'd forgotten
how green the South was even in the fall. The back roads
they were traveling down were bordered by a lush, verdant
landscape that was broken up here and there by abandoned
shacks and sagging barns. Every now and then they passed a
small cluster of homes with people sitting on the porches or

kids playing on the dusty cleared patches of dirt that served as the yard. She imagined that not much in the area had changed since the days of slavery, when this part of the nation was known as Deep South. According to statistics it ranked high in poverty, poor education, and teenage pregnancy, but because the South had a way of making lemonade out of life's lemons, she imagined there was a lot of joy around, too. She glanced at Devon, whose entire being seemed focused on the passing countryside. He was so convinced that he'd not be returning to Kansas, but she knew better and was not looking forward to the heartbreak she was certain he was going to have. As if Trent sensed she needed buoying, he closed his hand over hers, gave it a slight squeeze, and held on. She squeezed back to let him know how much it meant having him by her side.

A short while later, even though there were no road markers or signs of any kind to indicate their location, Harvey announced, "This is Ibo, folks."

From her place in the middle of the seat, Lily leaned over Trent to glance out the window at where they were.

Devon called out excitedly, "There's the church! Stop, Mr. Harvey. Stop!"

Mr. Harvey eased the car to a stop, and before Lily could open her mouth, Devon had the door open and was out. She sighed and said to Trent, "This is going to be rough."

"I know, but let's just go with it and see how it turns out."

So they followed Devon across the high green grass to a windowless cinder-block building with a weathered, hand-painted wooden sign nailed on the front that read: *Goodwill Missionary Church of God. All Welcome.*

Devon was wearing the happiest smile Lily and Trent had seen in months.

"This is our church."

"So I see," Lily said. "Lots of good memories here for you, I'll bet."

"Yes, ma'am," he replied proudly. "My grandma and I came every Sunday."

Trent asked, "How far away is your house, Devon?"

"Just up the road. Do you want to see it?"

"Yes, sir."

"Then come on." He grabbed Trent and Lily by their hands and ran with them back to the waiting car.

Once inside, he gave Harvey directions, and they were on their way.

"Where's Ms. Myrtle live, Devon?" Trent asked.

"Down this road a little ways. We have to pass my house before we get to hers."

"Then we'll stop by your place first."

"It'll probably be locked up, but we can peek in the window and see my room."

Lily said gently, "I believe another family lives there now, honey. Remember last year when we talked about Ms. Bernadine putting the ownership of the land away for you until you're eighteen?"

"Yes."

"She found someone to rent the place, and the money the family pays to live there goes into a bank account she set up for you."

Trent said, "So it might not look the same as it did when you and your grandma lived there."

He glanced between the two of them with dismay.

Feeling the need to soften the distress the news had caused, she added, "Maybe the people have moved to another house by now, but we'll see when we get there."

They drove a bit farther.

"Stop here," Devon called out.

They were parked in front of a brown wood-planked cabin. Three children in the front yard were playing with a ball, and the sight of the car made them stop their game and stare curiously.

"This isn't it. My house is blue."

"Are you sure? The new people may have painted it," Trent pointed out.

Devon studied the place for a long, silent moment. "It is my house."

"Do you want to get out?" Trent asked him. "We can go and ask if you can look inside."

"No, thank you." He looked so disappointed. "I'd rather go see Ms. Myrtle."

"Okay."

"I'll let Mr. Harvey know where to stop."

Lily shared a look with Trent and silently said a prayer.

In truth, Lily was secretly dreading the meeting with Ms. Myrtle because of the pain she was sure it was going to cause Devon, but Ms. Myrtle was one of the reasons they'd come to Mississippi. No sense in putting it off and have him continue to hold false hopes about the future.

Devon asked Harvey to stop in front of a small wooden shack with a lopsided porch set on short wooden stakes that looked like a mouth with teeth missing. It reminded Lily of the pictures she'd seen in magazines and on the news of some of the homes occupied by the poor. It sat alone on a lot bordered on one side by a tidy little fenced-in garden and an old white Buick with its back axle on the ground. Surrounding the house were trees and more wild, lush greenness that could have passed for Eden.

They could see that the front screen door was open, so they got out of the car and stepped into a silence that seemed almost alive. A heavyset woman came out onto the porch. She was wearing a sleeveless muumuu that hit her just below the knees and red slippers. Her legs looked swollen by age and maybe diabetes. It was easy to see by the wariness on her aged brown face that she was trying to figure out who they were and why they'd stopped. "You all lost?"

Before they could stop him, Devon shot out of the car and ran up to the porch. As soon as he reached it, her mouth dropped. "Devon! That you? My goodness. Look at you!" She gathered him into a hug that soon turned into rocking. The happiness on her face was clearly evident.

A smiling Lily and Trent walked up to join them.

She looked out at them and said, "I'm Myrtle Brooks."

Lily and Trent introduced themselves. Lily added, "We're Devon's foster parents."

"Is that your fancy car?"

Lily smiled. "No, ma'am. It's rented."

Myrtle looked down at Devon and said, "Looks like you fell into high cotton, baby boy. How are you?"

"Fine."

She gestured to them. "Pull up a piece of porch. Too hot inside for visiting. Devon, I'm so surprised to see you. Glad, too."

She sat in the big cane chair by the door, and Lily and Trent took seats on the lip of the sagging porch.

"So what brings you all to Ibo, Mississippi?"

Before either of the adults could respond, Devon said in a rush, "I came back to live with you."

She paused, looked at him, and then slowly took in the faces of Lily and Trent before saying, "Really? I'm honored, but looks like you're living pretty good with your new folks."

He shrugged. "I am, but I want to live with you. I don't like Kansas anymore."

"You came all the way from Kansas?"

The adults nodded.

She looked at Devon silently for another moment. "Do they treat you bad?"

"No."

"They must not be feeding you, then?"

"No, ma'am. Ms. Lily's a good cook, and I get to eat all the time."

"Then what's wrong? Because I'm going to tell you right now, you can't live here. I don't have the money or the patience to raise you, Devon."

He glanced down at the porch beneath his feet. "Oh."

"I'm just telling you the truth."

Lily felt bad for him, even worse than she thought she would, but she applauded Myrtle's upfront honesty.

Devon tried again, "But I won't cost a lot. I can help you with the garden, do chores, and I won't eat much. I promise."

Myrtle reached over and placed an arm around his waist and hugged him close. "I'm too poor and too old. Your new folks must love you a whole lot to fly you all the way back down here." She turned to them. "Both of you college graduates?"

Lily thought that an odd question, but she and Trent acknowledged that they were.

Myrtle set her attention on Devon and asked with a serious tone, "Do you know how blessed you are, boy? You have folks that went to college. You live here, you'll end up working at the meatpacking plant down the road, wishing you were somewhere else. These folks can help you get to places your grandmama and I could only dream about. God took our Willa Mae and blessed you with a new family so that you could grow up and become a presence in the world. Don't throw that blessing back in His face. It's not right."

Her wisdom reminded Lily of Tamar.

"But I don't like living there."

"Sometimes God gives you things not because you like them, but because you need them."

"But they won't let me preach."

"They're your parents, so I'm not getting in that, but from the beginning I never agreed with Willa Mae telling you you were anointed and all that other stuff, anyway."

He stared, surprised. "But why, Ms. Myrtle?"

"Because you're just a little boy, Devon. That's why."

Rather than think on that, or maybe because he didn't want to, he asked instead, "Then do you know where my parents are?"

She went still. "Why?"

"I want to live with them, then." He folded his arms across his chest.

Myrtle said warningly, "Never agreed with the way your grandma spoiled you, either."

Lily looked at Trent, and she wanted to laugh. It never occurred to her that Devon was a brat, but looking back at the way he'd been acting for the past few weeks, the signs were clearly there.

As if reading Lily's thoughts, Myrtle said, "Oh, yes. Spoiled the boy from the day he was born. He ran her, too. Anytime she tried to correct him, he'd throw those Bible passages at her, and she'd usually back down. Only one he never quoted was: 'Spare the rod, spoil the child.'"

Lily could see Devon starting to look a tad uncomfortable with the turn the conversation had taken.

"Ms. Myrtle, do you still have Missy?" he asked.

"She's in the barn. You can go say hello if you like. There's also sugar water in the fridge. Help yourself if you're thirsty."

Avoiding the eyes of Lily and Trent, Devon went inside the house.

"Who's Missy?" Trent asked.

"My cat. She just had kittens. That'll give him something to do while we talk. So tell me, what's going on with him?"

For the next few minutes they told her about all the madness Devon had been causing, his refusal to let go of his suits, and the stealing.

Ms. Myrtle listened and said, "Sounds to me like he doesn't want to grow up. Probably missing Willa Mae a whole lot, too, but that's natural."

"So do you know anything about his parents?" Trent asked.

She looked into the house to see if Devon was nearby. None of them heard him moving around inside the two-room place, so they assumed he'd gone to the barn to play with Missy and her kittens.

Myrtle replied, "I know where his mother is, but not his father. We never found out who he was."

"What do you mean?" Lily asked.

She sighed. "Devon's mama's name is Rosalie. She was born . . . different, shall we say. She didn't progress like normal babies. Took her a long time to sit up, even longer to crawl, and she didn't talk, not even the babbling babies do. Willa Mae took her to the doctor, and they did some tests and found out she'd had serious brain damage while in the womb, but they didn't know why."

Lily's lip tightened.

"They said she'd never progress past the mental abilities of a three-year-old, and that Willa Mae should think about putting her in one of those homes, but Willa refused. She kept Rosalie at the house with her until Rosalie was well into her mid-thirties. Folks around here would sit with her while Willa Mae was at work, but we were all getting older, and Rosie was needing more and more care, and then Willa Mae's sugar started acting up, so she was forced to have Rosie institutionalized at what the doctors told us was a real nice place."

"But it wasn't," Trent said, sensing a sad story ahead.

"No. About ten years ago, a man there did something unspeakable to Rosalie." She quieted for a few seconds, as if thinking back, and tears slowly filled her eyes. "Unspeakable," she whispered. There was another long pause while she pulled herself together before she continued. "The state's investigation never found out if it was an orderly, or a doctor, a guard, or just a visitor who slipped into her room, but she was pregnant, and Devon is the child."

"Oh, my God," Lily whispered.

Trent's anger flamed.

"Of course, Rosalie couldn't be a mother to him, so Willa Mae brought him home, and from the moment she did, she started him on the Bible. I believe it was her way of trying to make sure he didn't grow up to be as godless as the man who'd fathered him."

"Is Rosalie still alive?"

"Yes. Willa Mae sued the state for their neglect and won, and as part of the settlement they moved our sweet child to the best nursing facility in the state. She gets twenty-four-hour care, and the state pays the bill."

Devon stepped out of the door and said clearly, "I want to see her."

They stared, surprised. Lily wondered how long he'd been listening, but from the tight emotion evident in his posture and on his face, it must have been long enough. The adults were so caught off guard by his sudden appearance, he repeated the request louder and with more conviction. "I want to see her!"

Trent and Lily looked to Myrtle, who said gently, "I don't think that's wise, Devon. She doesn't know where she is or who you are."

"I don't care! She's my mom! I want to see her!" He started to cry angry, frustrated tears.

Lily instantly perceived that this was not the bratty child making selfish demands, but a little boy lost in a world not of his own making. She was tempted to put in a call to Reverend Paula and ask her for her professional opinion on whether Devon seeing Rosalie would be a help or a hindrance to his future development, but instead, she thought about Crystal and Zoey and Preston and Amari, all children with frayed ties to their real families, and she thought about Marie, but mostly, she thought about the motherless man next to her that she planned to marry. When she looked into Trent's eyes and saw the pain there, her decision was made. "Okay, Devon. We'll go in the morning."

He ran to her, and she held him tight while he cried.

Once Devon calmed down, Myrtle agreed to go with them, and so with a promise to be back to pick her up first thing the next morning, Trent, Lily, and Devon got into the car and were driven back to Jackson to find a hotel room for the night.

After saying good-bye to Harvey, they entered the hotel lobby. Seeing all the well-dressed people in tuxes and flowing gowns, Lily assumed there was a wedding reception somewhere in the building. "I'm starving," she said. "Are you hungry, Devon?"

He nodded.

Trent said, "Let's see what the restaurant looks like."

It was small and crowded with the noise and laughter of wedding revelers. The gaiety made Lily muse upon her own wedding and how festive it might be, and whether this situation with Devon would be resolved by then. She didn't want to begrudge the diners their good time, but after such a sobering visit she preferred to eat someplace quieter.

"Do you want to eat here, or would you rather eat upstairs in the room?" Trent asked.

"In the room."

Devon hadn't said a word since leaving Myrtle's, and looking at the emotionless mask he was hiding his feelings behind, she wondered what tomorrow might bring.

They ordered from the room service menu, and after the food arrived sat together in Lily's room.

Devon ate silently. Lily sensed he was thinking about the day, but she didn't push him to speak. Finally, halfway through his burger and fries, he asked, "How do you get brain damage?"

"The doctors aren't always sure, but sometimes it can come from an injury or bad medicine."

"Ms. Myrtle said my mom won't know who I am. Was she telling the truth?"

"I'm sure she was. I doubt she'd lie to us about something that serious. Do you still want to go and see her?"

He didn't hesitate. "Yes."

"Then that's what we'll do."

He finished his burger. "Can I go to my room now?"

"Yes. Your punishment's lifted for the weekend, so turn on the TV if you like." He'd be sleeping in the adjoining room. Trent was in a room across the hall.

"Okay. Thank you."

Trent and Lily watched him make his exit. They both wanted to save him from the pain he was sure to suffer tomorrow, but it wasn't in their hands. Life had to go forward.

CHAPTER
18

The following morning, Harvey drove them back to Ibo to pick up Ms. Myrtle, who came out to the car dressed like she was on her way to church. Her blue flower-print dress was topped off with a big blue hat, and a matching blue pocket-book hung from her wrist. In her hand were a pair of round-toed, short-heeled pumps, and on her feet the red house slippers she'd had on yesterday. Once she was settled into the seat next to the solemn Devon and carefully removed her hat, she greeted them, and Harvey drove them away.

It was a two-hour drive to the facility Rosalie now called home, and it was a beautiful place; from the well-kept grounds with their flowers and shrubs, to the stone statues of children playing, to the beautiful fountains, the complex gave off an air of wealth and calm. Wide walkways made of snow-white concrete crisscrossed the grounds, and patients in wheel-chairs were being pushed slowly along by staff members in green scrubs.

Lily said, "Looks like a very nice place."

"Used to be a mansion. State took it over when the owner went broke. Most of the patients here come from families with money."

Lily sent a discreet glance Devon's way and saw him staring silently at all he could see, and she wondered what he was thinking. She saw that Trent was watching Devon, too.

Inside, they followed Myrtle to the reception desk. They were met with a smile by a nice young man who looked like a grown-up Preston and were asked to sign in. As they did so, he gave them visitors passes that were meant to be stuck onto their clothing, and a warning: "Those passes have to be worn and visible at all times."

Lily was pleased by the security protocol and watched Devon stick the pass onto the front pocket of his suit coat. Once that was done, they were allowed to move on.

As they entered the elevator, Myrtle said to Devon, "Press four, please."

He did.

"She's on the top floor, and in the fanciest wing."

Trent asked, "Do you visit her often?"

"Not as much as I used to when Willa Mae was living, but I try to make it at least once a month. Hard to find somebody who'll drive me way up here."

The elevators opened onto an area holding another desk. The smiling woman sitting behind it checked their passes and then stood and gave Myrtle a hug.

Myrtle introduced the woman as Gladys, Rosalie's primary aide.

"How's she doing?" Myrtle asked as they walked down a quiet hall.

"She's fine. Rocking and humming as always."

Lily wondered if Rosalie had the entire floor to herself, because they didn't pass any other patients' rooms that she'd seen.

It was a sunny day, and Rosalie's room was filled with light. It looked like a child's room, with a banner of teddy bears on the wall below the ceiling. There was a huge four-poster bed topped by a white scalloped canopy, and around the room four white rocking chairs were all filled with bears and dolls and a ton of other stuffed toys. In a rocker, facing the sun-filled windows, sat a dark-skinned woman with long, snow-white hair. She had her back to them, but they could see her rocking in the chair and hear her soft humming. Lily looked around for Devon and found him standing beside Trent. His face was a mixture of curiosity and fear.

Gladys walked over to Rosalie and said gently, "Hey, Rosie. You have visitors. Myrtle's here, and she's brought some friends."

Myrtle walked over. "Hey there, Ms. Rosalie. How are you?"

For a moment the rocking and humming didn't stop, but after a few more coaxing words from Gladys, Rosalie looked up at Myrtle and held her eyes. Myrtle bent slowly and placed a kiss on her forehead. Only then did Rosalie glance around at the other visitors. For the first time Lily got a good look at her face. She appeared surprisingly young for a woman they'd been told was past forty, but more than that, to see Rosalie was to see Devon, because he favored his mother in every way. Same dark skin tone, same eyes, nose, and shape of the lips. Lily also noticed for the first time the little brown baby doll wrapped in a blue blanket Rosalie cradled in her arms. She tightened her lip at the implication of that.

Still rocking and humming, Rosalie studied Trent for a moment, but at the sight of Devon she stopped and went silent. Lily wasn't sure if it was her own imagination, but there seemed to be a distinct confusion in Rosalie's stare. It was almost as if she was trying to figure out if he was someone she knew, but a moment later she turned her gaze back to the window, and the rocking and humming recommenced.

Devon looked torn between hurt, confusion, and concern. It was as if he couldn't decide how he was supposed to feel, and Lily's heart went out to him.

He asked softly, "Can we go now?"

"Sure," Lily replied.

But to her surprise he didn't walk to the doorway. He instead walked over to his mother's side. He watched her for a long moment and then placed a kiss on her cheek. She didn't acknowledge him in any way. He had tears in his eyes as they left the room.

On the drive back to Ibo, Lily felt as if her heart had been sent through a shredder, but she was certain Devon felt worse. He was seated flush against Trent's side, and Trent had a fatherly arm around his shoulder. He hadn't spoken a word since getting in the car, and neither had Myrtle, but Lily could see her watching Devon with love and concern.

Lily said, "Thank you for telling us about Rosalie and taking us to visit her. Means a lot."

"You're welcome. We should stop by Willa Mae's grave before going to my place, and then you folks can fly back home."

Lily nodded. She saw Devon close his eyes for a moment as if the words brought pain. She looked over at Trent's eyes, and all she could think was how blessed she was to have him by her side. She knew she was strong enough to have handled this alone, but she was glad she hadn't had to.

The cemetery was nothing more than an overgrown field separated from the surroundings by a high, rusty wrought-iron fence. They entered the space solemnly.

Myrtle said, "Black folks have been using this cemetery since slavery."

As they followed the slow-moving Myrtle, Lily wondered about all the souls interred there. As at the Henry Adams cemetery, there were headstones so weathered and withered by time that the names they once held were gone.

Myrtle stopped and pointed to a mound of cleared earth. "I'm still trying to save up for a stone, but I get out at least once a week to keep the weeds away."

Trent was holding Devon's hand. "We'll take care of the stone. I'll give you a call when I get home, and we can make the arrangements."

"God bless you," she replied emotionally.

Devon walked over to the grave. After a moment of standing silently over it, he dropped to his knees and then spread his body out over the earth that separated him from his beloved grandmother. As he lay there in the thick silence with his arms outstretched, his sobbing was loud and heart-wrenching. Lily moved to go to his side, but Trent stopped her with a gentle hand and an even gentler voice. "Let him say good-bye."

He was right, of course, so through her tears, she watched

the little boy in the black suit lying on top of the mound of rich black dirt and listened to him weep.

Finally, after what seemed like a year of tears, he stood. He took off his tie and placed it tenderly atop the grave. When he turned to face them, he said in a hoarse voice, "I'm ready to go home now."

It was late when they arrived back in Henry Adams. Blessedly, Devon slept the entire flight. Lily knew he had to be exhausted, because she certainly was. Once at home, however, he went up to his room. Lily let him go, and she and Trent went to the kitchen. While Trent called Amari to let him know they were back, Lily looked around in the fridge for something quick to eat. She was still looking when Devon, now dressed in his pajamas, walked in.

Lily glanced his way and froze at what she saw. Neatly folded across his arm appeared to be every little black suit in his closet. Atop the pile of suits were five little clip-on ties. She straightened and closed the fridge door. In response to the quick questioning look she shot Trent, he shrugged in silent reply.

Devon asked, "Where should I put these? I won't be needing them anymore. Should I put them in the basement?"

"Um. Just leave them on the chair. I'll take care of them. You sure you won't need them? You might want to save a couple for church with Reverend Paula."

"I left two in my room."

Lily wanted to jump for joy at the metamorphosis, but knowing the painful road he'd had to travel in order to get to where he was now negated that. "I'll have Tamar take them to the Salvation Army next time she goes."

"Okay." He looked at the two of them and said, "I'm going to bed now."

Lily said, "Come give me a hug."

He walked over, and they hugged each other tightly. Lily whispered, "I love you, Devon."

"I love you, too."

When she finally turned him loose, he gave Trent a big hug as well. And when Trent finally turned him loose, Trent said, "I know how hard this weekend was for you, and I'm real proud of you, son. Real proud."

Devon nodded and said softly, "Night, Mom and Dad."

They wished him good night and watched him until he was out of sight.

After he left, Lily wiped at her eyes and said, "If I do any more crying, my eyeballs are going to turn into raisins."

"Mine are already there."

She walked over to him and wrapped her arms around him. They held each other silently. "You're a great dad."

"And you are a great mom."

"Think the fates can deal us some fun cards for a change? I'm tired of all these sad ones."

"So am I."

The fates heard them, but as the old saying goes: Be careful what you ask for.

Later, after Trent went home, a weary Lily doused all the lights and climbed the stairs. Her destination—bed, but she wanted to check on Devon first. He was asleep and snoring softly. The sight of his peaceful features filled her heart with love. He'd endured so much over the past two days, and she wondered just how much more sorrow a little boy could hold. His bringing down the suits had been a surprise. She took the offering as a signal that he'd finally made peace with his past and was ready to move on with his life, but she had no idea if that was the truth. Moving quietly to his side, she bent and placed a soft kiss on his cheek, then touched his head affectionately. After watching him for a few minutes more, she exited the room and left him to his dreams.

Lily, Trent, and the boys, along with everyone else in town, spent Sunday morning at Reverend Paula's first service. It was held in the kiva at the school, and they were all impressed with how serious and professional Zoey looked slowly walking down the center aisle wearing a long black robe with a short-waisted, long-sleeved white top over it as she carried the tall pole topped by a shiny gold cross. Behind her walked Reverend Paula in a voluminous green robe that was tastefully accented with a fancy gold cross appliqued on the front. She held a large red book reverently above her head as she solemnly followed in Zoey's wake.

Lily glanced down at Devon, who was watching all this with close interest. When the reverend and Zoey reached the foot of the stage, Zoey leaned the cross against it so that it would remain upright, and then Paula led the people in the auditorium in the prayers that were printed on the bulletins they'd all been handed by Zoey before the service began. Paula took a few minutes to explain how the service would be conducted and what part the congregation would play. After that, everything got under way. There were readings, done by Sheila; a sermon by the reverend that made them laugh and think; and then there was a part where they all were encouraged to get up and greet their neighbors. Paula called it the Peace. Lily thought that part was different and nice. After everyone took their seats again, Paula explained that church announcements usually followed the Peace, but since there weren't any, they went right into the offertory. Sheila and the colonel, both of whom were Episcopalians, passed the plates around and took them back to Paula, who blessed the plates by saying a short prayer. A short while later, it was time for communion, or the Eucharist as she called it, and anyone who'd been baptized could come up for the bread and wine that was meant to symbolize Christ's last supper. She'd explained earlier that communion was given every Sunday, not just on the first Sunday of the month as in some other denominations, and that they would be taking a sip of real wine from the silver chalice.

"Jesus changed water into wine. Not water into grape juice," she told them, and they knew it was okay to laugh after the humorous sermon she'd given. They were also shown what to do if they had an aversion to alcohol and didn't wish to sip from the chalice.

When the service was over, Zoey picked up the cross and silently led Reverend Paula in the recession. Lily looked over at Reg and Roni. Both were beaming.

All in all, everyone enjoyed the service. Mal in particular took a look at his watch and saw that they'd only been there an hour and fifteen minutes. "I like this," he declared. "I can go to church and be back home in plenty of time for the kickoff of the game."

Tamar smacked him lightly with her bulletin. "Behave yourself."

But many of the people in the line waiting to greet Paula heartily agreed with him.

When the time came for Trent, Lily, and the boys to shake Paula's hand, Devon looked at Zoey standing so proudly at the reverend's side and asked Paula, "Can I help with your church, too?"

Paula smiled. "You most certainly can. Usually there are three acolytes. One to carry in the cross and two to carry the candles. What about you, Amari? I could use a few more people."

He shook his head. "I don't look good in a dress."

Zoey snapped, "This isn't a dress, knucklehead. It's called a cotta and a cassock."

"Looks like a dress to me."

Paula said, "I talked to Preston, and he's game."

Amari looked around until he found Preston standing a few feet away, talking to Leah and her father. He called out, "Hey, Brain? You really going to wear one of these dresses?"

"It's not a dress, Amari. Good grief."

Amari still didn't appear convinced, but told the reverend. "Let me think about it, okay?"

"Will do."

Zoey said, "Come on, Devon, I have to hang up my robe."

Devon looked to Lily for permission, and she granted it gladly. "Go ahead. We'll wait until you get back."

Once they were gone, Paula said, "I have to greet the rest of the folks in line, but tell me quickly how the Mississippi trip went."

Lily said, "Rough. Are you coming to the Dog after this?"

"I'd planned to."

Trent said, "Then meet us there. We'll treat you to lunch and fill you in while we eat. Nice service, by the way."

"Thanks."

After lunch, Trent and Amari settled in for the second NFL game of the day. They'd seen the first game at the Dog on the new big-screen TVs that had been installed at the beginning of the season, but now they were home, and Trent was glad. Emotionally he was still drained from the Mississippi trip, and all he wanted to do for the rest of the day was veg out on the couch, watch some football with his son, and not have to think about anything other than maybe ordering a pizza later. So when his phone buzzed and he didn't recognize the number, he let it go to voice mail.

Only later, after crawling into bed, did he listen to the message. Hearing the voice of his cousin Griffin put a smile on his face. Unlike the eldest Julys, Griffin and Trent had always got along well, but Trent hadn't spoken to him in over a year. The call was to RSVP for the wedding and to let him know that Amari's father had been identified.

"I wanted to talk to you about it," Griffin said in the message, "but since you're not picking up, we'll have to do it when I see you for the wedding. I'm on my bike heading to Montana to see family. Be there about a month. There's no cell service, so you won't be able to hit me back. Tell Aunt Tamar I'll try and keep the family in line when we come for the wedding, but no guarantees," he added, laughing. "Oh, I'll contact the drummers. You get your team together so we can kick your tails. Later, man."

Trent fell back against the bed pillows and wished he'd taken the call. "Damn!" He reached over and turned off the lamp. Lying in the dark, he knew his mind wanted to analyze the call and speculate about Amari's parentage, but his weary body wanted sleep; his body won.

When he awakened the next morning, the call was all he could think about, so he got out of bed and made some calls of his own.

"Drummers?" Lily asked in a confused tone.

Trent had everyone connected with the wedding assembled in his office: Lily, Tamar, Mal, Bernadine, Sheila, and Reverend Paula.

"It's tradition," Tamar explained, even though she seemed deep in thought, as if mentally weighing what she'd heard from Trent. "How many did he say were coming?"

"He didn't."

"Singers coming, too?" Mal asked.

"I suppose, since singers and drummers go together."

"So what does all this mean, Trent?"

His answer to Lily was, "That we're going to have a lot more people at this wedding than we planned, and a lot more activity tied to the old ways."

"Can't you politely tell the drummers no thank you, we pass?"

"No, Griff's half Lakota. The drummers and singers are probably members of his family. We can't reach him by phone, so it'll be real bad manners to have them drive all the way from South Dakota and then tell them they're not needed."

Tamar said, "I used to have his mother's number, but that was so many years ago, I doubt it's current now even if I could find the old address book it was in."

"So will you still need me?" Paula asked.

"Yes," Trent replied, "but looks like we'll be adding some Native elements to the ceremony."

"Just let me know what to do and how you want to play it."

Sheila said, "I've never done anything like this before, but I'm looking forward to learning."

"Me, too," Bernadine echoed.

Trent took a moment to explain about the dancing and singing and that a ball game is usually played on the afternoon of the day before the wedding. "I'm guessing it will be football."

"What else would it be?" Bernadine asked.

"Lacrosse," Mal replied.

Trent shook his head. "We're not playing lacrosse. It's either football or nothing. Last time those Lakotas brought their sticks to town, they kicked our butts so bad, half of the Henry Adams team came back from the ER in casts."

"Goodness," Lily breathed.

Mal said sagely, "The Natives don't call lacrosse 'Little Brother of War' for nothing."

Conversation turned back to the wedding.

Tamar said to Sheila, "Tell Rocky she needs to have more meat on hand, and to add fry bread to the menu."

As Tamar and the ladies continued to plan, Mal threw in a few suggestions. Trent glanced Lily's way to see how she was taking the news that the simple wedding they'd both wanted would now be much more. "What do you think, Lil?"

She shrugged. "This is as much your wedding as it is mine, Trenton. I think the old-ways touch will be nice. Not sure how it'll turn out, but as long as we're man and wife when it's all said and done, I'm in."

"That's my girl," Mal said approvingly.

Trent nodded his approval as well. He hadn't talked about the other reason for Griffin's call but would do so now. Everyone in the room was family, and they all loved Amari as much as he did and needed to know. Although Reverend Paula was new in town, she was fitting in like a long-lost relative, and he was certain she'd come to love his son, too. "Griff's other reason for calling was to let us know that he'd found out the name of Amari's father." The room went still. "He didn't want to give me a name on the phone, but said we'd talk about it when he comes for the wedding."

Lily asked, "Are you going to tell Amari?"

"Think I'll wait until after Griff and I talk." Trent looked to Paula. "Sound good to you, Reverend?"

"Don't start doubting your parenting decisions simply because I'm here and have a bunch of letters behind my name. You've been doing an amazing job raising your kids. Go with your gut."

Tamar said, "Please don't let Amari turn out to be one of my brother's cubs."

"I think Uncle Thad's past the age of fathering kids, Tamar," Mal pointed out. "Although Amari was a car thief, and Uncle Thad's folks are the branch of the Julys that steals cars. It's in their blood."

"There is no car-stealing gene, Mal."

"That's not what you said when they stole Olivia."

"Stole Olivia?" Lily echoed.

Trent told the story and when he finished, a concerned-looking Lily asked, "We're having a family of car thieves at our wedding?"

Mal answered, "They're not so much car thieves as they are coyotes."

"What's that mean?" Bernadine asked.

"Tricksters," Paula replied with a knowing smile. "Right, Malachi?"

"Exactly. Forgot you were from Oklahoma, Reverend."

"Heard lots of Coyote tales growing up."

Mal explained the animal's role in Native mythology. "Coyote can take any form—male, female, another animal. Plays tricks good and bad. Sometimes brings gifts like corn, or meat."

"Or steals your truck," Tamar groused.

Mal chuckled. "But whatever Coyote's up to, he's always got an agenda."

"There are even stories from the Plains tribes that have Coyote in the night sky putting up the moon and the stars," Trent told them, trying not to laugh at Tamar's grumpy face.

"And let's not forget all those fair young maidens he impregnated," Mal tossed out slyly.

"When you all kept referring to coyotes, I thought you meant the real animal," Bernadine said.

"Same here," Lily echoed.

"Nope. These are the Julys time left behind," Trent voiced with amusement. "The outlaw blood still runs true in some of them."

Sheila appeared worried. "Are they dangerous?"

"Yes," Tamar declared flatly.

Mal rolled his eyes. "No, they're not. They just like to have fun."

"They're not going to screw up my wedding with this so-called fun, are they?" Lily wanted to know as she looked between the Julys.

"Don't worry," Tamar replied reassuringly. "If they get out of hand, a shotgun always gets their attention."

Trent wondered if Tamar was going to have to be tied up and tossed in a closet when Uncle Thad's clan arrived, but knowing such an action would also involve a shotgun, he turned his attention to Lily. "Weren't you the one who wanted the fates to bring on the fun?"

"I'm also the one who wanted us to elope. That option is still open."

The room filled with laughter, and they returned to the wedding plans.

When it was decided they'd done all they could for the moment, the meeting broke up. After the others departed, Lily lingered in Trent's office. "Do you have any idea who the father might be?"

"I'm guessing I do, but I'll find out for sure when I get with Griff."

"How do you think Amari will react when you tell him?"

"Don't know. We'll have to wait on that, too."

But Trent had been wondering about Amari's reaction, too. Whatever the reaction might be, Trent was certain he and Amari would be able to talk it through. There was something else he was wondering about. "Are you sure you don't mind the change in plans?"

She walked over and eased herself against his heart. "Positive. The first time I got married, it was done at the courthouse. We were in one minute and out the next. This one's going to mean more, so the service should, too." She leaned back and looked up. "Okay?"

He nodded. "Have I told you how honored I am to share your life?"

She gave him the smile that always melted his insides. "I'm honored to share yours, too."

They stood in the silence for a moment, holding on to each other while savoring the past, the present, and the future. Finally she asked, "So what other kinds of things are going to be happening with this very interesting wedding?"

"Have I mentioned the celibacy part?"

She snorted. "No."

"For the week leading up to the big event, I can't have any, shall we say, contact."

"What about me?"

He gave her a look.

"What if Bernadine brings in a hot young hunk of a stripper to my bridal tea? I can't throw him down on the table and have my way with him?"

When he didn't respond, she added, "I'm serious."

"I got your stripper, girl."

And for the next few moments the kiss he gifted her with rocked her world so long and hard, she forgot what the word *stripper* meant.

When he finally and lazily broke the contact, she said breathlessly, "You're way too good at this, Trenton."

"It's the July blood."

"Modest, too."

His eyes glittered. "Now that that's settled, you should probably get back to your office."

"Probably," she whispered softly, as if she wasn't sure she could make it that far.

"Go on before you wind up on a table."

She grinned and gave him a saucy, flirty look. "I like the sound of that."

"Out."

"You're such a tease."

He pointed to the door.

She leaned up and gave him a soft parting kiss. "See you later."

Trent watched her departure, proud to be the only man in Henry Adams to know how fabulous the Fabulous Fontaine really was.

CHAPTER
19

I n the weeks leading up to the end of October, the trees and grasses put on their yearly display and the countryside was painted with the vivid reds, golds, and oranges of autumn. In spite of the beauty, the weather continued its slow headlong march toward winter, still over a month and a half away. The daytime temperatures hovered in the mid-fifties, but on more and more nights the thermometers dropped to the low forties. The first snowfall could come any day.

Over at the Dog, Rocky's assistant chef, Matt Burke aka Sizzle, Siz for short, finally convinced Mal to let the jazz band he managed play on Friday and Saturday nights. The group made up of young twentysomethings went by the unlikely name of Kansas Bloody Kansas. They treated the audience to a mix of old and new, and were unbelievably good. Only the locals and a few friends of the band members attended the maiden performance, but Roni was so impressed by their talent that at the end of the first set, she gave them a few pointers on how they might tweak their onstage presence for an even better sound, and wowed the band members by promising to sit in when she finished up her CD.

The second weekend they played, word had gotten around, and the Dog was packed with people of all races, ages, and genders. Getting access to good jazz was difficult on the plains of Kansas, and lovers of the genre were ecstatic.

"The only complaint," Mal told the assemblage at the monthly town meeting, "no liquor. But I told the complainers to either drink the sodas we offered or find someplace else to go. A couple left in a huff, but the rest made do."

As the mayor, it was Trent's job to preside over the meeting, and he asked, "So are you booking them every weekend?"

"For as long as I can. The way they play, they won't be local for long, though."

Trent agreed. Siz's band was outstanding, and destined for larger and more lucrative venues than Henry Adams's Dog and Cow.

Siz raised his hand. His hair was the color of spinach this week. "I just want to say thanks."

Mal replied, "No. Thank you. And when the band goes big-time, we know we'll be losing you, so start looking for a replacement."

Siz grinned. "Yes, sir."

Trent saw Bing Shepard raise his hand. "What's up, Bing?"

"Got a letter from a gas company asking permission to lay a pipeline across my property. Want to know if anybody else got a letter."

This was the first Trent had heard of this, but he saw a few of the farmers in attendance raise their hands.

One man stated plainly, "Not selling them squat. My land's not for sale."

"Price they quoted me sounded fair," another farmer countered. "Especially when I was told the work wouldn't disturb my cows, and that the company would need only a few acres on the back of my plot. Told Leo I'd think about it."

"Leo Brown?" Bernadine asked.

"Yep. He's the front man on this."

From the coolness in Bernadine's eyes, Trent guessed this was her first time hearing about the offers, too.

The farmer who didn't plan to sell added, "Brown bragged that if I didn't sell now, his company would push for eminent domain in the courts, and once the judge ruled in their favor they'd put the pipeline on my land for free. You can imagine what I told him after he said that."

Bing asked Bernadine, "Can the court make us give him our land for free?"

"Sounds like a scare tactic, but let me ask my legal people about it and I'll get back to you as soon as I can. Promise."

Lily had been suspicious of Leo's motives, and she wondered if this might be the proof. The discussion brought to mind the prophetic last words of Ms. Agnes warning Marie to keep Leo away from her land. She wondered if Marie knew what Leo and his employer were up to. "When did you get the letter, Mr. Shepard?"

"This morning. Certified mail."

The others had received theirs over the past two weeks.

"Sounds like he's being selective about who he's targeting," Trent said. "I'll make some calls in the morning to see just how many people have gotten the letters, and we can go from there."

Bing seemed satisfied with that, as did everyone else, so the meeting moved on to the next item on the agenda.

On the ride home with Trent, Lily wondered aloud, "Do you think Leo came to town just to buy up land and used reconciliation with Bernadine as an excuse?"

"Maybe. I don't want to pass judgment without all the facts, but this doesn't smell right."

"When I get to the office in the morning, I'll look into his company and see what turns up."

"I'm sure Bernadine will have her people doing the same. Be nice if for a few months we could turn back the clock and become the sleepy boring little town we used to be."

"Then we'd all whine about what a boring sleepy little town it is. We did that a lot in high school, remember?"

"I do. I think I like this twenty-first-century version better, though."

"Why?"

"Got you back in my life."

"Aww." She hooked her arm through his and leaned her head tenderly against his shoulder. "You say the nicest things, Trenton July."

"Doing what I can to compete against hot young hunky strippers."

She laughed, and they basked in their feelings for each other for the rest of the ride home.

*   *   *

After dropping Lily off with a kiss and a wave good-bye, Trent pulled up into his garage and parked. In the bed of the truck were two boxes he'd retrieved from Tamar's barn.

Amari was watching television when he came in.

"Homework done?"

"Yep. What's in the boxes?"

"Some of my old stuff from high school. I'm looking for something I need."

Trent sat and opened the first box. Inside he found papers, yearbooks. He tossed one to Amari, who opened it and slowly turned the pages. "This is you!"

Trent leaned over and grinned. "I was pretty skinny back then."

"Is this Mr. Clark?"

"Yep." It was a group photo of the basketball team. They were lined up with their arms around each other and looked incredibly young. Trent played forward. Gary was guard. "That's Stevie Mills, Tommy Burton, and Bruce 'Big Head' Rice. We called him Big for short."

"They still live around here?"

"No. They all moved away. Haven't heard from them in years."

"Is Mom in here?"

"Should be."

They flipped a few more pages, and there stood the seventeen-year-old Lily Fontaine, surrounded by her many trophies.

"She was really beautiful, even then."

"What happened to her being hot?"

"She's my mom now. You don't call your mom hot."

"Oh, good to know," Trent answered with a straight face.

Trent left Amari to the yearbook while he returned to searching the box. He pulled out the ancient-looking pair of black track cleats he'd worn the year he won the state four hundred meters.

"Those look old," Amari remarked when Trent laid them on the floor.

Trent told him the story behind the shoes.

"You played football, too, right?"

"Along with basketball, baseball, and I ran track. I was a four-letter man." Trent opened an old shoe box held closed by a large rubberband and looked inside. VCR tapes.

"Those look old, too."

Trent read the labels. "Wow. Forgot all about these. Tamar had a video camera back in the day, and these are the tapes. We have track meets. My prom! High school graduation."

Amari grinned at Trent's reaction. "Do you think they still play?"

"Who knows? You'd probably need one of those real old machines, though."

Trent set the tapes aside and opened the second box. From beneath a plastic bag holding his orange-and-black basketball uniform he pulled out something wrapped in a roll of white cotton. "This is what I've been looking for." He unwrapped it to reveal the black flute inside. He placed it against his lips and blew, but no sound came out.

"You play the flute!"

"Used to." Trent scanned the instrument in an effort to determine why it wouldn't play and found the answer in the dried, cracked trill pads and the keys that were stuck closed.

He swallowed his disappointment. "There's a music store over in Franklin. I'll run over there tomorrow and see if they can fix it so it'll play the way it's supposed to."

Having the flute in his hands again made memories surface. "I took playing pretty seriously until I got heavy into sports, then I put it down because I didn't think it went with my four-letter athlete image."

"Why were you looking for it?"

"Need it for the wedding."

"You're going to play it for the ceremony?"

"Nope. I'm going to play it for Lily. It's part of the courtship tradition, and it's going to be a surprise, so you can't tell her. Back in the day, braves romanced their ladies by playing the flute."

"What?"

Trent gave Amari a short lesson in Native courtship traditions, finishing with, "In some tribes every male knew how to play. It was expected."

"Geez."

Trent laughed. "What's wrong?"

"Playing a flute for some girl? Not going to happen."

"You'll be surprised what you'll do when the time comes."

"You keep telling me stuff like that."

"Because it's the truth. Don't want you to be surprised."

"Thanks, but I'll be too busy racing cars to care about flutes or girls."

"I should make you write that down and sign it."

"I'm game."

His fearless acceptance of the challenge made Trent love him all the more. "Go grab a sheet of paper."

Amari hopped up and came back with a piece of lined paper and a pen. While Trent looked on, Amari wrote down his quote about cars and girls.

"Now sign your name at the bottom and add today's date."

Once it was done, Trent had him place the paper on the fridge with a magnet. He figured in a year or so, Amari would be snatching it down. For the moment, though, he'd let his son think he knew what he was talking about. Trent took a lot of pleasure in raising Amari and in finding his flute. After the trip to the music store, he'd start practicing.

The next day, Trent drove over to Franklin and left the flute with the clerk at the music store. She told him it would take a few days to restore it, and that they'd give him a call when it was ready to be picked up. On the way back to his truck, he passed the building where Leo was leasing office space and decided to pay him a call.

The receptionist greeted him with a smile. "Mr. Brown is on a conference call. He'll be done in a few minutes. Do you want to wait?"

"Sure."

Ten minutes later, Leo came out. Upon seeing Trent, he smiled and shook his hand. "What brings you here?"

"Your pipeline."

Leo paused and scanned Trent silently, then gestured him toward the inner office. "Come on in and let's talk."

Trent took a seat. The space was sparsely furnished and lacked the personal touches one might expect in an executive's office. There were no pictures of loved ones on his desk or any framed documents of achievements on the walls, which made Trent wonder how long Leo planned to stick around.

"So what would you like to know?"

"As much as you can tell me."

Leo pushed back in his chair. "My company wants to run a pipeline from the Canadian border to the Gulf Coast. It's almost complete, but a part of the line has to be in this area, so we're making very generous offers to some of the locals."

"I'm told you've threatened people who've turned you down."

"Threatened? I don't remember threatening anyone."

"You didn't say 'eminent domain'?"

Leo didn't respond at first as if maybe trying to determine how much Trent really knew. "I believe I did mention that, but we'd only go that route as a last resort."

"Some of the families in this area have been on their land for a century or more. They don't take kindly to being told you may take it whether they want you to or not."

"This pipeline is in the national interest, and we think the courts will agree. And it isn't as if the thing will be disruptive. We'll pay the owners market value. The strips of land we need will only be one hundred and two feet wide. We'll pay compensation for crop loss and any soil damage. The circumference of the pipe is only thirty-six inches, and it'll be buried five feet below the surface, so if they want to plant or graze their herds on top, no problem."

"What about ruptures and spills?"

He studied Trent again. "We don't anticipate any such problems."

"Neither did BP, but we all saw how that turned out."

"That was an extreme case."

"Which can be duplicated anywhere, am I right?"

Leo didn't reply.

"So what will the pipe be carrying, and how much?"

"Bitumen oil sand. About four hundred thousand barrels a day, and a capacity for double that once we get a few pumping stations built."

"That's some nasty gooey stuff."

Leo appeared surprised. "You know about it?"

"Worked in the Oklahoma oil fields when I was young, as have a lot of other folks around here. Makes us more knowledgeable about the industry than you might think." He could tell Leo was assessing that information, too. Trent decided he'd learned enough for the moment and that he'd put Leo on notice that acquiring the land for the pipeline was not going to be a cakewalk. "How's the build going on your new place?"

"Almost done. Marie and I should be moving in around Christmas."

"That's great news. She talking about selling her land?"

"I'm talking to her about it. She hasn't said yes, but hasn't said no, either."

Trent had no idea if Marie would be moving, but believed that Ms. Agnes would haunt Marie for the rest of her life if she sold even an inch of the Jefferson ancestral land, let alone the entire parcel. Trent stood. "Thanks for your time. I need to get back. Good talking to you."

They shook hands.

"Same here," Leo said. "If you run into anybody with any questions about the pipeline, have them stop by or give me a call."

"Will do."

Trent left the office and walked back to his truck. The conversation had put him on notice as well; Leo Brown and his pipeline would have to be watched closely.

Before heading to the office he spent some time riding around the countryside, talking to landowners and farmers to see how many of them had received Leo's letter. That a few had already signed on the dotted line didn't surprise him. Times were hard. Some farmers were desperately in need of cash to pay off debts for seed and equipment, and to prepare for planting in the spring. If they had to lease a swath of their land to the devil himself in order to keep title to their land, they would.

There were others who wouldn't sign, like Mike Freewater, one of Bing's neighbors.

"I worked forty-five years building track for the railroad, and bought this acreage with my sweat, my hands, and my back. I'll be damned if I sell any of it to a bunch of suits who never got their hands dirty. Told Leo if his people even look like they're coming on my land, I'll fill them so full of holes he'll be able to use them to strain spaghetti."

Trent laughed so hard he almost fell off Mike's porch. "Then I guess I can put you in the no column."

"You can put me in the *hell no* column."

Trent drove away still laughing.

*   *   *

At the Power Plant Trent found Lily and Bernadine in Bernadine's office. "Morning, ladies. Just got back from talking to folks about the pipeline. Talked with Leo, too." He filled them in on what he'd learned.

When he was done, Bernadine asked, "Did you ask him about the threats he made?"

"The ones he denied at first, yes. I'm pretty sure the locals are going to wind up fighting him in court. He thinks he's got it all figured out. Said the pipeline was needed for national security." He turned to Lily. "Also told me that Marie's going to be moving into that monstrosity he's building. He's says he's trying to convince her to sell."

"What? She hasn't said anything to me."

"Maybe Leo is just wishing," Bernadine replied.

"Either way, I think he's trying to get a foothold here, and what better way to put folks at ease than to buy the land of one of the town's oldest families?"

"If you're right, that stinks," Lily declared.

"To high heaven, but it's Marie's decision. Any luck on the search you were going to do on his company?"

"Not much. The company is a shell within a shell within a shell, so after an hour of looking and not finding the parent, I quit. Bernadine's people are going to take over now, but what I did find wasn't pretty. The subsidiary Leo's representing tried eminent domain in Illinois back in 'ninety-seven and lost in court. They have a spotty safety record, too. Two years ago, a fire along a pipeline in Wisconsin killed two welders, and three years ago in Minnesota, one of their lines ruptured and caused a hundred-thousand-gallon spill. According to an EPA report, the water table is still contaminated."

"Great."

"My legal people advise that we wait and see what Leo's company does. If they file for eminent domain, then the opposing landowners can cross-file as interveners with whoever the state's licensing body will be."

"Do you want me to put the word out on that?" he asked her.

"Please, and let Bing know, just in case we're not the only county being targeted. If he can spread the word across the state about what's going on through his ties to the Black Farmers Association, more people will know what Leo's up to when he comes knocking. I promised myself I'd ignore Leo when he started hitting on Marie, but on this, I'll fight him with everything I have. The last thing we need is a bunch of oil spills and fires just so he can turn more profit."

Trent agreed.

"In the meantime, we'll wait and see what my people turn up."

Lily said, "Sounds like a plan."

With that, they all went back to their offices and tried not to worry about what the future and Leo Brown might hold for them, their neighbors, and their town.

CHAPTER
20

At the conclusion of the workday, the town's managing triumvirate left their offices and worries behind and drove over to the field behind Tamar's place to watch the football team practice. The hastily put-together team would be defending their home turf against the Oklahoma July team during the traditional prewedding game. Bing Shepard, the high school football coach back in Trent's day, was on the field with his clipboard and whistle. For a man in his early eighties he was moving pretty good, but the team was a motley crew.

This was Lily and Bernadine's first look at practice, and as they walked over to the part of the field that had been designated as the sidelines, they joined a large group of onlookers. Lily was surprised to see Leah out on the field, too.

"They let Leah play."

Tamar said, "Bing knows they can't win, so he and Trent decided to just have fun with it and open up the team to anyone who wanted to play."

Leah came running off the field to grab a few sips of water. Lily couldn't remember seeing her sweatier or happier.

"Leah, I didn't know you liked football."

"Almost as much as physics. It's a really beautiful game if you know how to watch, and I've always wanted to play on a team. Daddy and I throw the ball around all the time."

"I'm impressed."

"Dad said you used to be a great athlete. You should join us. We could really use you. Eli can't catch a ball to save his life."

Bing was yelling, "Where's my receiver!"

Leah called back, "Right here, Mr. Shepard!"

"Excuse me," she said politely to Lily and the others before running quickly back onto the field.

Lily scanned the team members. Trent was quarterback, of course, and Gary was lined up as the running back. Barrett and Reg were blocking, and on the wings were Leah and Eli. Holding down the other wing were Preston and Siz, whose navy blue hair matched his hoodie and sweats.

She searched the area for Devon and found him sitting on the ground, watching Crystal, Zoey, and Tiffany Adele rehearse cheerleader routines. Seeing Devon made her smile, as it always did, but her smiles these days poured from her heart even more. The timid little boy who'd been afraid to change his life was making slow but steady progress. The suits had been replaced with regular kids' clothes like jeans, tees, and sweatshirts. He seemed to take pleasure in picking out what he would be wearing each day. Some of the clothes she'd purchased when he first came to town no longer fit, but they'd gone shopping after school earlier in the week, so now everything he had in his dresser and closet was the right size.

As she continued to watch the Henry Adams cheerleaders, an argument broke out among the girls. Zoey slapped her hand on her hip in a move reminiscent of her mama, Roni, or maybe her mother, Bonnie, and said something to Tiffany that made Crystal double over with laughter. Zoey stormed off with Devon on her heels. The howling Crystal took one last look at Tiffany's plainly angry face and, still laughing, left her standing alone.

Lily said to Bernadine, "I'll be back."

She had no idea what had transpired, but seeing the mad Zoey, the laughing Crystal, and Devon all talking to Roni, she made her way through the crowd and joined them.

She walked up just in time to hear Roni say to her daughter, "Zoey, that was not a nice thing to say. Don't say anything like that to her again. You hear me?"

Zoey looked mutinous. "But, Mama Roni—"

"No discussion. Now go with Crys and Devon and get something to drink and cool off. I want to talk to Lily."

The still smiling Crystal led them away. Roni's attention was focused on Reg for a moment as he blocked an imaginary opponent while Trent dropped back to throw the ball downfield to Eli, who promptly dropped it. "Reg hasn't played football since college. If he goes down during the game, who's going to patch up everybody else?"

"No idea. Is the CD finished?"

"Hallelujah, yes. I'm home until after the new year, I hope."

"What happened with Tiffany?"

Roni rolled her eyes. "She didn't want to do any of the cheer routines Crystal worked up."

"Why not?" Lily could see Tiff sitting alone, looking mad.

"She said they were ghetto girl cheers."

"Excuse me?"

"Uh-huh."

"And Zoey told her?"

Roni chuckled and said, "That the reason she didn't want to do them was because Tiff couldn't dance. Zoey said she knew pigeons in Miami that had more rhythm than Tiffany."

Lily immediately clamped her hand over her mouth to keep from laughing aloud. "No, she didn't."

"What am I going to do with this child of mine? I thought Crys was going to have a heart attack, she laughed so hard."

Lily's smile peeked out. "I suppose you heard what Zoey told Trent and Marie about painting the fence?"

"That tradition needed to get a clue? Yep, Reg told me. Now that Zoey's talking, raising her is turning out to be even more than a notion."

"She's a tough little girl."

"And I wouldn't want her any other way, but being with her makes me remember to take my blood pressure meds every morning."

Eli dropped another ball, and Roni cracked, "Would somebody please go out and drag that boy off the field? He can't catch a cold."

"You like football?"

"Love it. Big Jets fan."

Lily liked football, too, and yes, their team was bad. She watched Bing yell at Amari for running the wrong pattern.

"Cut to the left, boy! No, not that way! Your other left!"

"Reg must be glad to have you home again."

Roni shrugged.

Lily saw that Roni wouldn't meet her eyes for some reason, and as her friend, Lily found that a cause for concern. She asked gently, "You okay?"

"Not really. This is the first CD I've done since he and I have been together. He had no idea of the time involved. My being away from home for so long got real old for him, real quick. We're trying to rekindle the magic, but he's been flat-out mad at me for the last month or so. Not sure how to deal with it."

"But you two love each other so much."

"True, but music is my lover, too. He's having issues with that."

"I'm so sorry."

She shrugged again. "We'll figure it out. Maybe being able to record here at home next time won't be so hard on him."

"If you need anything, let me know. I'm here for you, girl."

"I know."

Leah ran downfield, cut left, glanced back over her shoulder, and caught a long spiraling pass from Trent that made her look like Jerry Rice catching one from Joe Montana. The sidelines erupted. She was doing a funky victory dance in the end zone when Trent ran down and gave her a hug that lifted her off her feet while the other team members mobbed her with congratulations.

Roni drawled, "We really ought to see if we can play the Oklahoma folks with just Trent and Leah. If the rest of our team goes anywhere near the field, we're going to get creamed."

On that note, practice ended for the day, and a smiling Lily went to find Devon so she could drive them home.

The first day of November dawned with two inches of beautiful white snow. That evening Trent came out of the basement after finishing his flute practice.

Amari was working on homework at the kitchen table. "Sounding much better, Dad."

"Is that why you've stopped wearing headphones when I practice?"

"You were making my ears burn."

"Thank you," Trent offered with affectionate sarcasm and walked to the table to see what Amari was working on. He was drawing the United States. Trent also noticed their small egg timer sitting in the center of the table. "What are you doing?"

"We're having a geography contest at school. The person who can draw a map of the United States the fastest doesn't have to take the test on Friday."

"What's your best time so far?"

"I finally got it to under three minutes, but I know Leah and Preston can do it in under a minute and a half because they were bragging about it at lunch."

"That's a great way to learn the states, and it'll be something you'll know how to do for the rest of your life. Win you a lot of bets at the bar when you're old enough to go. And girls like great parlor tricks."

Amari rolled his eyes.

Trent laughed. "Just teasing."

Not looking up from his drawing, Amari asked, "When do you start playing the flute for Mom?"

"Ten nights before the wedding, and I do it every night until the night before we get married."

"I still think it's dumb."

"That's okay, love is dumb."

"I guess."

"I'm going to turn on the TV. You finish practicing. Almost time for bed. And good luck on getting your time down. Keep me posted on how you do."

"I will. Oh, by the way," he said nonchalantly, "I beat Preston in chess today."

Trent had been on his way out of the kitchen, but hearing that caused him to stop and turn back. "You did?"

Amari beamed. "Took his pawns, his rooks, his queen. Took everything from him but the pencils in his backpack."

"Congratulations. I didn't know you two were playing."

"We've been playing at lunch and after school. He taught me how so that he could get in enough practice to beat the colonel."

"But you beat him today?"

"Like he stole something. Leah was a big help. She gave me a book a few weeks back that was real easy to understand because it showed pictures of the moves and the strategies I needed to get better. She said her dad gave it to her when he taught her to play."

"How'd Preston take being beat?"

"Not sure. He gave me a high five just like I do when he

beats me, but he was real quiet for the rest of the day. He hasn't called or texted me tonight, either. Do you think he's mad?"

"I don't know. Shoot him a text and see."

"Maybe I'll wait until I see him at school tomorrow. I never got mad when he was beating me all the time."

"Could be he's not used to losing at chess."

"That's not it. Leah whips him all the time."

Trent thought maybe Preston was having issues with being beaten by Amari. For as long as they'd been friends, Preston had been Brain, and Amari had been—well, just Amari, but Trent didn't say any of that aloud. "I'm sure you guys will work it out. Real proud of you, though. Maybe you can teach me to play."

"Whenever you're ready. I'm good now."

"That's great," Trent said, and left him to his drawing.

The depositions that were due to take place later in the week in the case of *Curry v. Curry* didn't. Rumor had it that Eustasia had left Kansas with Chocolate and gone back to her spread in Texas with her fancy, high-priced lawyers in tow. Nobody knew why, or when she'd made her exit, or even if it was the truth. All they knew for sure was that everyone on the list had been called and told not to show up because the charges against Genevieve had been dropped.

The only person who might have had the answer was Genevieve, but she and Marie celebrated the news by hopping a plane to Vegas early the next morning. According to Cliff Dobbs, the two best friends were going to be gone five days.

In the interim, Lily found a suit she loved at one of the

high-end stores at the mall. It was made of ice blue silk and perfect for the wedding. She also found some killer shoes. As an afterthought she purchased a pair of dressy boots, too, just in case it snowed on the big day.

Genevieve and Marie arrived home right on schedule, so Lily drove over the next day after work. Once they'd caught her up on their Vegas trip, she asked the question everyone in town had been buzzing about.

"She left town because she finally got the truth about what happened to my home, and she got to see the real Riley," Genevieve said frankly.

"How'd she find out about the house?"

"Gen told her on the day she came over for a visit," Marie replied.

"Eustasia came over for a visit?"

"It was the morning after Riley and I got into the argument at the movies," Genevieve said. "I asked him point-blank, had he told her the truth? He said he had. I knew he was lying, so I challenged her to come over and see the pictures the coroner and the police had taken of the house on the night Prell died, and she took me up on it. When she saw them, she was appalled. She said Riley had explained to her all about Prell but hadn't told her he was married. She didn't know I even existed until the extradition hearing down in Louisiana."

Marie added, "She also said Riley had gotten real bossy since coming back to town. Ordering her around, being snippy for no reason. Fussing about the shows she watched on TV. Wanting her to fetch this and that. I guess she'd had enough and left."

"You think she's gone for good?"

Gen shrugged. "All I know is that she is gone. Not sure whether Riley's still living in the trailer or not, and I don't care."

Lily turned to Marie. "I've been meaning to ask if you'll need any help packing."

"Packing? Why am I packing?"

"Leo told Trent you were moving in with him as soon as his house is finished."

"He wants me to, but I'm not."

Marie had on her poker face, making it impossible for Lily to know what was really going on or how the relationship between them might be faring. "You heard about the letters his company is sending around."

"I have. I tried to tell him that only a few people would take the money, but he's kind of a know-it-all."

"Maybe he should ask Riley to move in with him, then," Genevieve cracked. "They'd probably get along great."

Even Marie had to laugh.

"You and Leo okay?"

Marie shrugged. "Not sure, but if it ends tomorrow, I can say I've been to Paris and Bermuda. New York City. Not bad for a sixtysomething country girl. He's been in Pittsburgh for the past week or so at company headquarters. He wasn't sure when he'd be back."

Lily's lips thinned. Once again it was difficult to tell how Marie was really feeling, but she decided not to ask anything else.

On the evening that Trent picked to start his flute courting, it snowed. Hard. Coat on, he stood in the doorway watching the white stuff come down in blinding blowing sheets.

"You aren't really going to go over there, are you?" Amari asked from behind him.

"No. She'd never hear me over the wind, and I'd probably freeze to death." He closed the door.

"Why don't you just play for her in her kitchen? Does it have to be outside?"

"Supposedly." Suddenly, Zoey's assessment of the fence-painting tradition came to mind. This tradition needed to get a clue, too. It was November. He doubted any brave would be out playing the flute in such terrible weather.

He pulled out his phone and called Lily to let her know he was coming over for a few minutes.

On his way out the door, he heard Amari yell, "Good luck!"

When he entered, she gave him a kiss and took his coat. He stepped out of his hikers and left them on the mat by the door. Wearing his socks, he followed her into the kitchen. "Where's Devon?"

"Upstairs, taking his shower. What brings you over besides wanting to see a good-looking woman?"

"This," and he took the flute out of its case and played a few notes.

"Why don't I know that you play the flute?"

He played a few more soft trills. "I'd quit by the time you moved to town."

"You came over to give me a concert?"

"No, to court you."

"Court me?" she asked.

He could see the confusion in her face. "Yes, darlin'. Court you. It's part of the wedding tradition."

She had her hand over her mouth now, and he thought she might be starting to cry. For once he didn't mind her tears, because these weren't from pain or sadness. "Have a seat."

When she complied, he began.

Lily had no idea he could play so beautifully. From the first note, she was enthralled. The skill, the tone, the intense look in his eyes as his fingers moved skillfully over the keys, left her breathless.

"I'm going to play for you just like this on our wedding night," he promised, and Lily went weak in her chair. He set his lips against the instrument again, and she wondered how many women could claim to have been seduced at their kitchen table by a man playing a flute. She was glad Devon was upstairs.

Trent continued playing long enough for her to wish he'd go on forever. He played songs that were familiar love songs from the likes of Stevie, Luther, and Teddy, interspersed with classical choices that he must have learned in school, but it was the free-form improvised tunes that she felt the most. They rose and fell, soared, flirted, and teased. And when he was done, the notes slowed and faded into the silence.

The air in the room was electric.

"Next time you play for me, we need to be in the house alone."

Eyes shining, he said, "After the wedding you got it. Right

now, I'm on the celibate diet, remember, but I'll come and play for you every evening until the night before the wedding."

"Thank you for the great music."

"Anytime."

Neither wanted to move. The music had touched them both.

He stood. "I need to get going so Amari can head to bed."

She walked him to the door and waited for him to put on his boots and coat before opening the door. "See you in the morning."

He gave her a kiss and held her close. "Living in separate houses is about to kill me."

"Me, too."

He placed a solemn kiss on her head and stepped out into the snow.

Lily leaned back against the closed door and sighed with contentment.

CHAPTER
21

Thanksgiving was a little over a week away, and the town geared up for the double treat of a holiday and a wedding. Trucks arrived at the Dog filled with the meat and other items Rocky had ordered for the meals. The kiva was being readied for the ceremony. Bing and Cliff used tractors to clear the snow from the field where the football game would be played and then covered it with tarps so it wouldn't have to be cleared again if it snowed.

The kids were on break and spent most of their free time helping out wherever the adults needed them. Trent continued to serenade his fair maiden every evening, and Lily tried not to make herself crazy wondering whether her son would show up for the wedding or not.

The answer came the next day. He called to let her know he was in town and coming in the door of the Power Plant. Ecstatic, she stuck her head in Trent's office. "Davis is here!"

She ran off to meet him, leaving Trent to follow or not.

Lily's mood changed as she saw the tall, well-dressed

woman walking beside her son, but Davis's familiar smile reignited her happiness. He gave her a big hug. "Hey, Mom."

She squeezed him tight. "Oh, baby. I'm so glad to see you."

When she finally let him go, she extended her hand to the woman with him. "Hi, I'm Lily Fontaine. Welcome to Henry Adams."

"Jessica Harris. Pleased to meet you as well."

By Lily's estimation, Ms. Harris was a good ten years older than Davis and had on a suit that gave off the air of an executive. Lily wondered what she did for a living but held on to the question when Trent and Bernadine joined them. Lily did the introductions.

Davis shook Trent's hand firmly. "Pleased to see you again, Mr. July."

"Same here, but please call me Trent."

"Thanks."

Once the formalities were over, Jessica intoned, "I'm starving. Is there a restaurant here somewhere, preferably Italian?"

Lily saw Bernadine raise an eyebrow.

"No Italian," Lily told her. "Just a small-town diner, sorry."

"Why am I not surprised?"

Davis's tightly set jaw told Lily a lot. The coolness in his gaze on Jessica told her even more.

Trent asked, "How about I drive? Lunch's on me."

"I have some work I want to finish," Bernadine replied, giving Jessica another once-over. "I'll see you all later."

Lily went back to her office to grab her coat and muttered to herself, "This is going to be a long visit."

Or maybe even longer, she decided after the ride to the

Dog, which Jessica spent complaining about the flight and the woman who'd been sitting beside her. She complained about the weather and how cold the day was, and that she hated snow. Then they even had to listen to her gripe about getting mud on her expensive brown boots during the walk across the parking lot.

Trent held the door open so Davis and Jessica could enter first. When Lily moved past him, they shared a speaking look before he followed them inside.

Crystal was their waitress, and she stood patiently waiting to take orders while Jessica studied the menu with a disdainful eye. "I've never been in a restaurant that didn't serve chicken cordon bleu."

"Welcome to Henry Adams," Crystal replied, rolling her eyes. While she waited for Jessica to decide, Crys went ahead and took everyone else's orders. She turned her attention back to Jessica. "Are you ready?"

Jessica sighed with what sounded like resignation and ordered a burger and fries. Crys thanked her and departed.

The silence in the booth was awkward. Lily wanted to know more about this woman, but was afraid to ask anything for fear of what she might start complaining about.

Davis must have sensed her thoughts. "Jessica is in real estate, Mom. In fact, she was the person who sold me my condo."

"So that's how you two met. I was wondering."

"And since he knew nothing about decorating, I handled that as well."

"I see." Lily wondered if she was making sure he cleaned his plate, too, but kept that to herself.

Trent asked Davis, "You play any ball? There's going to be a football game before the wedding, and we could use a good player."

"I'm more of a track man, but I played a little wide receiver at Rutgers."

While they talked, Lily used the moment to study Jessica more closely. She wasn't bad looking. Lily checked out the gold hoops in her ears and the bracelets and rings. Everything looked expensive. From the way she'd been acting, it was obvious she was accustomed to being in charge, which made Lily wonder again why Davis was letting this woman be in charge of him. And what in the world was Jessica doing with someone so young?

Reverend Paula walked into the Dog. Lily waved her over and invited her to sit with them. Jessica was rude, condescending, and turning out to be a real pain in the butt. Lily hoped having Paula's Christian presence at the table would help Jessica be more charitable.

Crystal returned with their orders and set everyone's food down. After handing out straws for the soft drinks, she turned to leave.

"Excuse me, young lady."

Crystal sighed and directed her attention at Jessica. "Yes, ma'am."

To Lily's displeasure, Jessica sent her food back to the kitchen three times; the burger wasn't cooked properly, the fries were too greasy, the bun didn't taste fresh. As it went on and on, and poor Crystal was run to death trying to satisfy the demands, even Paula shot Jessica a few testy glances. Lily looked over at Trent, who pretended to be concentrating on his food, but she could tell he wasn't happy with the woman's self-important act, either. Davis's jaws were so tight, Lily wondered how he was even managing to eat.

The Dog was packed with the lunch crowd. The waitstaff was hustling. The jukebox was jumping to Fontella Bass singing "Rescue Me," a title Lily found highly ironic, when the music went dead. Everybody looked up to see what the problem might be, and there stood Tamar in the middle of the room. She didn't appear pleased.

In the midst of the silence, Mal came out of the back. "Why'd you turn off the box?"

"Listen."

"To what?"

"Listen!"

Mal cocked his head as if using his ears to search the air; then, as if finally hearing whatever it was she was referencing, he immediately went still. Lily could see that Trent had stopped eating and appeared to be listening as well, and then he smiled knowingly.

"What is it?" Lily asked.

"Drums. Can you hear them? You might not be able to, because it sounds like they're still miles away."

Lily listened hard but didn't hear a thing. Paula, either.

"Listen for the rhythms," he told them.

Davis's face lit up. "I hear it."

Suddenly, Lily did, too. She had to listen hard, but there it was again, like the faint boom of thunder from a far-off storm, the cadence too even for it be a natural occurrence.

Soon everyone in the diner had picked up on the sound, and a buzz began. Lily noticed that some of the older locals like Bing and his friends hastily paid their bills and departed.

Mal called out, "Trent, take those flags and pictures off the wall over by you."

The colorful flags encased in glass frames had been designed by Crystal for the August First parade. The pictures were of various subjects. One in particular was of the old Dog and Cow, with its hole-filled roof and duct-taped booths. Lily wondered why Mal wanted them taken down.

"So they won't be broken," Trent explained, handing them down to her and the others in their booth.

"By what?" Paula asked.

"The Oklahoma Julys. Those drums you hear are theirs. They'll be here shortly."

Lily and Paula shared a surprised look. Under Mal's orders the waitstaff collected all empty glasses from the diners and took them into the kitchen. Tables were moved to open up the center of the room. Tamar had taken a seat at the booth vacated earlier by Bing and sat as unmoving as the Sphinx.

Meanwhile, the sounds of the drums seemed closer. Lily could hear what sounded like voices accompanying the unceasing but ominous-sounding beat, though they were still some distance away.

Jessica said, "Davis, I insist you get me out of here."

He ignored her for the moment as he asked Trent, "How many do you think there are?"

"Uncle Thad had nine kids, so anywhere from a dozen to thirty—who knows?"

"It sounds like hundreds," Paula said, and Lily agreed.

"During the wars, that's what it sounded like to the enemy. They'd hear the thunder getting louder and louder and closer and closer and be scared big-time, not knowing how many braves they'd be facing. The Julys come in this way because it's tradition and fun for them."

"It's sorta like waiting for Godzilla," Davis said, smiling while looking out the window like an eager kid hoping to catch sight of Santa.

Trent laughed. "Pretty much, but they're mostly harmless."

Lily noted the word *mostly*. Apparently Jessica had, too, because she'd tensed like she wanted to get up and run.

Ten minutes later the drums were so close, Lily swore the walls of the Dog were vibrating in sync with the noise. Suddenly they were inside, entering en masse and filling the air with their drumming and chanting as they slowly danced their way around the room, bent at the waist and doing a stomp step that shook the tables. This was her first look at Trent's relatives, and they were a sight to see. Most were wearing shirts and jeans, but some were shirtless and wore traditional vests that appeared to be made of embellished leather. Some were carrying long clublike sticks decorated with paint, bells, and feathers, which they beat against the tabletops in time with the drums. There seemed to be waves of them, so many in fact that the center of the room was filled with chanting, dancing men. The sound was deafening. It was the wildest and craziest thing Lily had ever witnessed. Davis was grinning, but Jessica had shrunk back against the booth as if the sight of the men snaking their way in a line to the beat of the drums was terrifying.

Mal was yelling for them to stop bashing his tables, but they ignored him and kept up the beat. The singers were in full voice, chanting in a foreign-sounding language while Mal continued to yell. Crystal was caught in the aisle near their booth. Lily saw her being smiled at by some of the younger members dancing by. One July with the face of a brown-skinned god and a body encased in worn black leather grabbed her around the waist, dipped her, and asked with a grin, "You old enough to be kissed?"

Crystal's eyes popped, and she grinned. "Yeah."

Trent grabbed him by his leather collar. "Don't make me shoot you, Diego. Back off."

Diego smiled sheepishly. "Sorry, cousin, but she's gorgeous."

Trent let him go. Diego gave the wide-eyed Crystal a wink before dancing away to rejoin his relatives.

Mal was still yelling.

Tamar apparently had had enough. Raising a shotgun that made Lily's eyes go wide, she aimed it above her head and fired. The loud blast took out one of the lights and a portion of the ceiling. Then all the electricity died.

She'd been right about shotguns getting their attention. One moment there'd been pandemonium, but now you could hear a pin drop.

In the silence, Mal looked up at the damage and whined, "Dammit, Tamar!"

"I'll pay for the damage." She stared balefully around at the momentarily cowed but smiling members of her brother's clan. "Where's Thad?"

"Right behind you, Tammy."

He was in a wheelchair pushed by one of the most gorgeous men Lily had ever had the good fortune to see. He, too, was all in leather, and the black hair flowing down his back rippled like a stream.

Paula asked in an awed voice, "Who is that behind his chair?"

"My cousin Griffin, and thank God he's here."

"Why?"

"He's the only one who may be able to keep these knuckleheads in line." What Trent didn't say aloud was that Griffin might possibly be Amari's biological father, too. It was the only reason he could come up with to account for the presence of the Lakota men sprinkled in with the crowd of Julys. Their only connection to Trent's family was through Griffin. His mother, Judith, was Lakota, but his late father, Neil, had been Uncle Thad's youngest son. Were the Lakota there to help Griffin welcome Amari into the clan?

Trent's thoughts were broken by Davis saying, "The knuckleheads certainly know how to make an entrance."

"I agree," Lily said, watching them. Many of them were talking to the now-smiling Mal. Others raised hands of greeting to Trent before taking seats at some of the unoccupied tables and conversing with the patrons nearby.

Jessica seemed to have pulled herself together enough to snap, "Davis, get me out of here! I've never been so terrified in my life. Bunch of heathens should be arrested."

Apparently Davis was as through with her as Tamar had been moments before. "How about I take you back to the airport, and you just fly home?"

Lily wanted to cheer, even as she pretended not to be listening.

"If I go, that'll be the end of us, Davis."

"Then by all means, let me call you a cab. It'll take you back to where we parked the rental car, and you can cut me out of your life right now."

Without a word, Trent handed him his phone. The number of the local taxi company was highlighted.

"Thanks, Trent." Davis made the call.

"I'll wait outside." Jessica grabbed her coat and purse and pushed her way past the Julys to the door.

Lily gave her son a high five.

Paula said, "I love this town!"

Now that some semblance of calm had been restored, the electricians in the crowd went with Mal to see what could be done about getting the electricity back up, while Trent told Lily and the others, "Come on. I want you all to meet my great-uncle."

Up close, Thad looked very much like Tamar. He had the same lean build and the familiar hawk-black eyes. He was dressed like a gentleman rancher in a blue long-sleeved shirt and matching pants. Around his neck was a silver bolo tie, and on his knees sat an ivory-colored Stetson.

Trent made the introductions.

Thad looked Lily up and down. "You sure you want to marry him? July men have a hard time holding on to their wives. I know. Had and lost three. How many times you been married, Trent?"

"Twice, but the third time will be the charm."

"That's what I thought with my third one, until she caught me and her sister one night. Man can run pretty fast with buckshot going off around him."

Trent and Griffin both shook their heads.

A perturbed Tamar asked, "Why would you tell her that?"

Lily could see his eyes sparkling with mischief.

"Because it's the truth."

"Since when have you ever told the truth?"

"Oh, here we go."

"Don't oh-here-we-go me, Thaddeus July."

"Tammy, if you want to fight, let's save it for later when I'm not so tired. You got my room ready?"

"What room? You're not staying with me."

"The hell I'm not."

Trent attempted to be peacemaker. "Uncle Thad, you can stay with me."

"Nope. Came all this way to stay with my sister. You get Griffin. She gets me."

Tamar looked mutinous but gave in. "Griffin, bring your grandfather and follow me in whatever it is you're driving. He does not get to ride in Olivia."

"Like I want to ride in that old relic. Damn truck's old as she is." Thad ignored the anger on her face and said politely, "Ms. Lily, Davis, Reverend Paula, nice meeting you all."

Griffin nodded farewell and turned the chair to follow the already departed Tamar out the door.

"Sounds like maybe he should stay with you, Trent," an amused Lily noted as they all walked back to their booth.

"What concerns me is that they're both armed."

For the next little while, Trent held Lily's hand as he introduced her to his cousins and the members of Griffin's family whom he was familiar with. The Julys had numerous Neils, Madisons, Harpers, and a couple of Edwards, but only one Diego.

Later, as he drove Lily and Davis home, she asked, "Why all the same names?"

"Uncle Thad named them after the original family members."

"Why only one Diego?"

"Because the world can only hold one at a time. He's been arrested more times than Amari."

"For what?"

"Car theft."

"Lord. He isn't Amari's father, is he?"

"Hope not, but I should know more on that tonight after I've had a chance to talk to Griffin."

He drove up into her driveway and left the motor running while they got out.

"I had a good time, Trenton."

"Glad my family didn't scare you off."

"No chance. You are signed, sealed, and delivered." Leaning in the window, she gave him a kiss. "Love you."

"Love you, too."

Davis whined, "Come on, you two. The California boy is cold!"

Lily let her freezing son into the house, and Trenton drove home to wait for Griffin.

Inside, Lily called over to the Garlands and was surprised to hear that Amari had come and gotten Devon so he could hang with him and Preston.

She hung up. "Looks like Amari's playing big brother. Can I ask you a question?"

"Sure," Davis said.

"Why you and Jessica? We won't even talk about her age, but she didn't seem to be your type."

Davis sighed. "At first I was trying to be nice. I was new in town, I liked jazz, she took me to a few clubs. I told her I liked plays, and she got tickets. Next thing I knew she was planning my weekends. I didn't want to hurt her feelings, and she was fun, sorta, but there was a lot of what you saw today, too."

"Women don't like pity, Davis."

"I didn't know what to do."

"You handled it today, though."

"I couldn't take it anymore."

She walked over and gave him a hug. "So good to see you."

"And with no Jessica around, I can enjoy myself."

"Hear, hear. Come walk with me over to the Paynes'. Devon is going to flip, meeting you in person."

Trent didn't get a chance to talk with Griffin until much later that evening. They were in Trent's kitchen, catching up over a beer.

"My guess is that you're the father. Right or wrong?"

Griffin saluted him with his glass. "You always were smart. How'd you figure it out?"

"I didn't until I saw the Lakotas with my cousins. Figured Amari had to be the reason they were along."

Griffin then told him the story behind their son Amari's conception and about Griff's meeting with the mother.

"Sounds like she had to make some hard choices after she found out she was pregnant."

"I just wish she'd called me, written, something. I never would have let him be taken into the welfare system, you know that."

"I do."

"I feel like I failed him."

"He's back where he belongs now, so don't beat yourself up."

"I can't believe he was a car thief."

"That shouldn't be a surprise. Wants to race NASCAR when he grows up."

"I like that. Have you talked to him about any of this?"

"Only that the family was looking into his parentage. I wanted to wait until I learned who it turned out to be before saying anything." Trent searched Griffin's face for a moment. "So what do you want to do about his raising? He's legally adopted, and I will fight you in court if you're planning on contesting my rights."

"Please. Where would I raise him, on the back of my bike? No, he's your son. All I ask is that my mom be able to call him grandson, and that he come to Pine Ridge and stay with her for a week or two during summers. I am her only son, you know."

"I have no problem with that. In fact, I think it's a great idea. Is she coming for the wedding?"

"Yes. She wants to meet Amari and your Lily—who is gorgeous, by the way."

"Thanks—just keep your distance. She's mine."

"Be glad you met her first."

"I am."

"Can I meet Amari?"

"Sure. He's across the street, hanging with his friend Preston. Let me send him a text."

When Amari walked in, he said excitedly, "Dad! Mom said the other Julys tried to trash the Dog, and Tamar shot up the ceiling."

He noticed Griffin for the first time. "Sorry. Didn't know you had company." Amari studied the man closely, especially his leather jacket, pants, and long hair. "I'm Amari."

"Griffin July. Great to meet you, Amari."

"Same here. You with the Oklahoma clan?"

"I am."

"You hair looks like that Samoan dude's that plays defense for Pittsburgh."

"He's an awesome player, isn't he. I'm Seminole and Lakota, though."

Amari turned to Trent. "Did you need me for something, Dad?"

"Yeah, just for a minute. Pull up a seat."

Amari was pretty intuitive, and as he sat down, Trent could see him trying to determine if something was wrong.

"This isn't bad news, is it?"

"No, son. Just wanted you to meet your biological father."

"This is him?" He studied Griffin for a longer moment. "I'm not going to have to leave and go live with him, am I, Dad?"

Griffin answered first. "No, Amari. I'd never separate you from your dad."

Amari sighed audibly with relief. "Good, because I'd only wind up running away a thousand times. Do you ever see my birth mom?"

"Saw her a month or so ago, which is when I found out that she and I made you. I'm sorry about not knowing before."

"That's okay. Does she know I live in Kansas?"

"No."

"She want to be contacted?"

Griffin shook his head solemnly. "I'm afraid not."

Amari shrugged. "Doesn't matter. I have a real mom now."

But Trent could tell that deep down inside it did matter.

"And that real mom is very pretty, too," Griffin added.

"Yep," he replied proudly.

"Your mom and mine are probably the prettiest ones I know. My mom would like to meet you. I'm her only child, which makes you her only grandchild."

"That okay, Dad?"

"Yes. You'll like Judith."

Amari asked where she lived, and when he learned she lived on the Pine Ridge res and wanted him to spend some of the summer with her, he replied, "I might like that, but is it okay if I meet her first before I decide? Not trying to offend her or anything."

"Absolutely. You just let me know," Griff replied.

"You said you were Lakota? That's the Sioux Nation, right?"

"Yes. I'm impressed that you know that."

"Blame it on our teacher Mr. James. He makes us learn a lot about Native culture."

"That makes him a great teacher in my book. Maybe you can introduce me to him while I'm here."

The conversation moved on to many subjects after that: Amari's dream of being a racer, his newfound finesse at chess, and his Spirit Quest.

Griffin said, "I did my Quest twice. Once as a Seminole

with my grandfather, and then the next year as a Lakota with my uncles."

Amari told him about catching a fat trout with his hands, and how a hawk had swooped down and stolen it from him.

"You have to watch those hawks," Griff added.

Then came sports, favorite foods, and movies. They even walked out to the garage and spent a few minutes looking over Griffin's vintage Harley, which impressed Amari the most.

"This is awesome. How fast will it go?"

Griffin told him what the top-end speed was, and Amari's mouth dropped. "Man. The cops would've never caught me on this. Can you give me a ride before you leave?"

"Will do, if it's okay with your dad."

"As long as he wears a helmet."

Back inside, Trent happened to glance up at the clock on the kitchen wall and saw that it was almost 11:00 p.m. They'd been talking for hours.

Amari yawned and asked Griffin, "Where are you staying while you're here?"

"Your dad wants to put me upstairs in the guest room, but I wanted to make sure it was okay with you first."

"It is."

"Then I'll grab my stuff off the bike and head up. It's been a long day. I'll see you two in the morning."

When Amari and Trent were alone, Amari said, "It's pretty sweet meeting him. I like him."

"I'm glad. He's a good person."

"But just so you'll know, he may be my father, but you're my dad."

"That means a lot."

"Don't want you getting it twisted."

"I won't." Trent was glad the meeting had gone well. "You go on to bed. See you in the morning."

After Amari went up to his room, Trent sat in the silent kitchen and thanked God and the Ancestors for all the blessings in his life. Finally getting up from his chair, he put on the locks, turned out the lights, and climbed the stairs to his own bed.

CHAPTER
22

On the Saturday before the wedding Lily drove over to Tamar's for the bridal tea. All of the women in her circle of friends were in attendance, including Zoey and Crystal. They ate the tasty little appetizers Rocky had brought, drank tea and sodas, and ate cake. For Lily, the highlight, besides all the support and love she received, was the bestowing of what Sheila called Borrowed, Blue, Old, and New.

The Something Old was a blue-and-white carved cameo that Tamar explained had originally belonged to Mayor Olivia July. "I had it restored back in the eighties, hoping you'd wear it back when we all thought you'd marry Trent the first time, but when it didn't happen, I put it away. Guess it's been patiently waiting for you all these years."

"I'll wear it proudly. Thank you."

The Something New came from Bernadine. "You know how much I love to multitask, so what I have is something that fits the Something Blue category as well as the Something New." She handed Lily a slim black velvet box. Inside lay the most beautiful gold and sapphire bracelet Lily had ever seen. The exquisite detail and craftsmanship rendered her speechless.

"And if you start fussing at me about it being too expensive for you to accept, I swear I'll never speak to you again."

Lily couldn't take her eyes off the beautiful bracelet. "This is gorgeous." The spendthrift side of Lily did want to fuss—the bracelet had probably cost more than her car—but she accepted it in the spirit in which it had been given. "Thank you, Bernadine."

Roni presented the Borrowed gift. "You and Trent are going to need love songs while on your honeymoon, so here's a copy of my new CD. I borrowed it from the studio when Sheila told me what my category for the tea would be. You don't really have to return it, but it was all I could think to get. Sorry."

"Sorry? Are you kidding? Trent and I were big fans of your music before we even met you, and for us to have this before anyone else? Makes me feel real special. Thanks, Roni." Lily couldn't wait to stick it in the CD player.

Crystal and Zoey stepped up. "Zoey and I didn't know what to get, so Ms. Bernadine suggested we get you something that might help you relax and work off the stress. Like maybe she doesn't need something like that her own self."

The ladies howled. Bernadine, too.

"So I thought about what helps me relax, so we got you this."

Lily undid the beautiful hand-painted purple paper and found a large art set inside. There were watercolors and oils, brushes and inks. She was touched by their thoughtfulness. "I've never had anything like this before, girls. Who knows if I can paint, but I will give it a try. Thank you."

Zoey asked, "You don't think it's dumb, do you?"

"No, Zo. It's real cool."

Paula stepped up. "I'm new here, and because I didn't know anything about this party until yesterday"—she looked over at Sheila, who smiled and dropped her head as if guilty as charged—"so I guess my gift will have to be something I know how to do well, which is pray. Grab hands, everybody."

The women circled up, and Paula said reverently, "Dear Lord. Creator or all things male and female. Bless this assemblage of women. Help them continue to support and lift each other up in this great sisterhood they have created. Offer them Your guidance and keep them in Your heart as we keep You in ours. We ask this in Jesus' name. Amen."

"Thank you, Reverend Paula."

"Anytime."

Marie stepped out of the circle. "I know we already did the Something Old, but I have something to add." She took a sealed envelope out of her purse and handed it to Lily.

The envelope appeared to be very old. "What is this?"

"A letter from your mother. She wrote it before she passed and asked that I give it to you on your wedding day."

Lily found it difficult to breathe. "My mom?"

"Yes. Funny, though, I couldn't find it the first time you got married, so I never mentioned having it, but about a week after you and Trent announced your engagement, there it was in a box I knew I searched through a dozen times before. It was as if the letter wanted to be found when it did."

Lily's heart was pounding so hard, she thought it might burst through her blouse. Her name, Lily Renee, was written across the front in the familiar scrolled handwriting she knew all too well. Her hand shook. Tears filled her eyes. She gave Marie an emotional hug. "Thank you," she whispered. "Thank you so much." She'd never expected to receive something so precious. The urge to tear it open and read it there and then was strong, but she held off because she wanted to read it alone. After taking one last teary glance at it, she gently placed the envelope in her purse and took in a few deep breaths to pull herself back together. It was difficult. All she could think about was what it might say and how much she still missed her mother.

"Cass was a very special lady," Marie voiced.

"Yes, she was."

Every person in the room viewed Lily with fond eyes. They all knew how much the letter meant.

Later, they were helping themselves to the buffet again when Tamar asked Rocky, "Are the Oklahoma clan running you ragged?"

"Lord, I can't wait until they're gone. They are some meat-eating men, my goodness. We ran out of bacon yesterday, and they took poor Siz outside and tied him to a tree as punishment. Had him roped up like one of those old movie heroines tied down on the railroad tracks. It was all in fun, of course, but I had to use a butcher knife to cut him loose because they refused to untie him."

Tamar asked, "Where was Griffin? He's supposed to be the ringmaster of this circus."

Rocky shrugged. "Not sure, but Mr. July was there. He just laughed."

"He would," Tamar pronounced sourly.

"Tamar, why are you two so mad at each other?" Genevieve asked.

"Secrets, right, Tamar?" Marie tossed out.

Tamar studied Marie. The air between the two had been strained since Agnes's deathbed confession, and Lily wondered where this conversation might be heading.

Roni took one look at the two women and said, "Crys, do me a favor. Take Zoey outside so she can get some air."

Zoey looked confused. "I don't need any air."

Crystal took her by the hand. "Come on. I think some grown folks stuff is about to jump off, and they don't want us to hear."

"What?"

Once they were gone, Tamar and Marie continued to eye each other coolly. "You're still mad at me."

"Yes, because you of all people should know how wrong it is to keep secrets."

"Agnes told you?" Tamar sounded surprised.

"Yes, but I don't know why you're surprised. You were more a friend to her than she was to you."

It was difficult to glean Tamar's true reaction, but she looked caught between anger and disappointment.

Marie asked pointedly, "How can you be mad at Thad for not telling you Mal's father was already married when he married you, but think it was okay to keep the truth about my mother from me?"

That bombshell made the other women in the room share stunned looks.

"Tamar, you're my godmother, for heaven's sake!" she declared heatedly.

Tamar looked away from Marie and off into the distance. She sat silently for what seemed a long time. When she finally turned back, there was a bleakness in her eyes none of them had ever seen before. "Forgive me."

Marie had tears in her eyes. "I do, because you thought you were doing the right thing, but it still hurts."

Tamar's eyes were wet as well. "Been a long time since anyone's called me out."

"I know." Marie took the tissue Genevieve offered and showed a watery smile as she blew her nose. "But every now and then somebody has to risk decapitation to set you straight."

That broke the tension. Lily was glad. The rest of the women appeared to be relieved as well.

"When I married Joel Newton, he and Thad were best friends. Thad had to know he was already married, so why didn't he tell me?"

"Have you asked him?"

"Yes. He said he didn't know how to tell me."

"Just like you probably didn't know how to tell me."

Tamar's lips thinned.

Marie hunkered down before Tamar's chair and said with sincerity, "You are the wisest, most caring person I know, and you've been more of a mother to me than Agnes ever was. I don't want you to go to your grave with this anger on your soul. Talk to your brother."

Tamar didn't respond at first, then said grudgingly, "I'll think about it."

After tucking Devon in for the night, Lily slid the letter from the envelope and read: *My dearest Lily. When you read this, I'll be gone, but I wanted to send my love to you on this momentous day. My baby girl is getting married, and I'm in tears just thinking about how beautiful you will be. May the Good Lord bless you with a child that fills your life with the same amount of joy that you gave to mine. Stay strong, my Lily. I may not be able to love you in the flesh, but I'll never stop loving you in spirit. Your mother. Cassandra Fontaine.*

For the next hour Lily was a mess as she cried over the loss of such a remarkable woman and over the joy of receiving such a precious gift. She reminisced over the good times they'd had and how fearlessly Cass had approached chemo and the final walk to her demise. Lily missed her so much, and rereading the letter brought home again just how much. "Thank you, Mama," she whispered.

Finally, after pulling herself together, she called Trent to ask if he'd come over.

"What's up?" he asked as he entered. "You sounded like you'd been crying."

She handed him the letter. "Read this."

"You have been crying. Your eyes are all red."

"Just read, please."

He searched her face as if checking for more signs of distress, then lowered his eyes to the letter. When he finished reading, he asked in a voice filled with wonder, "Where'd you get this?"

"Come on in the kitchen."

Once they were both seated at the table, she told him the story. He read the short but moving note again. "This is very special."

"I know. I've been bawling like a baby since I got home."

He handed it back. "Always wanted something like that from my mother. Gave up on that eventually, though. No idea if she's living or dead."

Guilt washed over her. "I didn't mean for this to open old wounds. I'm sorry."

He waved her off. "It was just a comment, that's all."

She wasn't sure whether to believe him or not. His mother had been a teen when she got pregnant by Malachi, then she and her parents moved away. A few months after the birth, her mother had showed up at Tamar's with the infant Trent in her arms, handed him to Tamar, and driven away. As far as Lily knew, there'd been no further contact between the two families. "Maybe she's waiting for you to contact her."

"Maybe."

Because he said nothing else, she sensed the subject was closed, so she didn't push him for more.

"So how was the tea?" he asked.

"Interesting. You probably already know, but I had no idea why Tamar is so mad at her brother."

He cocked his head. "She told you?"

"No, Marie did." And she related what happened.

"Mal's father was a bigamist?"

"You didn't know?"

"No. I kinda figured there was more to their feuding than what Thad did to Olivia, but I never imagined it would be something like that. She must have been furious when she found out."

"Heartbroken, too."

"More than likely. The one time I asked Dad about it, he shrugged, said his father found somebody else, and left it at that. I just assumed Tamar had gotten a divorce. I wonder if he knows the truth."

The only way to get the question answered would be to

ask Mal, but because Lily knew it wasn't her place, she left it for Trent to handle as he saw fit. "So how was your day?"

"Would've been a lot calmer if Griff and I hadn't spent most of it running back and forth paying fines and bailing knuckleheads out of jail."

"What?"

"Well, let's see. We had to bail two cousins out of jail over in Franklin for drag racing through the middle of town last night. Then this morning a different knucklehead bet his knucklehead brother that he wouldn't hop out of the car and run over and kiss a woman they saw walking down the street."

"Oh, my goodness."

"Gets better. He did it, of course. Grabbed her just as she was going into the mayor's office, dipped her back, and kissed her good. He said later that she grinned, but at the time, her husband—the mayor—didn't."

"They kissed the mayor's wife while he was with her?" Lily couldn't help it; she laughed. "Oh, no."

"Oh, yes. The mayor's so mad, he takes a swing at the knucklehead, misses, falls down, and breaks his arm."

Wide-eyed, Lily put her hand over her mouth.

"Ambulance is called. Sheriff Dalton was called."

"Did they go to jail?"

"Nope. The wife refused to press charges. The mayor is on the stretcher, yelling and screaming at her. He was still yelling when the medical people closed the doors and drove him away."

"Oh, my goodness."

"She told me it was the best kiss she'd gotten in all the years she'd been married."

Lily hung her head.

"All Oklahoma Julys are now barred from even looking at the city of Franklin, let alone entering. Dalton says any of them set foot in town again, he's going to throw them in jail for being a public nuisance."

"Lord."

"No kidding." But he was smiling.

"Your people are a mess, Trenton July."

"And it doesn't take them more than a day or so to prove it. There's a week between now and the wedding, and all I see ahead is mayhem."

"At least no cars have been stolen."

"That we know of. There's a jack and a bunch of my tools missing from the garage. I know they'll be returned eventually, but only the Ancestors know what they'll be used for in the interim."

"Olivia okay?"

"Far as I know. Tamar's probably sleeping in the front seat with her shotgun." He paused for a minute. "I keep thinking about the story you told me about her marriage."

"That's something, isn't it? I always wondered why her last name was still July."

"I figured she went back to it after the divorce. You don't have any secrets you're keeping from me, do you?"

"Not that I can think of. How about you?"

"Nope."

"Good. The last thing we need around here is more intrigue."

"You got that right."

She spent the next few minutes showing him the wonderful gifts she'd been given at the tea.

"These are nice. Bracelet's gorgeous. Tamar said this belonged to the original Olivia?" He studied the cameo.

"Yes, and that she had it restored back in the eighties because she wanted me to wear it at what she hoped would be our wedding back then."

"This time is better."

"I think so, too."

He handed everything back. "I need to get home. Griffin and Amari spent the evening together with his Lakota family. They should be back soon."

"The two of them doing okay?"

"Yes, they are. Griff's a good man."

"I'm glad it was him."

"So am I. His mom, Judith, is coming to the wedding, also."

She walked him to the door. He gave her a kiss. "See you tomorrow."

"Love you."

"Love you more."

And after his departure, she was left alone with her love for him, her gifts, and the memories of her mother, Cassandra.

Later, when Davis came home from hanging with the younger Julys, Lily showed him the letter, and her waterworks started all over again.

"Wow, Mom."

"I know."

"You think she would've liked Trent?"

"I do. How about you, do you like him?"

"He's pretty awesome. I saw the car he and Amari are working on. You'd told me that you and he went together during high school, but you never said why you two broke up."

"Did you ask Trent?"

"I did, but he said to ask you."

Lily sighed. "Let's just say I treated him like crap. It wasn't my best moment."

"You broke his heart?"

"More like I trashed it big-time."

"Really?"

"Yes, but that's all I have to say. No sense in letting you know I have feet of clay."

"Already do."

She laughed.

"Trent's a good man. Glad you found someone who makes you happy."

"Me, too. And one day you'll be calling and saying you're getting married."

"Maybe, but it won't be Jessica."

"Hallelujah."

"I'm going to bed," he said, smiling. "Love you, Mom."

"Love you, too, baby."

As he climbed the steps, Lily decided that she had to be the happiest woman on planet Earth.

CHAPTER
23

The Henry Adams Julys had always gathered at Tamar's for Thanksgiving dinner, but this year, because of all the extra folks in town, the meal was shared at the Dog. Julys of both clans filled the diner from front to back, and everyone appeared to be having a good time, even Tamar. She was sitting next to her brother, and they were both laughing. Whether they'd reconciled was still a mystery, because no one wanted to risk Tamar's wrath or her shotgun by asking. Diego was sitting next to Crystal in a not so discreet effort to hit on her. Lily could see Bernadine giving him the eye, but he appeared to be on his best behavior. Eli and Jack were seated nearby, and the scowl on Eli's face was one he'd been wearing since Diego and his clan came to town.

Speaking of scowls, the colonel seemed to have put his away for the dinner, but it was common knowledge that he was still having issues with Sheila's job. She, on the other hand, was practically glowing. She'd helped Mal with the arrangements for the dinner and seemed to have finally found her niche, even as the quest for something to keep Barrett occupied continued.

Reverend Paula had found her niche, too, and was seated with the Henry Adams kids. Earlier in the week, she read in the Franklin newspaper that the sanctimonious Pastor Donovan had been picked up in a sweep at one of the rest stops out on Highway 183. The police had been having a problem with men engaging in lewd behavior in the stalls. Donovan swore he'd been there to pray the men back onto the straight and narrow, but Paula was skeptical, and so was the sheriff, since Donovan had had no pants on when the police swooped down.

The day after Thanksgiving was the day of the big football game. The sky was sunny and bright, and the temperatures had warmed, as they sometimes did during the last days of autumn. The team representing Henry Adams got whipped so thoroughly and totally that nobody but the other team wanted to talk about it when it was over. The only rays of light for the home team were the two touchdowns Leah scored. The final score in the hour-long game: Oklahoma 56, Henry Adams 14.

The beautiful weather held for the wedding the next day. It was almost as if the Ancestors felt the need to throw Henry Adams a boon after they'd taken such a licking on the ball field. Lily was in her room getting dressed when Marie, acting as mother of the bride, went downstairs to answer the doorbell. She returned with Tamar and a beautiful brown-skinned woman wearing biker leathers whom Lily didn't know. Tamar introduced the woman as Judith Windsong, the mother of Griffin July.

"I'm honored to meet you," Lily said with sincerity. She'd known that Griffin's mother would be coming to the wedding, but hadn't expected her to show up on a motorcycle. She also knew about Judith's desire to be a grandmother to Amari. Lily was of the belief that there was no such thing as a child having too much love, so she was totally supportive of Judith's wish to forge a bond with her only grandson.

The wedding ceremony was a mix of Christian and Native. There were drums and crosses, prayers and Lakota chants. Sweetgrass burned alongside Episcopalian incense.

The beaming Lily was escorted down the aisle by Davis on one side and Devon on the other. Both of them looked handsome and very serious as they left her at the kiva stage and silently stepped back.

Reverend Paula, draped in beautiful red and gold vestments, began the ceremony, and when the time came for the vows, Trent's softly spoken words, "Share my life and I will love you until time is no more," made tears flow not only from Lily's eyes but from the eyes of women all over the kiva.

She responded with, "You are my sun, my nurturing rain, my life. I will love you always."

Reverend Paula asked for the rings. Amari, Trent's best man, passed his ring to him. The gorgeous sapphire that he gently pushed onto her finger was so beautiful, Lily's knees wobbled. The matron of honor, Bernadine, handed Lily the groom's ring, Lily pushed the diamond-accented gold band onto Trent's finger, and the ceremony continued.

When it was done, Paula spread her arms wide and called, "Ladies and gentlemen, I present to you Mr. and Mrs. Trenton July."

Applause shattered the air on the heels of her words, and cheering greeted the kiss the newlyweds shared. The drummers began pounding their instruments and a happy Lily locked hands with an equally happy Trent and headed down the aisle.

The reception took place at the Dog, but before the festivities began, Lily looked out over the crowd until she spied the smiling Judge Davis and beckoned her to the front of the room. Judge Davis waited until the crowd quieted, then said, "Devon Watkins, will you join me up here, please?"

Confusion on his face, Devon did as the judge asked, then stood beside her as he and everyone else wondered what this was about. As soon as she began to speak, Amari smiled. The words were very familiar to him because they were the same ones she'd spoken the day he'd been officially adopted, and now Devon was going to be official, too. It took Devon a few moments to understand what was happening, but once he did, and Judge Amy declared that from that day forward his name would be Devon July, he went crazy, and so did the guests.

Lily leaned down and gave him a big hug. "We can't have an official family if everyone isn't official, so is this okay with you?"

Over the pounding of the drums and the low-toned chants and high-voiced calls of the singers, he nodded happily. "Yes! Thank you, Mom and Dad! Thank you."

After that, the party began in earnest. Toasts were proposed, the first dance taken, and when Trent and Lily sat down, Amari stood on a chair and yelled over the din, "May I have your attention, please!"

Trent and Lily shared a look. Neither of them knew what this meant.

Once everyone quieted, he announced, "Preston and I, with the help of Tamar and my OG, prepared this special presentation. Please turn your attention to the big screen."

Suddenly, Lily's seventeen-year-old face from the high school yearbook came on the screen, and she screamed with surprise. Next came Trent's. The crowd went nuts again. To his delight, Amari and his coconspirators had somehow transferred the images from Tamar's old video camera to the screen. There was Lily, blazing her way around the track, and Gary and Trent, wearing their basketball uniforms, flexing their muscles, and mugging for the camera. Lily started crying again as picture after picture slowly flashed by. Getting up, she embarrassed Amari totally by giving him a big thank-you kiss, then did the same to Preston.

The food was set out, folks lined up, and Lily was so touched and happy after all she'd seen and done that she couldn't stop crying.

At midnight, Nathan came and whisked them away to the airport. Davis would be flying home Sunday morning, and Mal would be staying with the boys at Trent's house until they returned. Lily and Trent didn't find out where they were going until Bernadine's jet was in the air.

Pilot Katie Sky said over the speakers, "Lily, Ms. Brown left you an envelope in the galley."

Lily retrieved the envelope. With Trent beside her, she looked inside and found a photo of Tina Craig's sprawling patio. The sticky note attached read: *Lily. You and your hunk will have the place all to yourselves for a week. My staff will take care of everything. Enjoy being in love—Tina and Bernadine.*

Trent pulled her onto his lap and held her as the happy tears flowed once again. "You planning on crying all week?" he asked affectionately.

"I just might. Who would've ever thought we'd end up together again?"

"I certainly didn't, but I'm glad we did. Have I told you I love you today?"

"I'm not sure. Maybe you should tell me again."

"How about I show you?"

Seven o'clock Monday morning, when Bernadine pulled into the Power Plant, she was surprised to find Preston out front. "Hey, Brain. What brings you by so early?"

"Need to talk to you about something."

"What is it? That was a real nice photo show you and Amari put together, by the way."

"Thanks. It was fun." He handed her what appeared to be a printout of an e-mail message. "Can you read this, please, and tell me what you think I should do?"

Bernadine read the words, and when she was finished, she looked at him with surprise. "She says she's your grandmother and wants to get in touch."

"I know. What should I do?"

"She included her phone number. Do you want me to call her?"

"Would you?"

"Okay. Come by after school, and I'll let you know what I find out."

"Thanks, Ms. Bernadine."

"You're welcome."

Preston left her to walk over to the school, and Bernadine went inside. She set her purse down, opened her phone, and punched in the number from the e-mail. When the call went through, she said to the woman who answered, "Mrs. Crenshaw. My name's Bernadine Brown. I'm calling you on behalf of Preston Mays. Do you have a moment to speak with me?"

Tamar was getting ready to go to the rec. Her brother and his clan had headed home sometime before dawn, so she pulled the curtains back to take a quick peek outside and make sure Olivia was still parked where she'd been left last night. What she saw widened her eyes and shot her temper through the roof. Olivia was in the same spot, but she'd been turned over and left upside down. She looked like a beetle on its back, and all her tires were gone. A bunch of tools lay on the ground beside her, including a jack. Steaming, Tamar ran outside to get a closer look and found a sticky note on the door that read: *I know we called a truce, but I couldn't resist. Your coyote brother.*

Tamar opened her mouth and screamed, "THADDEUS!!"

A⁺

AUTHOR
INSIGHTS,
EXTRAS &
MORE...

FROM

**BEVERLY
JENKINS**

AND

WILLIAM MORROW

Book Club Questions

1. How did the title, *Something Old, Something New,* manifest itself in the story?

2. Besides Trent and Lily's relationship, who else did the title represent?

3. Which character's back story surprised you the most and why?

4. How best can Barrett contribute to Henry Adams?

5. Which scene(s) made you laugh? Which one(s) broke your heart?

6. If you were a resident of Henry Adams, which of the children would you most like to parent and why? Which one would you least like to raise?

7. Was Tamar's anger at her brother justified? What about Marie's at her mother and at Tamar?

8. Should Marie's son have contacted her?

9. Talk about Trent's role as father to Amari and Devon.

10. Should Devon have been made to paint the fence alone, per tradition?

11. Discuss tradition in your individual families.

12. What should Jack do about Rocky?

Author's Note

Something Old, Something New marks our third visit to modern-day Henry Adams, Kansas. This installment is filled with humor, heartache, and a bit of mayhem in the form of the Oklahoma Julys. I hope you had as much fun reading it as I had writing it. I especially enjoyed working in the traditional flute played by most Native cultures, which is more akin in form and fingering to the Western clarinet. The *siyotanka*, as the Lakota flute is known, played a prominent role in my first Henry Adams historical romance, *Night Song*, and I couldn't resist resurrecting the concept for Trent and Lily.

Over the course of the series one of the main questions readers have been asking is: When will Zoey speak? That has now been answered and I'm looking forward to learning more about her multifaceted personality in the future.

As with the previous two books, *Bring on the Blessings* and *A Second Helping*, we leave Henry Adams with many still-unanswered questions. Will Leo and his company run roughshod over the rights of the farmers and lay their pipeline anyway? Is that e-mail really from Preston's grandmother? Will Rocky ever give poor Jack the time of day? And what about Riley—will he have to act as his own lawyer at the upcoming trial in order to save Cletus's bacon? In the words of the great Rocket J. Squirrel: Stay tuned, girls and boys.

Once again, I want to say thanks to all the foster parents and adoptive parents who've e-mailed me their stories, forwarded me pictures of their kids, and sent me blessings for writing a series that has touched their hearts. You've touched mine also with your commitment and love. Keep doing what you're doing.

According to statistics compiled by the U.S. Department of Health and Human Services, 424,000 children were in state-run foster-care homes or facilities in 2009, and of that number, 57,000 were adopted. In many ways that's great, because in 2002, there were 520,000 children in foster care and 51,000 were adopted. However, you don't need a degree in math to figure out that if 57,000 were adopted in 2009, more than 360,000 are still waiting for a permanent home. Many of these children will age out of foster care on their eighteenth birthday and be forced to deal with a world that often lacks the support system they'll need to succeed. And yes, there are wonderful stories of children who have the smarts, drive, and tenacity to surpass even their wildest dreams, but unfortunately these stories seem few and far between.

As I noted in *Bring on the Blessings*, most of the children in the foster-care system are children of color, and the hardest to place are groups of siblings, children with special needs, and teens. My son was five when we adopted him. He'd been taken out of his home at the age of three because of abuse that left him hospitalized and encased in a body cast to heal his broken ribs and limbs. Although his maternal grandmother wanted custody, she was denied by the courts and he went into the system. But in social worker speak, he's called a survivor—a child who has come through the fire relatively whole.

When he came to live with us, he had issues. He had a very limited vocabulary for a child of five, had never gone out for dinner as far as we knew (not even to McDonald's), and had become accustomed to sleeping on a bare mattress due to bed-wetting problems. In those first few months, he wore us out. I have two younger brothers, so I was well aware of how much wild energy boys can have, but this little guy must have been drinking jet fuel after we put him to bed at night, because he got up every morning turbocharged. It made me tired just watching him. It was like having a curious wolf cub in your home: lots of zooming around and lots of destruction, from the antennae on my then twelve-year-old daughter's boom box to the odometer on my hubby's exercise bike. Nothing was safe, and it wasn't because he was destructive. It was because he wanted to touch everything in his brave new world, and sometimes knobs that look like they should turn and other things that look like they should bend don't. My daughter wanted to bury him in the backyard every day.

But we survived, as families tend to whether the children are biological or not. Although he was age ready for school, the rest of him wasn't; too much jet fuel for a classroom. When he did start kindergarten a year later, my husband and I tag teamed. Three days out of the week, I was in the classroom; the other two days, my husband was. Nothing like watching a labor consultant dressed in a suit playing in a sandbox with kindergarteners.

We got it done, however, and by the time our son started high school, the little wooden boy who came to us with a vocabulary that was limited to the word *motorcycle* and the phrase *gotta use it* had transformed himself into the Fresh Prince of our small, semirural town.

He was sixteen when cancer took my husband, his dad. His life was shattered, and during the eight years since, he's performed more stupid kid tricks than a mother can shake a stick at. For a while, I was the one wanting to bury him in the backyard on a daily basis.

Do I regret adopting him? Not in the least. His grief at losing his dad had nothing to do with being adopted and everything to do with love and how lost he felt when his guiding star dimmed. Getting him through senior year and beyond turned into such an adventure that my daughter suggested I write a book about him titled *You Did What?!*

I'm sharing his story to say parenting is parenting, no matter where your children originate. Biological kids have been known to give their parents fits, too, so don't let the fact that a child may have issues deter you from opening your home and heart.

In traveling over the last two years to promote this series, I've cried a lot. Upon hearing stories from adoptive parents, foster parents, and adopted children about how much the Blessings series has hit home, or how much the Henry Adams kids remind them of the children they are raising, or the joy the entire family experiences reading the series, crying was all I had.

The folks in Henry Adams have readers and book clubs all over America talking about adoption, fostering, and volunteering, and I hope the discussions lead to some positive action on behalf of those 360,000 left behind. However, if only one person steps up, it gives one more child a shot at a life most of us take for granted. So if you can help, do so. The rigid rules that used to apply as to who can be an adoptive parent and who can't are finally changing as society realizes that only two questions are truly paramount: Will you love this child? Can you provide for this child? If the answers are yes, all that's left is the shouting.

So if this series has touched you enough to consider helping out a child in need, then my job here is done. Take it from me, you will be blessed.

Until next time,

B

BOOKS BY BEVERLY JENKINS

BRING ON THE BLESSINGS

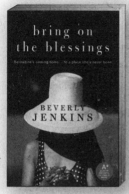

ISBN 978-0-06-168840-9 (paperback)
The town of Henry Adams is falling apart.
Bernadine Brown is a woman with money to spend,
and she has some ideas about how the town should
be run. But will the townspeople be willing to shake
up their comfortable lives to save their home?

"*Bring on the Blessings* is a tasty reading confection
that you'll savor long after the story ends."
—Angela Benson, *Essence* bestselling author of
Up Pops the Devil and *The Amen Sisters*

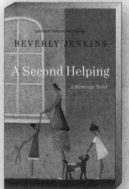

A SECOND HELPING
A Blessings Novel

ISBN 978-0-06-154781-2 (paperback)
A lot has changed in Henry Adams since Bernadine
Brown saved the historic community from
bankruptcy. Now she's turning her attention to
revive the diner that was the town's former bustling
hub and meeting grounds. But life in Henry Adams
gets even more interesting when her ex-husband
comes crawling into town and stirs up trouble.

SOMETHING OLD, SOMETHING NEW
A Blessings Novel

ISBN 978-0-06-199079-3 (paperback)
Former high school sweethearts Lily and Trent are
finally getting married, and all they want is a nice,
simple wedding. But as always, nothing in Henry
Adams is simple. With the "help" of well-meaning
neighbors and family members, their no-fuss
wedding starts turning into the event of the decade.
But amidst the bustle of everyone around them, one
thing is certain . . . happiness is meant to be shared.